LUCKY TOWN

a Clarke & Clarke mystery

PETER VONDER HAAR

CONTENTS

ACKNOWLEDGMENTS

A relative of mine (who shall remain nameless) who'd made a career of writing once told me this was a "lonely pursuit," which I suspect was a way of justifying his lack of friends and why his cousins never visited him. And while it's probably true that solitude is more conducive to the act of completing a novel, it's something I never could have accomplished without a huge number of people in my life.

First, let me thank everyone who dropped their hard-earned money for a copy of *Lucky Town*. I know how many options there are for your reading dollar, and I'm honored you picked this one.

To my editors, Mason and Kathy Hart: thank you for doing the work I should've asked y'all to do in the first place. Dinner's always on me.

To the "beta readers" of *Lucky Town* – Jami Anderson (who also created the excellent cover art), Tracy Croom, Kristy Kincaid, Dana Losey, and Melissa Turnquist – as well as Mom, Dad, and my sister Jessica: thank you for your patience and for fixing some occasionally embarrassing plot holes.

And sorry to Dad for naming one of the less pleasant characters after you. I was thinking of someone else, honest.

Finally, to my wife Tory: I rarely feel confident about anything, but I'm certain this never would have happened without you. Your encouragement, sacrifice, and feedback that occasionally veered into brutal honesty were integral to getting this done (to say nothing of solving every plot problem I had). I love you, and now I can finally say "I'm a writer" wasn't just a cheesy pickup line.

For Kathryne, Erin, and Sydney

PROLOGUE

Ever woken up in a hospital room?

It's not an experience I recommend to … well, anyone, but if you've had the pleasure, there are things you'll always remember. Even before opening your eyes: first the glare of fluorescent lights piercing your closed eyelids, then the aroma of industrial cleaning agents heroically masking the accumulated odors of decay and rot, followed by the feel of sheets and pillowcases worn threadbare by hundreds of bodies and industrial wash cycles.

It's all right if these things are unfamiliar to you. Outside of pregnancy, an average person probably gets through life without a hospital stay. But I'm the wrong person to make that call.

This wasn't my first rodeo. I'd seen more emergency rooms than birthdays by the time I was in my twenties. I was oddly proud of this until I entered my third decade and started experiencing the kind of chronic aches and pains that aren't supposed to show up until years later. I thought it was hardly fair to experience all the disadvantages of middle age without even buying a new Corvette.

Cracking my right eye open (the left one was still being stubborn), I took comfort in the familiarity of my surroundings. I'd been in this particular room now for almost a week, but I again confirmed my neck worked by turning my head, taking in a TV tuned to a Richard Dawson-era episode of *Family Feud* and the expected array of life-preserving machinery.

Oh, and also my mother.

If I'm an old pro at regaining consciousness in medical facilities, my mom could give a TED Talk about waiting patiently for others to do so. All six of her kids (five boys, myself included) were involved in sports, most of them subsequently embarked on careers with potential for injury, and at least one (hello) has proven uncannily prone to taking beatings. Mary Clarke would be Norm from *Cheers* if he hung out in the various hospitals in the metro Houston area instead of a bar run by an ex-Red Sox pitcher.

Attempting a smile, my jaw felt like it was held in place with razor blades. Though it couldn't be too severe, because the doctors hadn't bothered to wire it shut. In my mind, the grinding of misplaced bone on bone caused Mom to look up from her book. Realizing I was awake, her expression shifted from middle-grade maternal concern to resigned anticipation.

Feeling the need to reassure the woman who gave me life, I spoke: "Hrrggkkkk." It sounded (and felt) like my mouth was full of gravel.

Setting her paperback down on the bed, she said, "Can you talk?"

I tried swallowing and only tasted a hint of blood. There was a cup with a straw next to the bed, but when I reached for it, Mom got there first, holding the straw to my lips like I was an invalid, which — in a sense — I was.

I felt better after some water. Mom leaned forward in her chair.

"Tell me everything."

ONE

One week ago.

I woke up in my bed, in a considerable amount of pain.

Neither eye was swollen shut, so it was with normal vision that I absorbed the daylight and saw my bloody clothes from last night draped over my dresser.

And then I remembered I'd been in another fight.

I sat up, tentatively self-evaluating my pain points before going to the bathroom mirror and confirming the worst. Legs: fine. Groin: fine, except I had to go to the bathroom — hardly unusual after just waking up. Abdomen: sore. Ribs: no problem.

That was generally good news. It meant I'd taken only a few shots to the body, and no one had kicked me in the balls. I wasn't a religious man, but I willed a silent thank-you to whatever deity was in charge of genital protection. The Greeks probably had somebody.

I noticed some abrasions on my knuckles, but not too many, indicating the fight hadn't lasted long. Unfortunately, my head was one big mass of throbbing, so after dragging myself into the bathroom, I took a look.

It wasn't pretty (even less than usual, I mean): My left eye was swelling nicely, with some purpling already evident around the socket. My nose didn't look broken. This time. Though the lump on the bridge provided plenty of confirmation it had already happened three times before. The back of my head stung and was tender to the touch, but no blood came away on my fingers. Finally, I had a cut on my chin, which brought flashes of a class ring. Whoever clocked me had graduated high school, at least.

All told, the damage didn't look too bad. Clearly there'd been no ER visit, and Charlie hadn't felt the urge to bust out the first aid kit. Between that and the lack of ball-kicking, we had all the hallmarks of a successful evening.

After brushing my teeth (gingerly, my jaw still ached) and shaving, I gathered up my bloody clothes before going downstairs. The physical evaluation was complete; now it was time for the psychological ordeal. Namely Charlie, my twin sister.

The coffee smelled good, and I was grateful that she had bothered to make some. She was a tea-drinker herself, probably thanks to some unknown British ancestor. I didn't see her in the kitchen, so I went into the laundry room and prepared to dump last night's soiled fashions into the machine.

"You'll want to soak that shirt."

I turned. Charlie stood in the doorway, arms crossed. She was decked out in her version of business casual: a Dead Kennedys' T-shirt and jeans that could charitably be referred to as "distressed." Her long brown hair was pulled back in a loose ponytail, and she completed the ensemble with red suede Pumas. Few places would consider that suitable work attire. Fortunately, we were self-employed.

And I knew the soaking trick, for crying out loud.

"Uh huh," I said, throwing the shirt into the old iron laundry sink. I ran cold water until it was submerged, "Can you hand me the dish soap?"

An unreadable look passed over her face, but she retrieved the bottle from the kitchen and gave it to me. Grunting my thanks, I squeezed a healthy dollop into the water and stirred everything with my hand until it was sufficiently frothy.

There was still a decent chance the shirt was ruined. It wouldn't be the first.

"What do you remember, Cy?" she asked.

Being a former detective and current private investigator, I summoned my formidable powers of recollection. There was a bar — pretty sure it was the Wing Joint over on Washington, but they all tend to run together in your mind after a time — and a fairly dense weeknight crowd. McHugh was pitching against the Angels. It was an away game, on the West Coast, so the evening was already fairly far along by the first pitch. I'd gone there by myself (as a mostly non-drinker, Charlie was the smarter twin), but was only two beers in when something happened.

I relayed all this to her. "This sounds suspiciously like one of those 'I was just minding my own business' introductions," she said.

"But I *was* minding my own business," I protested. "A guy can't go catch a game at a bar without looking for trouble?"

Charlie laughed. "If you just wanted to watch the game, you'd have gone to Rudyard's or Alice's Tall Texan."

"Alice's doesn't have TVs," I said.

"You know what I mean. You weren't looking for a quiet evening's contemplation; you went to a sports bar packed with meatheads because you knew it was the easiest place to start shit."

The evening was coming back to me. "I wasn't the one who started it."

"You never are," she said.

The meathead in question had been talking trash all night, I remembered. He especially liked bagging on George Springer whenever he was on screen, but his vitriol wasn't limited to the TV, as he was increasingly argumentative with his group's waitress. His friends and someone I assumed was his girlfriend tried several times to get him to calm down, with little success.

Noting his position in the establishment relative to mine, I filed it away for future reference. Belligerent drunks were tiresome and unpredictable, but they tend to be the only prospects when the night wears on.

"See?" Charlie jumped in, 'Right there, you talked about 'prospects.'"

"And?"

"And?! You were obviously sizing up the crowd. Unless your romantic target profile has completely changed and now you only hit on drunk bro assholes."

I said, "Wow, 'romantic target profile' sounds a lot less serial killer-y when you say it."

No response to that, but maybe her patience was running out. Sisters, right?

"May I continue?"

I took her eyeroll as a "yes."

McHugh was taking a 4–3 lead into the eighth inning when the "drunk bro asshole" in question hovered into my peripheral vision, returning unsteadily from the restroom and scanning the room. His eyes settled on his embattled waitress and he hailed her in the fashion customary to his kind.

"Yo, bitch!"

The bar was loud, so only a handful of people heard, fewer still knew who he was bellowing at, and the two bouncers had disappeared downstairs, doubtless to deal with the Very Serious Threat of college freshmen trying to sneak in to deplete the bar's domestic beer reservoirs.

Without turning my head, I watched the waitress's reaction. She tensed up but didn't acknowledge him, perhaps hoping he was directing his charms elsewhere. No such luck.

He lumbered past me with the bovine grace you'd expect from a person who'd been downing pitchers of Bud Light for three hours and grabbed her by the arm, tugging her toward him.

"Where are my mozzarella sticks?" The act of speaking clearly took a lot out of him, as he was concentrating like she was about to reveal the riddle of the Sphinx.

The young woman shook out of his grasp and strode off, probably to get the manager or the bouncer. I figured this was as good a time as any, left $20 for my beers, and got up from my stool.

"Why didn't you wait for the manager?" Charlie asked.

"Why do you keep interrupting my story?" I countered.

She said, "This was a completely avoidable situation. She did the right thing, de-escalating tensions by leaving to get help. You initiated contact for no good reason."

"I had good reasons," I said.

"You got something against fried cheese?"

"Can I finish?"

The guy was taller than me, but not by much. Bigger guys tend to put too much faith in their size, which can lead to a mouth overdraft of their ass's checking account. I was counting on that, as well as my own (relative) sobriety.

"Don't you think it's about time you called it a night?"

He spun around, mostly without stumbling. "Who the fuck are you?"

I smiled. "I'm the guy telling you to go home, chief."

In my experience, calling a guy "chief" — or "buddy" or "champ" — is almost guaranteed to get a rise out of them, and this dude wasn't defying expectations. He laughed and tried to shove me in the chest, so I put him in a wrist lock and started bringing him to the floor. He swung with his left but mostly caught shirt as it glanced off my ribs. Before he could bring his arm around again, I elbowed him in the nose, releasing his wrist as I did so.

He started wailing and brought both hands to his face as I stepped backward. One of the bouncers was coming up the stairs and made straight for us.

"What happened?"

I shrugged. "Must have walked into the *Golden Tee* machine," I said. "He looks like he's had a few."

I stepped around the drunk dude, who was now bleeding freely from his hopefully broken nose. His friends were slowly rising to see what was going on and I saw their waitress walk up behind the bouncer. She gave me the briefest of nods and returned to cashing out her checks, while I walked down the stairs and out of the bar.

TWO

"Back up," Charlie said.

"What?"

"You took the drunk dude down in two moves and left? That's it?"

I said, "I mean, he really wasn't in any condition to fight."

"And the blood on your shirt? The black eye? Did you stop at another bar on the way home?"

"Oh, that," I said. "Nah, his friends jumped me in the parking lot."

Charlie said, "Seems like a significant part of the story to leave out."

I was unlocking the front door of my trusty 1998 Toyota Corolla when I heard a footstep on the gravel behind me. I turned to my left and the beer bottle that had been aimed at the side of my head caught me on the thicker occipital bone of my skull. At first, I was more relieved than angry that I hadn't gotten any glass in my eye.

Then the anger came.

There were three of them, two dudes I recognized from socializing with the asshole upstairs hanging back while the bottle-wielder looked equal parts surprised and disappointed that his bar-brawl tactic hadn't worked.

Use a whiskey bottle next time, junior, I thought, as I aimed a straight jab at his face. I put my hip into it and was rewarded with

6

the crunch of bone under my knuckles. He staggered back, cursing, and I bull-rushed the bigger of his friends, hoping to take him by surprise.

Charlie said, "It didn't occur to you just to get in the car and drive off?"

"You know the locks on that thing," I replied. "Hell, the driver's side door barely closes all the way."

"Of course."

The big guy recovered from his shock faster than I would've liked and didn't go down when I hit him. He landed a sloppy punch to my ribs that might have caused some damage if he hadn't been fighting gravity as well as me. I stomped on his foot as hard as I could, then kneed him in the groin.

Hey, I didn't say *everyone* had a successful evening.

I looked up just in time to see a fist come looping in. I ducked, so I only caught most of it. That one hurt, but he'd only gotten enough weight behind it to carry him forward. I spun around as he overextended and nailed him in the back of the head with my elbow. He groaned and dropped to the ground.

Red and blue lights suddenly illuminated the lot. I heard rapidly receding footfalls I deduced belonged to the bottle guy (former detective, remember). Then others approaching with cautious authority.

"Hands where I can see them," came the expected voice. [More. Need to justify "**the** voice" vs. "**a** voice" — e.g., "the cop's voice." Or "the expected voice."]

"Obviously, you weren't arrested. Or it was the fastest trial since Judge Roy Bean," Charlie said.

"One of the cops was Jeff Ramsey. He was a rookie during my last year on the force."

"And he convinced everyone not to press charges?"

I said, "I assume so. They talked to the bouncer and the waitress while I was sitting in the back of his cruiser."

She looked at me in a manner disconcertingly similar to our mother's. "Naturally, it didn't occur to you to mention this when you rolled in last night."

"Why?" I said. "The EMTs said I didn't have to go to the hospital, so what were you going to do?"

"Maybe you should take some kickboxing classes. Anything would be better than white-knighting your way through neighborhood watering holes looking to get your ass kicked."

"The bouncer actually offered me a job," I said.

Charlie rubbed her eyes, "You got into a lot less of this kind of trouble when Emma was still around."

"Watch it," I cautioned. It had been almost a year, but hearing my ex-girlfriend's name was still enough to sour my mood.

She smiled, but raised her hands in mock surrender, and I elected not to escalate.

"Look, I'm sorry," I said at last, "I bore easily. Plus, I'm good at it."

"You can take a punch," she agreed, "but your superhero shtick needs work. Batman doesn't make a habit out of getting the shit beat out of him."

"Sure he does. And when he gets home, Alfred has cleaned the house and made him a hot meal," I said.

"I know you didn't just call me a butler," Charlie said.

I smiled. "You'd have to learn how to load a dishwasher before I went that far."

She shot me the finger and returned to her desk.

"I'm going to get the *Chronicle*," I said.

"Cy Clarke: the only person not employed by the journalism industry who still reads an entire newspaper," she said.

"Not true," I replied. "Those guys at the doughnut place do as well."

"The doughnut place."

"Yep."

"Those guys are eighty years old if they're a day," Charlie pointed out.

"I … fail to see your point."

She rolled her eyes. "Fine, journalists and retired postal workers are the only people who read the newspaper anymore. Happy?"

"A rare and special breed," I agreed as I went to the driveway. I needed some air. The mention of Emma was a gut punch I hadn't anticipated. Ours hadn't been a particularly nasty breakup, just the bifurcation of two lives going in different directions. But the ache was still there.

I picked up the paper, mildly curious to see if my evening's exploits had made the news, but it was a long shot. Murders barely made the front page, and then mostly if they involved innocent bystanders or kids.

The article that eventually caught my eye wasn't something most people would notice, buried as it was on the eighth page of the *Houston Chronicle*'s Metro section. I only came across it because of what Charlie describes as my archaic habit of reading the entire thing every morning.

Charlie is my sister. My twin sister, to be precise. She and I were the youngest of six kids, though she's older by two minutes, that being the amount of time it had taken my mother's obstetrician to arbitrarily pull her from the womb ahead of me. Not that I'm bitter or anything. Charlie is as deliberative as I am impulsive and has forgotten more about computers and technology than I could ever hope to learn.

All six of us were named after baseball players. Specifically, we were named after Major League pitchers who've thrown perfect games. It started with my older brother Lee, named for Lee Richmond, the first player ever to accomplish the feat, though Lee had been dead for three years now (my brother, that is; the pitcher died in 1929). My other three brothers, in chronological order, were Mike, Jim, and Don, named after Witt, Bunning, and Larsen respectively.

I lucked out in getting what was maybe the most recognizable name: Cy. Even non-baseball fans have heard of Cy Young, thanks to the award bearing his name and given to the best pitcher in either league each season.

Thankfully, Mom and Dad didn't use Young's real name. "Denton" Clarke doesn't really have the same zing.

My sister gets her name from Charlie Robertson, who threw his perfect game against the Tigers in 1922. Robertson would unfortunately go on to own the worst winning percentage (0.380) of any pitcher who'd thrown a perfecto, for which my brothers and I would give her no end of shit.

Not that she had any control over it, but it obviously pissed her off. "Why Charlie?" she'd complain. "Sandy' (meaning Koufax) was *right there*."

Growing up, Mom was always the sports fan, and our home was littered with memorabilia from the Houston Astros, Oilers, and Texans. To his credit, my dad Al — may he rest in peace — never fought it. More analytical than confrontational, I think he secretly enjoyed being married to a woman who loved baseball and football more than he did. Besides, it wasn't like the names were that objectionable. Charlie could whine about it until she was blue in the face; at least she wasn't named "Catfish."

That honor went to the dog.

I didn't know why I was thinking about my brothers that particular morning. It was mid-May, far from any sibling birthdays or, more poignantly, the anniversaries of Lee's or Dad's deaths. Still, almost as soon as I turned to the page in the Chronicle, my eyes found the name "Mike Clarke."

And while there are undoubtedly several men by that name sprinkled among Houston's estimated population of six million, the article's headline removed any lingering doubt:

DHS OFFICIAL SOUGHT IN MURDER

I skimmed the text. A Department of Homeland Security officer named Bob Ramirez had been found dead in his office near the Port of Houston. One of Ramirez's fellow officers — Mike Clarke, an ex-Marine — was being sought after witnesses put him at the scene. According to the report, Mike hadn't been heard from in two days.

Unless another of the region's Mike Clarkes was also working for the DHS (following a highly decorated career in the USMC), they couldn't be talking about anyone but my brother. I tried to recall the last time I'd spoken to him when Charlie burst in.

"Did you know about Mike?"

I nodded, "Where did you see it? Don't you famously reject printed media?"

She said, "I have a search agent for our names. It fed me the story as soon as I booted up the computer. When was the last time you talked to him?"

"Four, maybe five days ago," I said. "You?"

"About the same."

We looked at each other for a minute. I could feel dread spreading like poisonous vines in my stomach, the instinctual reaction when your gut immediately starts anticipating the worst even as your rational mind tries to intercede. I imagined Charlie was feeling the same way.

As one, we said, "We gotta tell Mom."

THREE

Let me tell you about my brother Mike.

He's my second-oldest brother. Technically, *the* oldest now that Lee was gone. And while Lee was firstborn chronologically, Mike always fit that mold better anyway.

There's a long tradition of movie characters who are effective in spite of (perhaps because of) the fact they don't speak much. Clint Eastwood's "Man with No Name" from Sergio Leone's spaghetti Westerns comes to mind, as does Red Grant in *From Russia With Love*, or Max in the Mad Max movies.

Mike is like that.

Charlie and I never got to know Lee all that well. He was eight years old when we were born, and by the time we were old enough to conceivably have a relationship with our eldest sibling, he was a teenager and barely around. He enlisted in the Army when we were still in grade school, and though we saw him occasionally when he was on leave, his influence was more by way of reputation than actual presence.

Mike was only a year younger, and therefore also subject to the existential vagaries of adolescence, so he stuck around for a while. He lived at home while he went to Rice University for two years before enlisting in the Marines. I still have a hard time comprehending that, considering there were four other kids tearing around (Don was a one-man demolition crew in his own right), but the mayhem never seemed to faze him. If I didn't know any better, I'd swear he enjoyed it.

It wasn't until we got to high school, by which time Mike was already enjoying the hospitality at Parris Island, that Charlie and I learned of Mike's rep there. He'd played baseball and basketball at Reagan High (now Heights High, since the school district finally realized they shouldn't name buildings after dudes who served in the Confederacy), and featured prominently in several photos of District and State Championship teams from the eighties. Even though he'd graduated six years before Charlie and I started school, the teachers and faculty still spoke of him with great fondness.

Unlike Lee, who'd coasted through school almost unnoticed and bugged out to the military almost before the ink on his diploma was dry, Mike was remembered as both a helpful kid and one who brooked no tolerance for bullies or assholes.

As you can imagine, this put him at odds with a not insignificant portion of his fellow students.

There's a possibly apocryphal story about Mike that Don would sometimes tell when he'd had a few. It would've been Don's freshman year, before he'd earned his own reputation. He says he walked into the boy's restroom by the band hall, the one farthest from the office, and three older boys were thumping another freshman, calling him "faggot" and generally being teenage assholes. Don says he tried to stop them, but one of the kids sucker-punched him and shoved him out of the restroom.

Where who should he see heading to baseball practice but Mike?

To hear Don tell it, he gave Mike a quick rundown on what was going down in the restroom. Mike told him to go tell the school security officer there was a fight going on, then turned and walked in to the restroom.

By the time Don returned with the security officer, the bullied kid was gone, and the three assholes were lying on the bathroom floor, bleeding from assorted facial contusions. None of them never said who beat them up (likely to avoid admitting one dude had handled the three of them), and Don knew better than to fink on his older brother. Don said no one ever messed with the other freshman after that. I'd like to believe him.

Mike also wasn't a "teacher's pet." He didn't raise his hand or shout out answers to questions. But if a teacher needed someone to stay late and help clean up after biology lab, or partner up with a student who was having a hard time with their trigonometry homework, Mike would be there for them.

Mike's spirit of giving, or charity, or basic human decency, whatever you wanted to call it, spread to our home as well. As did his general reticence. To say the Clarke household was loud would be like saying dogs aren't overly fond of cats. I can't recall a time when the average decibel level wasn't somewhere around "AC/DC concert" levels, but Mike was never a contributor.

On those rare occasions when the rest of the family did appear to finally aggravate him, he'd simply get up and go to his room (which he shared with no one, benefits of being the oldest).

But his silence didn't mean he wasn't paying attention. With Lee gone and Dad having the home improvement skills of a guy whose idea of "kicking back" meant rereading biographies of Al-Khwarizmi and Tartaglia, it fell to Mike to keep our century-old house from falling apart.

Mom would mention loose boards on the porch or a leaky laundry room faucet at dinner, for example. And while no one would acknowledge this (well, my dad might make some comment about "looking into it"), Mike would be up before school the next day, nailing the porch back together or taking the faucet apart. If Jim was the weird one, Don the troublemaker, and Charlie and me the smart-asses, then Mike was the doer.

Is he my favorite brother? Can all of us with siblings just admit we have favorites? If so, then … probably. Like I said, I never really got to know Lee before he died, and I regret that to this day. Jim was and still is a deeply odd dude, but I don't begrudge anyone their adolescent nerd phase (I myself have been known to sling a few D20s in my time). Don is the guy you'd want to have your back, whether kicking down doors in Tikrit or walking into a sports bar.

Charlie is our favorite sister, which goes without saying.

But if I'm telling the truth, then yeah; Mike's probably my favorite. All those movie characters I mentioned were like him in the strictest "actions speak louder than words" sense, but all of them also had an agenda. I never got the sense from Mike that he wanted anything from me. If he offered to help me move some boxes into the attic or push my shitty Corolla to a gas station, it was never followed by "You owe me one, bro."

Then again, I'm told still waters supposedly run deep, so it's possible Mike was harboring homicidal tendencies all along.

I was on the phone waiting for Mom to pick up. Charlie was already on her own phone, simultaneously calling Mike's wife Kayla and clicking through other local web pages to see if there was any more information.

"Any other news?" I asked.

"Hold on," she said to her phone. To me: "No. It's the same AP boilerplate. The story doesn't seem to have a local reporter attached to it yet."

My phone connected: "Hello?"

"Hey, Mom, it's Cy."

"I know who it is," she said, "your name shows on the screen when you call."

"Kind of takes all the suspense out of it."

She sounded bemused now. "Do you think I still have one of the old candlestick phones with the separate earpiece? I'm not *that* old."

I cut to the chase. "Mom, when was the last time you heard from Mike?"

"Mike? About a week ago. He was helping me move boxes into the attic." Her tone changed, and the hardass I'd grown up with replaced the affable grandmother she was now. "Why? Tell me what's happened."

"He's missing. According to the news, he's a person of interest in a murder at DHS."

"What?"

"It didn't say he was a suspect ..." I started.

"Oh, bullshit. You know what 'person of interest' really means."

She had me there. "Look, Charlie's calling Kayla, Don, and Jim to see if they've heard anything. I'll keep you posted."

"See that you do," she said. "And Cy?"

"Yes?"

"You both be careful."

"We will, Mom." I ended the call.

"We will what?" Charlie asked. She was off her phone.

"Be careful."

She smiled without humor. "Always easier said than done."

"Any luck?"

"Don hasn't heard from Mike lately," Charlie said. "I left a message with Jim's service."

Our big brother Jim spent a lot of time overseas in his State Department job, though I feel like we should put "State Department" in quotes, because everyone in the family is convinced he's continuing the spook work he began in the Air Force's Intelligence, Surveillance, and Reconnaissance Agency.

Even Mom.

"What about Kayla?" I asked. Mike's wife wasn't a big fan of mine for a variety of reasons that are pretty much entirely my fault.

"She and Tyler are going to Mom's."

"When did she find out Mike was missing?"

She said, "That's what's weird; she didn't know he was. She found out right before I called, when another paper-reading weirdo, a neighbor this time, called to ask what was up."

I said, "Maybe we should go to Mom's."

"No. Don's on his way there now," Charlie said. "He said he'd stay with her. I think he and Carlos are on the outs."

I didn't have a response for that. The Clarkes were notoriously difficult romantic partners.

Charlie turned her monitor to me. "Look at this."

I walked over to her desk. "You found something about Mike?"

"No," she said, "it's a story about an HPD raid in a house in southeast Houston three weeks ago."

Knowing Charlie, she had a reason for showing me an apparently unrelated story, so I scanned it. "What were they raiding it for? Drugs?"

"Human trafficking," she said. "They found a couple dozen women who were apparently in transit to wherever they were going to be turned out."

I exhaled. Seeing the treatment of women and children victims had always been the worst part of being a cop. "Okay, and?"

She pointed to a paragraph. "DHS was there, too.

Recognize the name?"

"Bob Ramirez," I said. "That's interesting."

Charlie nodded. "And now he's dead."

We exchanged another look. "What was that about being careful?" I asked.

FOUR

I mostly became a private investigator because of a promise.

Being the youngest of five brothers carries certain challenges, especially when you also happen to be the smallest. I'm not a dwarf, by any means, but when every other male in your family is over 6' 3" tall, nicknames like "Runt" follow naturally. Such was the case throughout my childhood and into my adult years, even after I'd topped out at a hair over six feet tall.

All the older men in the family are/were ex-military, just like Mom. Mary Duncan was one of a dozen women to receive the Bronze Star in Vietnam. While stationed as a nurse in Hue City, she rescued eight Marines from a downed, burning helicopter. After the war, she attended the University of Texas on the GI Bill and met Al Clarke when she took his math class. They were married in 1974. The kids, starting with Lee, followed at irregular intervals over the next ten years.

Dad passed 12 years ago from a heart attack. A legitimate academic genius, he nevertheless refused to heed warnings about excessive red meat consumption. A year later, as if God decided to add an exclamation point, an IED would claim the life of my oldest brother Lee in Fallujah.

My other older brothers were already in the service at that point (Jim and Don both signed on after 9/11), and I had just finished college. And while Mom pleaded for all of them to resign their commissions, Charlie and I were persuaded not to enlist in the first place.

"Promise me, you two," she said, at my father's wake. "Promise me you won't join up."

We'd been hearing both Mom and my brothers bitch about military bureaucracy, REMFs, and mission creep since before we could walk, so we weren't exactly enamored with the idea of a military career at that point (Charlie even less than me). Therefore, while we may have done so with exaggerated reluctance, it was an easy promise to make.

Still, Mom and Dad had always impressed upon the Clarke kids the merits of public service. Charlie went into the Peace Corps after college, which earned her some gentle ribbing from her oo-rah older brethren. But if we're being honest, helping provide network and Internet access to African villages seemed pretty worthwhile to me.

Anyway, that promise wasn't the one that led me to become a PI, but it was the reason I became a cop.

Like I said: public service. I had a degree in Criminology from the University of Houston and thought I could make a difference in my community. And I like to delude myself that I did so for about four years as a patrolman and three as a homicide detective. Until I was shot in the line of duty.

I woke up in the hospital (sound familiar?), only this time Mike and Charlie were there with Mom. People sent flowers, they talked about me on the local news for a few nights (the stories always accompanied by my none-too-flattering Academy graduation photo), and I was given the citation handed out to cops unlucky enough to get shot but fortunate enough to live.

Mike, stateside by then, was at my bedside at 7:30 a.m. on the morning after my surgery. He had driven six hours straight from training with the Marine Corps detachment in Goodfellow San Angelo to Houston. When I asked him why he didn't just catch a flight, he said the first one wouldn't have gotten to Houston until 10 a.m. The gunshot in question, courtesy of a drunk who took offense at my interrupting him in the act of beating the shit out of his girlfriend outside a country bar called the Rhinestone Cowboy, broke a rib and punctured my lung. Non-lethal it may have been, but it still ended up killing my police career. Seeing the anguish on Mom's face, I promised for the second time to make a (hopefully) less dangerous career choice.

I'd been weighing my career options already at that point, but that's a story for another time.

Charlie had by then returned from the Peace Corps and was making a killing doing computer security consulting (what they call "white hat hacking") for various energy companies. One afternoon, while clicking channels in my hospital bed, I happened upon a *Magnum, P.I.* rerun. Inspiration struck, and the rest is history, though convincing Charlie to sign on likely kept the whole thing from going under in the first year. Not only had she managed to hold her own growing up in a house full of boys, she was probably smarter than the rest of us put together.

We were currently set up in an old house on the north side of town, in the quote-unquote "up and coming" Lindale neighborhood, where we maintained a steady if not lucrative practice running skip traces and taking surveillance photos of unfaithful spouses. Though, if we're being honest, we caught people by their own dirty text messages about as often as with my long-range zoom lens. Use burner phones, people.

Gumshoe work may not dovetail as neatly into the Clarke family's proud tradition of public service, but at least I (usually) wasn't getting shot at.

My sister's office was in the house's converted master bedroom. She got the biggest of the three so she could have room for her computer equipment. Our electricity bill could support a house twice the size, probably with a pool to boot, but if her hacking into someone's iPhone meant I didn't have to take hanky-panky photos in the Houston summer sun while sitting in my Corolla with the twitchy air conditioner (remember what I said about "not lucrative"?), it was all good.

FIVE

Mike served with distinction in the Marines from 1996 to 2016. He earned a Silver Star and a Purple Heart in Afghanistan for a battle that no one was allowed to talk about (officially) and which he himself described as a "colossal shitshow."

As I've said, Mom and Dad were big on public service, so when Mike retired from the Corps, he signed on with the Department of Homeland Security. The Port of Houston is the sixteenth-busiest port in the world, handling well over 200 million tons of cargo per year. It also provides smugglers, traffickers, and terrorists convenient access to the Gulf Coast in order to do Bad Things.

Mike's reasons for joining DHS weren't entirely altruistic. Working at the Port also gave him some stability for his wife (he and Kayla got married right before his first deployment) and son (Tyler was ten), and helped keep him close to Mom, who was past 70.

After talking about it, Charlie and I realized we weren't entirely clear on what Mike did on a day-to-day basis. He was rarely in his office and spent the bulk of his day on the docks, inspecting shipping containers and the ships themselves.

"Don says he hasn't talked to Mike in the last three days," Charlie said, "and you said Mom hadn't either, so that burns up the sibling end." Mike was the only one with an official spouse. Charlie, myself, and now apparently Don, were single.

Jim, for all we knew, had multiple wives.

I thought for a second, "His office ought to have a personnel listing on its site," I said. "Can you pull up his supervisor's name?"

"Shouldn't be a problem," she said, navigating to the DHS website and clicking through a succession of online menus. "Here's Mike. He's listed as a Technical Enforcement Officer." She looked at me. "Sounds sinister."

I shrugged. "It's basically a cop; he gets to kick down doors, testify in court, all that fun stuff. And at the end of it, he gets a government pension."

"There's an address and a phone number," she continued. "Supervisor is an Assistant Director David Hammond. Do you want to call him or should I?"

"Neither," I said, getting up. "I'm going over there."

"Want me to come with?"

I said, "Tempting as the thought is, I doubt government security personnel are going to be very forthcoming when confronted by your Dead Kennedys T-shirt." I took the blue sports coat that was perpetually draped over my chair and shrugged into it. I'd forgo the tie, since my recollection was that few Port of Houston guys wore them.

Charlie affected a hurt look. "This is practically a classic. And what about you?"

"What about me?"

"You look like you got into a fight in the parking lot of a bar," she said.

I laughed. "These guys are law enforcement. All I have to do is add a few stylistic touches to my story and they'll be offering to buy me beers after work."

"That's just pathetic enough to be true," she said. "I'll see if I can find anything about what Mike was working on."

Grabbing my keys, I said, "I'll be back. Text me that address."

She paused. "You're taking *your* car?"

I stopped at the door. "Yeah. Why?"

She smiled. "No reason. But rather than worry about the reception my DK's shirt would get, you should be concerned they'll laugh you off the property when you pull up in that piece of shit."

I gave her a sincere finger and walked out to my car.

I have a few talents. For starters, it turns out I'm pretty good at the detective stuff (I had the highest clearance rate of my unit when I was on the force), I can also — as my sister already pointed out — take a punch (and occasionally deliver one). What else? I also possess an almost encyclopedic knowledge of James Bond movies, and I have a pathological inability to let things go. It's what Black Flag singer Henry Rollins once referred to as the "tenacity of the cockroach," though referring to it as a "talent" rather than a "mental defect" might be a stretch.

One thing I still haven't been able to let go of is my car.

My 1998 Corolla is my first car. Bought when I was still in high school with the proceeds of countless hours spent bagging groceries and trundling them to cars in the sweltering southeast Texas heat. It spends nearly as much time in the garage as it does on the street. And yet it's never (okay, rarely) occurred to me to go out and get another because I'm afraid to confirm my suspicion that the problem isn't the car, it's me.

The heap started on the third crank of the ignition, which is about average. It belched out a cloud of black smoke that eventually ran clear-ish, as if it were exhaling a particularly powerful bong load, and settled into what could charitably called "idling" as the engine veered between alarmingly high revs and near-death sounds.

Figuring it wouldn't get any better, I reversed out of the driveway and tentatively gave it gas.

Contrary to expectations, the Port of Houston isn't on the coast. Not exactly. The Houston Ship Channel runs from the Gulf of Mexico almost into downtown, and the Port proper is actually just off the east side of Loop 610, which is the innermost of the (now) three concentric freeway rings encircling our ever-expanding city.

Charlie texted me Mike's office address and I committed the cardinal sin of copying it and pasting into my phone's map app while driving. A disembodied, vaguely feminine voice eventually guided me to one of a seemingly endless series of warehouse complexes off Industrial Park Road. The thoroughfare is mostly free of trees, which is both atypical for the city itself and par for the course for the Ship Channel area. And it's hard to say whether this is a conscious landscaping choice or the by-product of the area's proximity to dozens of refinery complexes.

I parked in front of a building that was bigger than most, with a large American flag and new-ish letters indicating the agency's name over the entrance. I deduced the sign's age by noting it hadn't yet been stained brown by the combination of rain and pollution that hovers over East Houston.

The parking lot held a smattering of cars. Plenty of pickups, of course, and even an old H2 Hummer, the vehicle for the man with everything but self-esteem.

Being a weekday, the door was open, so I walked in like I had business there (which was actually true, when you got down to it). I strode up to the reception desk, where a nameplate informed me the woman looking at me with naked suspicion from under a distressingly large amount of hair was named Dot.

"Can I help you?" she asked, resigning herself to the fact I hadn't wandered into the wrong office by mistake.

I let loose with my biggest shit-eating grin, hoping it offset the black eye. "I certainly hope so, Dot. I'm here to see Dave Hammond."

She swiveled to look at her computer monitor, the distrust never leaving her face. "Do you have an appointment with Mr. Hammond?"

"I'm afraid this is more of an unofficial visit." I produced my wallet and flipped it open to my badge. "My name's Clarke, and I have some questions about the murder of Bob Ramirez."

Before you say anything, the badge is fake. Since it's a felony to impersonate a law enforcement officer, it's a good thing I made no such claim. I turned in my HPD badge when I resigned from the force. The one in my wallet was purchased for $19.99 from a police supply store just a few blocks from where I'd gotten into an altercation last night. It says "Investigator," which is technically accurate.

I took an exam and everything.

Dot ratcheted the glare back about thirty percent when she saw the badge, and she picked up her phone. "Mr. Hammond, there's an Officer …" She looks at me.

"Clarke, but it's not officer, thanks."

A look of puzzled irritation crossed her face, but she continued, "… Clarke to see you. It's about Bob." A pause. "Yes, sir."

She waved me to a door behind her. "He's right that way."

I rebooted my shit-eating grin as I walked past. "You're a peach, Dot."

She responded with what may have been a human vocal response and buzzed open the door to Hammond's office.

SIX

"Dave Hammond. Pleased to meet you."

My brother's boss was a large man that authors of a certain vintage would have described as "florid" but was now best described as "pre-cardiac." He pumped my hand with the kind of crushing grip affected by politicians with undisclosed sex scandals. I disliked him immediately.

"Cy Clarke. Likewise," I said, hoping my insincerity wasn't too obvious.

"That's a hell of a shiner, son."

I touched my eye like it was a mostly forgotten inconvenience. "Aw hell, you should see the other guy."

Hammond laughed and motioned me to a chair opposite his desk. "Please, have a seat."

I did so. On a hunch, I said, "Hey, is that your H2 out there?"

"It sure is," he beamed.

I liked him even less. "Hell of a vehicle," I lied.

He said, "I should tell you, I already told you HPD boys everything I know."

"Let me stop you right there," I said. "I'm not HPD. Used to be, but … well, that's a long story. No, I'm a private investigator. Mike Clarke is my brother."

It was difficult to read the full spectrum of emotion running across Hammond's face, but I'm pretty sure I caught relief, suspicion, and gradually, anger.

"Look, I don't know what you're trying to pull …" He began.

I held a hand up. "I'm just trying to find my brother, and to do that I need to know what he was involved with, or if there was anything going on at work."

Hammond's expression softened somewhat, but I could tell he was still pissed off and defensive. "I'm sorry about your brother. And if I knew anything that would help find him, believe me, I'd have already told the police."

"Yes, they said you were very cooperative," I lied, "but I was more interested in anything beyond the official record."

He seemed pleased by my bullshit. "Naturally I can't speak about current DHS cases," he began.

"Naturally," I said. I didn't care. Charlie could find all that out for me.

Hammond steepled his fingers in a way I'm sure he felt gave him extra *gravitas*. "Do you know what my division of Homeland Security does, Mr. Clarke?"

"I do not." It was true: I did not.

"We're one of many organizations attempting to put a stop to human trafficking in Houston. As you're no doubt aware, Texas is second only to California in the number of people — mostly women and children — brought to our country illegally, and thanks to our proximity to the Port and the I-10 and I-45 corridors, Houston is a major hub. DHS is very serious about changing that."

I nodded. "I think that's admirable, and I'm proud that my brother is part of that effort." That much was true.

"Well, we were — are," he corrected himself, "very proud of Mike as well. What did you say your name was?"

"Cy."

"Of course. Mike spoke of you often," Hammond said, his eyes avoiding contact with mine. Even if Mike wasn't my brother, I'd know he wasn't telling the truth.

"I know you can't speak about current investigations with a civilian," I said, "but can you talk about Mike? Did he seem himself in the last few weeks?"

He leaned back, crossed his legs, and thought for a moment. "Now that you mention it, he was acting more preoccupied than usual."

There are at least a dozen physical cues indicating when a person is lying, and Hammond had demonstrated nearly half of them in a few short minutes. Might as well try for all of them, I figured.

"Did he ever say why?"

"No, he didn't talk about his personal life all that much."

Except to sing his little brother's praises, I thought.

"Did he mention any problems with Kayla or Tyler? If he was going to confide in anyone, it would be you," I said this knowing full well Mike was not the kind of person to spill his guts to anyone not in his immediate family. And even then …

Hammond frowned. "Sometimes I'd hear him shouting at someone I assumed was his wife, but the door to his office was always shut."

"Why did you assume it was Kayla?" I asked.

He shrugged. "Who else do people yell at?"

I didn't feel like giving the guy an alphabetical list. Partly because I wanted to avoid the appearance of being a total sociopath, and partly because it wouldn't have mattered anyway. The day Mike Clarke yelled at his wife in front of other people would be the same day you could drive a Zamboni on the Lake of Fire.

"Like I told the police, I didn't notice anything off." Hammond shrugged. "I wish I could help you."

Here goes nothing, "I don't suppose I could take a look in his office?"

"The police have already been in there," he smiled, "and since you're no longer with HPD, I'm afraid it's out of the question."

I figured as much. This wasn't going anywhere, and I needed to leave while I was still barely on his good side. "Mr. Hammond, thank you for your time."

He stood, unable to hide the relief on his face. "I wish I could've been more help."

Oh, you were, I thought; *just not the way you were expecting.*

I left Hammond's office and, on a whim, approached Dot's desk again. Her expression would've daunted all but the most determined of suitors, but this was about my brother, dammit.

"I trust your meeting went well?" she asked warily.

I nodded. "Very well, thank you. Dave was very accommodating, I'm happy to say. In fact," I reached into my coat, as if I'd just remembered something, "he asked me to give you this."

I handed her my business card. One hundred for eight bucks, and I still wasn't sure it was a wise use of resources.

"He said if there were any new developments for you to please keep me in the loop," I said. "My email and office number are on there, but also my personal cell phone, should the need arise."

I gave Dot what I hoped was a sufficiently non-creepy grin and was rewarded with a look somewhat short of total disgust. It was hard to blame her after seeing my battered mug in the mirror that morning.

It was time to go, so I inclined my head to Dot and walked out. Once I'd cleared the office proper (and any potential hot government mics), I called Charlie.

"How'd it go?"

"About like you'd expect. He claimed not to know anything and clammed up about any current cases."

"I'm already on that," she said.

"I figured."

"You had to drive your ass all the way to the Ship Channel to get stonewalled?"

"No, I expected that," I said. "But I wanted to give him a chance to lie to my face."

"And did he?"

"Yeah, he told me Mike used to talk me up all the time."

She snorted. "Are you kidding?"

"He just assumed the Clarkes are your normal touchy-feely family, I guess."

"And not tremendous assholes," Charlie said.

I unlocked the Corolla — the fob had given up the ghost years earlier so I had to insert the key in the door like an animal — and said, "See what you can find out about what Mike was working on. I'm going downtown to see if any of my old buddies on the force feel like grabbing a beer."

The car started easily, probably because it hadn't had the

chance to cool down completely, indirectly proving what a waste of time my trip had been. I put it in gear and lurched back out of the parking lot, heading west into downtown.

SEVEN

There are benefits to being an ex-cop PI, just as there are disadvantages. The obvious perks include established contacts in the department. Several friends from the Academy were still on the force, and a few had been promoted to positions of real importance. I hoped one of them could point me to who was handling Mike's case and the Ramirez murder, if it wasn't the same person.

One drawback was I could no longer use the department's parking garage.

I parked on Travis Street downtown without feeding the meter ... a passive-aggressive move calculated to provoke the city into towing my heap to the impound yard, where I could let it die an undignified death.

Kate, the HPD receptionist, wasn't much friendlier than her counterpart Dot, but we had a passing acquaintance, so she approximated a smile as I approached.

"Uh oh, we have a Clarke sighting."

I grinned back. "Hey, they haven't put a Wanted poster of me up on the wall yet, I hope."

"What can I do for you?" she asked.

I leaned on the formidable granite counter that served as a barrier between Kate and the general public. "Can you page Roy DeSantos for me? See if he's in the building?"

"Sure thing." She pushed some buttons and spoke into her earpiece while I stood back and tried to look like I wasn't attempting a mild breach in law enforcement protocol.

Kate looked up at me. "Lieutenant DeSantos is not currently in the office, but I can send a message to have him call you. Does he have your number?"

I was pretty sure Roy did, but I gave it to Kate anyway. We exchanged pleasantries until someone came up in line behind me; I thanked her and walked out of the building. As I was walking to my car, my phone rang. Wonder of wonders, it was Roy.

"Hey, *Lieutenant* DeSantos." I emphasized his rank. "How's it hanging?"

"Clarke," he growled, "and just when I thought my day couldn't get any worse."

I laughed. "Lighten up, you big grump. I was going to see if you wanted to grab a beer."

"You buying?"

I sighed. No one in the department could remember when — if ever — Roy DeSantos had paid for a drink. "Don't I always?"

"Yeah, but you always bitch about it. Warren's?"

"See you in a few." I hung up.

May is when the Texas summer usually starts sinking its fangs into Houston. By mid-month you've probably seen 90-degree highs a few times, and the next cool front likely won't be until you're picking out Halloween costumes. Even so, there are still occasional pleasant days, and today didn't feel like it was going to top 80, so I decided to forego the car and walk the nine or so blocks from HPD headquarters to Warren's Inn.

One of the oldest remaining bars in downtown, Warren's was known for lethally heavy drink pours and near-crypt-like darkness, even at afternoon's peak. As a result, continued patronage was mostly guaranteed, especially from the city's chronically alcoholic population of lawyers and municipal employees.

My eyes took several seconds to adjust to the bar's gloom after leaving the sunlight outside. As they did, I saw the bar was doing a fairly brisk business for a Wednesday afternoon. About half the old booths were occupied, and an older woman I didn't recognize stooped behind the bar. It wasn't until I approached that I realized this was apparently a permanent condition. She glanced up at me expectantly.

"Lone Star?" A question rather than a statement, given the bar owners' lackadaisical approach to resupply.

She nodded and shuffled off to the cooler to fetch a can. I usually prefer draft but was glad to forego that to enjoy a drink in a bar that didn't feel the need to put TVs every five feet or play music at jet engine decibel levels.

The bartender brought my beer and I handed her a five, assuming that was enough. I once paid ten dollars for a pint of the same beer on vacation in Washington, DC, where I was told it was an import. Texas really is like a whole 'nother country.

I left a dollar of my change on the bar and she scooped it up with a speed belied by her arthritic frame.

Making my way to the rear of the bar, I spotted Roy entering; his bulk and close-cropped red hair were hard to miss. Nodding in my direction while peeling off his sports coat, he headed to the bar. In what had become an increasingly by-the-book city police operation, Roy still cultivated a reputation for playing fast and loose with regulations. The fact he'd made lieutenant meant either his superiors didn't care, or — more likely — he knew where in the bayou some key bodies were buried.

After a minute, he joined me at a booth with a clear drink that would pass for club soda if any of his HPD superiors were watching.

"Roy." He could've been one of my brothers; Roy Halladay threw a perfect game for the Phillies in 2010.

"Cy. You look like shit."

"But I have a song in my heart."

We sat down. "How's the dick life?" he asked.

I ignored the jab at my chosen profession. "Thanks for meeting me," I said. "I assume you heard about Mike."

He nodded. "I did. And all the guys wanted me to tell you they're going to do everything they can to bring him back safe."

"All the guys, huh?" I raised an eyebrow.

He shrugged. "Some of your so-called brothers in blue are always going to be down on you for leaving. Fuck 'em."

"Fuckin' A." Only a few years off the force had mostly cured me of the cop's penchant for constant profanity, but it was easy to get back in the groove.

Roy raised his glass and I clunked my can against it.

"Still, plenty of guys come back after getting shot," I said.

"And plenty more don't. Don't get caught up in that macho bullshit; you were lucky. Nobody with any sense would expect you to tempt fate again."

"You know that wasn't the whole story," I began.

He cut me off. "You had your reasons, and nobody who wasn't in your shoes can say they wouldn't have done the same goddamned thing."

The sentiment wasn't entirely unexpected, but good to hear nonetheless. "I appreciate it. So who's investigating Mike's disappearance?"

"I am."

Okay, *that* was unexpected, "You're shitting me."

He shook his head. "I shit you not."

"And the Ramirez murder?"

Roy was in mid-drink, so it took him a second to respond. "Homeland Security is handling it in-house."

"Is that … can they do that?" I thought for a second. "He's a federal agent. Doesn't the FBI have jurisdiction?

"Technically, but in case you hadn't heard, we're approaching record numbers of murders this year. It's technically a 'joint investigation' between us and the Feds, but I'm sure HPD is happy to share the load."

I nodded. "Still, it's good news you're on the disappearance." I caught the look on his face. "Or is it?"

Roy put his drink down. "Honestly? I don't know. They put me on it because I've been with the task force for a year or so and figured I'd know some of the players."

"Do they know about your connection to my family?" I asked.

"This is HPD bureaucracy you're talking about," he said. "Someone higher up might be aware you and I went to the Academy together, but I doubt whoever's handing out assignments has the free time to run down my tenuous attachment to the Clarke family."

That made sense. "Lot of Clarkes in Houston," I ventured.

"Are there?" Roy took another drink. "I hadn't noticed."

I switched gears. "Can you tell me anything about the case?"

34

"Not much. And I'm not being coy; we're still trying to put the pieces together."

"What have you got?"

"DHS raid on a compound in southeast, near Pasadena." He spread his hands. "On the order of twenty to thirty subjects being held within. Caretaker — or whatever you want to call him — clams up as soon as they kick the door in. '*No parlez Anglais*' or some shit."

I laughed. "Don't get many French smugglers around here."

"It was a joke, but you know that. Anyway, Ramirez is clearing the area with two other agents, one of whom is your brother, and ends up getting shot."

"By one of the smugglers?" I leaned forward.

Roy shook his head. "Don't know yet. All we know is Ramirez is toe tagged and nobody can seem to find your brother or this other agent."

"Cartel operation?" I asked.

"Possibly, but no way to be sure. The women were from all over, but primarily Central America."

"What's the other agent's name?"

He smiled. "Nice try, but I've already pushed the envelope of friendly interagency chatter. Hell, you're not even legitimate law enforcement."

"I'll have you know I'm fully accredited by the Texas Association of Licensed Investigators."

Roy made a gesture with his hand commonly referred to as a "wanking motion."

"Meaning you showed them a valid driver's license and their fifty-dollar background check didn't turn up anything. Look, Cy, I respect you, and I respect the hell out of your family —"

"Thanks for the qualifier," I said, a touch of bitterness creeping into my voice.

If he noticed, he gave no sign. "But you're not a cop anymore, and I'm not at liberty to discuss particulars on a murder with civilians, whatever esteem I may hold you in personally."

"Fine," I said, "there are always alternative methods to access that information, after all."

Roy offered the first genuine smile I'd seen since he came

in. "And how is Charlie?"

"Still out of your league."

"Ah, well."

As if receiving the same signal that the conversation was at an end, we rose. I offered my hand, and Roy gave it two vigorous pumps with his own trademark bone-cracking grip, very alpha male.

"Roy," I said, "I appreciate you meeting me. Take care of yourself."

He nodded. "You too, dick."

I sat down and finished my beer as he left, not looking forward to the walk back to my car. But it was only mid-afternoon, and if I hit the road now I could beat the bulk of the evening rush.

Convinced of the cunning and possibly foolproof nature of my plan, I walked back to where I'd parked the Corolla.

It didn't start.

EIGHT

The tow truck said they'd be at least 30 minutes getting to my location, which was something to be thankful for; I had waited upward of four hours in the hinterlands of West Texas during previous breakdowns.

There being no convenient places to cool my heels, I rolled the windows down on the car and called Charlie.

"Hey." Her enthusiasm was apparent.

"Hey," I said, "find anything out?"

"Some," Charlie said. "It turns out ... where are you?"

"Why?"

"It sounds like you're on the highway with the windows open. Corolla's AC shit the bed again?"

"Not exactly," I said, and explained my current predicament, which drew the expected laughter.

"I have never known anyone who needed to move to a city with mass transit more than you," she said, her chuckles gradually fading.

I nodded, watching a passing panel truck spew exhaust from a faulty muffler through my passenger window. "What did you find out?"

"That DHS raid where Ramirez got killed was a last-second thing."

"That's not unusual," I said. "Sometimes a tip comes in and they only have a certain window of time to act on it."

"Right," Charlie continued, "but that's usually indicated on the op request. There's a field on the standard agency form where you're supposed to reference the instigating contact, or the LEO or informer, but there's nothing like that here."

I considered that. "But at least it was a sanctioned raid, right?"

"Yes, but that's where it gets weird."

I was starting to regret leaving my windows open but heroically decided to soldier on through my impending carbon monoxide headache. "Weird how?"

She said, "First, contrary to what we've been told, Mike, Ramirez, and an agent named Chet Hanford took part in the raid."

"Go on."

"Before these reports are submitted, all agents and officers present are supposed to sign them. Hammond's signature is here, so is Hanford's—"

"But not Mike's," I finished for her. I knew how much she loved that.

An irritated exhale. "But not Mike's. For whatever reason, even though he's listed on the action plan and the summary write-up has him on site and entering the house, he never signed off on it."

I frowned. "Does the write-up say anything about what happened after they went in?"

"No. It mentioned Ramirez's shooting, but is mostly vague. Quote: 'DHS officer Ramirez was engaged in clearing ops and was fatally shot by assailants unknown. Perpetrator may have escaped through rear of property.' That's it."

"That syncs up with what Roy told me." I gave her the rundown on what I'd talked about with DeSantos at Warren's.

Charlie said, "You think you can trust him?"

Good question. "He always seemed like solid police when I was on the job. But he joined the trafficking task force not too long after I left, and there's a lot of opportunities for enterprising young officers there, if you know what I mean."

"But he was solid when you were there." A question masquerading as a statement. Charlie knew I had a tendency to withhold information and wanted me to testify to something I wasn't sure of.

I shrugged, even though she couldn't see me. "You heard

rumors about everyone, and Roy admittedly got more than his fair share, but I never personally saw any evidence he was on the take."

"You still haven't answered my question."

"Can I trust him?" I thought about that. "He could have blown me off instead of meeting me. And since what he told me is in line with what you found, it seems like the intel he gave me was legit. So, short answer … yeah, I trust him." About as much as I would any cop, I didn't add.

"He still gambling?"

"It didn't come up," I said, irritated. "Did you really expect me to ask about that?"

"Easy," Charlie said, "I'm just thinking of going to Vegas and wanted to know the skinny on the Texans' win totals."

I knew what she was getting at and ignored her. Alone among our siblings, Charlie was a Dallas Cowboys fan. A forgivable offense for Houstonians during the dark times between the departure desertion of the Oilers in 1997 and the arrival of the Texans in 2002. Charlie, however, had been a traitor since birth. It's a wonder Mom didn't leave her at a fire station.

"I'll bet you a hundred dollars straight up Houston wins more games than Dallas this year."

Her laughter was cruel. "You sure you want to risk that much? Don't forget, I can access your bank accounts."

That reminded me of something. "Speaking of access, do you think you can get into Mike's email?"

"Work or personal?"

"Did he have a personal email?" I honestly couldn't remember.

Charlie said, "Sure he did, he just never emailed you on it."

I sighed. "Work, then."

She thought for a moment. "It'll be tough. Government server, government encryption, and that's not even counting getting into the system in the first place."

I saw emergency lights in my rearview and turned to see a wrecker approaching. "I have faith. Gotta go, sis; my ride's here."

She said, "Okay, let me know what the damage is and I'll see if I can release some funds from petty cash."

"Cute."

"Talk to you later—wait!" Charlie said. "Did he ask about

me?"

"Who?"

"Who?" she mimicked. "Who do you think, jackass? Roy."

I smiled, "You're cutting in and out, sis. Must be all these skyscrapers." I ended the connection before the entirety of her "Asshole" came through, then stepped out into the increasingly sticky downtown afternoon to greet the tow truck driver.

As luck had it, I didn't need a tow, just a jump. The driver — real name Gabriel — told me I wanted to get a replacement battery before too long, but admitted a new DieHard battery might be more than the Kelly Blue Book value of the Corolla. We both had a good laugh over that.

Well, he did. I grimaced and paid him the $50.

My automotive hiccup had cost me more than just half a Benjamin: I was now firmly ensconced in Houston's dreaded rush-hour traffic. I avoided I-45 out of downtown and snaked my way north via North Main Street, which ran parallel to the interstate, before turning onto Quitman and avoiding the light rail by going all the way to Hardy and swinging north again to the office.

I didn't save all that much time, what with the stoplights, but there was something to be said for avoiding the freeways, where the concrete barriers always made them feel too much like a slaughterhouse passage for my comfort.

I walked into the office and tossed my keys onto the table with more force than was probably necessary. Charlie didn't look up.

"You've had a day."

"Occasionally productive," I agreed, "but now I have more questions than answers." I took off my sports coat and dropped it back on its usual perch, then took my chair, grateful that the living room's window air-conditioning unit had kicked in.

Charlie threw a wad of paper at me. "You have a message."

I retrieved it from the floor, where it had come to rest after bouncing off my head. "From who?"

"Someone named Dot," she said.

"Hammond's receptionist?" I asked.

"If you know more than one woman named Dot, we may

need to find you a therapist."

This was unexpected. I sat up and smoothed out the paper on my desk. "Isn't this a little analog for the likes of you?"

She smirked. "I know you don't like being texted while you're driving."

The message just had Dot's name and her phone number. I created a new contact in my phone with the information, then called her.

"Homeland Security, Assistant Director Hammond's office."

"Could I speak to Dot, please?"

"Speaking."

"Hi, Dot," I said, trying to sound convivial. "This is Mike's brother Cy Clarke. I was in the office speaking to Assistant Director Hammond a few hours ago."

"Yes, Mr. Clarke. I remembered you saying the Director wanted to keep you informed of new developments regarding your brother's case."

I *did* say it, that much was true. Hammond had said nothing of the sort, but there was no point confusing the poor woman.

"That's right. Has something happened?"

Something had. I let Dot give me the details and jotted them down as fast as I could. I thanked her for her time and promised I'd be in touch. Hanging up, I noticed Charlie had rolled her chair over to my desk.

"What's up?"

"Oh, nothing much," I said, "except it turns out Chet Hanford has been reassigned by the Department of Homeland Security."

Charlie wasn't at a loss for words very often, so I savored the occasion until she said, "Reassigned where?"

"Joint task force with the TSA, working out of Brussels. He's apparently in the field and won't be reachable for the foreseeable future."

She whistled low. "Wow, that's …"

She said "Suspicious" at the same time I said "Convenient." We could both be right.

NINE

It was the first time this many of the Clarke siblings had all
been together at Mom's since ... I couldn't remember. The last
Texans game, maybe. And since Houston's perennially
underachieving football team failed to make the playoffs (again),
that meant it'd been almost four months.

My mother's house was in The Woodlands, which wasn't
quite BFE but was far enough to count for Inner Loopers like
Charlie and me. And yet, even though we had the farthest to drive,
we were still the first to get there.

Mom's wasn't an especially big place, though larger than
she needed. Her military benefits (she'd gotten Lee's pension as
well as her own) meant she could afford a house with enough
bedrooms for grandkids, though at the moment she just had the
one. A fact that she never failed to gently remind her childless
(and, by definition, ungrateful) children.

Charlie threw her bag on the dining room table, an act
which normally would earn a rebuke, except the rebuker wasn't
currently at home.

"Where is she?" she asked.

I was idly going through the mail on the off chance there
was a clue to be found in a stack of AARP letters and coupon
mailers. "What?"

"Where's Mom?"

"She's over at Kayla's." I went back to the mail. "Maybe
she wanted to comfort herself by sitting shiva with her grandson

and daughter-in-law while us siblings come up with a plan."

Charlie asked, "Can you sit shiva if you're Episcopalian?"

"If you're as nonobservant as most of us are, I think it's fine."

"Poor choice of words, though."

"Why's that?" I asked.

She said, "Because 'shiva' is the first stage of the Jewish mourning period, and Mike's not dead."

I was proud of how sure she sounded.

"You learn something new every day," I said. "I thought it just meant 'hanging out with someone in uncomfortable chairs.'"

"*Oy gevalt.*"

My phone rang. I was surprised to see it was Jim calling.

"Hey," I said.

"Cy?" Jim said after a second.

"Who else? We're at Mom's. Let me put you on speaker." I did so and set the phone on the dining room table.

Charlie and I had supplanted him as youngest sibling when we were born, but if he was grateful for that he never showed it. Although he was as large as the rest of my brothers, he'd always been the most reserved.

"How you doing, big brother?" Charlie asked.

"Just working," he said. "The usual."

We exchanged a look. "What's the State Department up to these days?" I asked with half a smirk.

Jim said, "The usual. Diplomacy is never pretty. How's the private investigator business?"

"The usual," I said. "Car chases, running gunfights, hot chicks."

"And dudes," Charlie said.

He ignored both of us. "Is Don there?"

"I am now, big bro," Don said from right behind me. He was ex-Special Forces and moved like a goddamned panther when he wanted. I envied the bastard that, if not his taste in clothes. He dressed like a 20-something MMA fan with an NBA player's salary.

"Don, how much did those shoes cost?" Charlie asked. Don had parlayed his elite military training into a job providing executive security to oil and tech bigwigs, and CEOs were shockingly willing to pay much more handsomely to protect their own asses than they were to provide a living wage to their employees.

"Well, I was going to say 'more than Cy's car,' but I think the Keds I saw hanging from a telephone wire down the street are worth more than that piece of shit."

I hugged him, and Charlie followed suit. Here we all were, more or less; the last surviving/non-missing siblings of the Clarke family. It was becoming an exclusive club.

We took seats around the dining table without fanfare or prelude. We sat for a moment, looking around. The house looked like it always did: Mom's china displayed in her antique hutch, tastefully subdued cherry wood furniture, and more family photos than you could count, encompassing over seven decades of Clarke family history.

But every time our eyes fell on a picture of Mike, it felt sinister, like looking at a picture of a ghost. I wish I had Charlie's confidence in his well-being.

"So," Don said, direct as always, "what's the plan?"

I was about to speak when Charlie beat me to the punch. "Cy and I are on it."

"What does that mean, exactly?" asked Don.

Charlie looked at me, so I said, "I've already talked to Mike's boss, and we're looking at his case files and should have his emails shortly."

Don's eyes narrowed. "Mike's boss just gave those to you?"

"Not exactly," Charlie said.

Jim spoke up. "How legal is the course of action you're describing?" Whatever Jim's real job was, he did a fine job presenting as a by-the-book bureaucrat.

I said, "I'm not a cop anymore, so I'm not worried about warrants or probable cause."

"Damn straight," Don said. "Our brother's missing."

"It's not like we need to concern ourselves with rules of evidence," Charlie said. "Even though we're assisting the cops, it's in an unofficial capacity."

Don looked at my phone. "Jim, what's the problem?"

"None yet," Jim said, "but if they find whoever took Mike

and need to build a case against him, I don't want it fouled up because our two Columbos broke into something they weren't supposed to."

"Hey, Jim," Don said.

"What?

"You were in the Judge Advocate General's Corps when you were in the Navy, right?"

From the phone, Jim said, "Yeah, for six years. Why?"

"Because you're really acting like a JAG-off now," Don said, smiling without humor.

Jim didn't respond, as I knew he wouldn't. Don had a habit of provoking people, and it frustrated him that our older brother never took the bait.

"Look, Jim has a point," I said, and when I saw Don's nostrils flaring, I held a hand up. "But we have a little leeway from the police going forward, so don't worry about that." Charlie raised an eyebrow, but thankfully didn't do anything else, since what I was saying was mostly bullshit.

"Charlie thinks she should be able to access Mike's email," I continued. "And I'm going to meet with a lead I got from the Department. Meanwhile, the cops are all over this. I'm confident we'll find Mike before long." I wasn't, but no use telling them that.

"Who's your lead?" Don asked.

"What does that matter?"

He affected a thoughtful look. "Maybe I want to come with."

Jim cut in. "I don't think that's such a great idea."

"Why not?"

"Talking to people is a skill you never really mastered," Jim said.

Before Don could respond, Charlie said, "To be fair, some of Jim's concerns might actually come about if you start roughing up third parties."

Don smiled, then looked me up and down. "You look a little roughed up yourself, brother."

"That was an unrelated matter," I said.

"Oh, I'm sure."

"What happened?" Jim asked. "Cy, are you hurt?"

I said, "It was just a bar brawl, Jim. Nothing to worry

about."

"Ah." He'd heard this tune many times.

Charlie said, "Look, Cy and I do this for a living, and we're actually pretty good at it. Don, you've got your hands full with Kayla and Tyler. In fact, in many ways you have the toughest job of any of us."

Whoa, she was good.

"And Jim," she said, "it'd be great if you could check in with Mom every so often — do you mind?"

Jim said, "Of course not." That was magnanimous of the bastard.

Don spread his hands, the peacemaker now. "I just want Mike found. I'm happy to babysit while you and Cy run down what happened to him," He leaned forward. "On one condition."

"What's that?" I asked, though I already knew his answer.

"That when you find out who's behind this, you turn me loose."

"You talked to Carlos about this?" Charlie asked.

"We aren't married, and he's got plenty to do with the new law practice," Don said. "And you said it yourself: we all have to play to our strengths."

I said, "So it's agreed: Charlie and I do the legwork, Don keeps an eye on the wife and kid, and we all help with Mom."

General murmurs of assent all around.

"I'm signing off," Jim said. I hung up and pocketed my phone.

"Off chasing Bigfoot again," Don muttered.

"Are there Bigfoots in Belgium?" Charlie asked.

"You know what I mean. If Jim isn't working for the X-Files, I'll eat my shoe."

"You know that was a TV show, right?"

"Anyway," I said. "Who wants a drink?"

Now it was Don's turn to roll his eyes. "This is Mom's house. You going to pour some shots of cooking sherry?"

Charlie stood up. "The bottle of Grey Goose I brought for the Texans game should still be up there."

"Where?" Don was already up.

"Look behind Dad's martini setup." Al Clarke was the only one in the family who drank martinis, and the ancient shaker and strainer combo had sat mostly undisturbed on the top shelf of a kitchen cabinet for many years.

The vodka was there, so we drank a toast to Mike, and I had a sudden, unwelcome premonition of a wake.

TEN

In a general sense, I have faith in the institutions of our government. I believe the three branches, as conceived, were intended in good faith as effective checks and balances against each other. Certain events in our nation's history have demonstrated significant weaknesses in the conceptual framework, but — and call me an idiot — I still believe in the fundamental willingness of the majority of Americans to *want* to do the right thing.

But I'm also a realist, and I understand my experience is at odds with those who didn't grow up with the same benefits and support I had. Their relationship with their government is likely much more antagonistic than mine and colors their perceptions with distrust. Or even fear.

And it's because I'm able to hold both ideas in my head that I found myself once again in the Corolla, driving to Chet Hanford's house.

I wasn't entirely dim; I waited until later in the evening to venture onto the freeways. This after Charlie found his address in a matter of seconds, without even having to use confidential sources. "I'll be damned," she'd said. "He's on the appraisal district website."

I looked over her shoulder (which I knew annoyed her) as she pulled the address up. "Maybe it's a different Hanford."

Charlie shook her head, "'Chester A. Hanford.' Matches his paperwork with DHS. Parents must've been big fans of the twenty-second president."

"Twenty-first president."

She turned to look at me.

I returned her glare. "Chester A. Arthur was the twenty-first president."

"How the hell did you know that?"

"*Die Hard With a Vengeance.*"

Shaking her head, she scrolled through Hanford's residential listing. "Looks like he's been living in the same house since 2011. No other owner name, so either he's single or ..."

"Or he's one of those dudes who isn't comfortable letting a god-damned female cosign a mortgage," I finished. "But let's not jump to conclusions. Maybe he just hasn't found the right girl."

Charlie smirked. "Or maybe he putts from the rough."

"Such a smooth talker. Still, it is odd that he never scrubbed his name. Most LEOs take care of that pretty quickly."

"Maybe he doesn't know about it. Or maybe he wasn't in law enforcement when he bought the house."

Without waiting for my prompting, she went to LinkedIn and entered Hanford's name. "Not only wasn't he law enforcement before 2011, he hadn't even graduated college."

I pulled up a chair, because I was tired of standing behind her, and looked at Charlie's monitor. Hanford graduated from Texas State University (formerly Southwest Texas State, and a host of other names) in 2010, with a degree in business administration. DHS was his first employer, and he'd moved up the chain from analyst to technical officer in short order.

"He interned with the Border Patrol?" Charlie said, reading further down. "How does that work?"

"Maybe he changed batteries on the drones," I said. "This might work to our advantage, though."

"I'm all ears."

"Hanford's profile suggests he's someone who's going to toe the company line," I said. "DHS is the only job he's ever had, the only employer he's ever known, so maybe he hasn't developed that mercenary attitude that comes with realizing you're a disposable cog in the capitalist machine."

I could practically hear Charlie's eyes rolling. "When do we smash the means of production, comrade?"

"The point is," I ignored her, "if he didn't actually ship out, which I'm betting on, he might just stick close to home."

Charlie nodded. "You heading out there?"

"Yeah."

"Taking the Corolla out again?" she asked. "What does Princess Leia say to Han Solo? 'You're braver than I thought.'"

I said, "I can't justify buying a Corvette until my midlife crisis hits." Getting up, I said, "I have a hunch Hanford might still be hanging around his house.

"His name's on Hammond's official report," Charlie said.

"Meaning the police have it," I agreed. "Maybe I can poke around a little and see what turns up."

She stuck her fingers in her ears. "If you're planning to commit a crime, I don't want to hear about it." Pretty rich coming from someone who made a living out of virtual B&E.

I rose and grabbed my keys, smiling at her. "Since when have I ever planned anything?"

The sun was dipping below the downtown skyscrapers and I headed south on Lockwood. Hanford's place wasn't very far from the office, as such things in Houston are measured, and it was just nearing dusk as I pulled up to the East End house.

He lived in the solidly working-class neighborhood of Denver Harbor — a typically misleading name, as there was no harbor of any kind in sight. Many of the houses had chain-link fences or better around the yards to discourage interlopers. His pier and beam home on Sherman looked to have been spared from flooding by Hurricane Harvey, but a handful of neighbors weren't as lucky. Some homes were still boarded up, and water lines not cleaned by pressure washers were evident here and there.

I parked a few houses east of his, facing downtown, and rolled down my windows. Hanford's driveway was empty, which I'd expected, and like just about every other house on the street, there was no garage. Unless Hanford was one of the handful of suicidal types who biked to work in this town, he wasn't home.

When cops and folks in my line of work talk about the drudgery of the job, they're referring to stakeouts. I admit, it was one of the aspects of being a detective that really drove me nuts. Unfortunately, there's only so much one can do with record searches and online sleuthing. And at the end of the day, it's all about bringing in an actual human being and pressing charges.

But waiting for those human beings could be maddening.

Full dark came on as I stared idly at the house. There was no illumination there aside from the bulb on Hanford's porch. A group of kids rode by on bikes, coming from the direction of Eastwood Park. Traffic was light this time of evening, most folks were home from work and ensconced in evening routines of meals and TV. The first wave of dog walkers was likely to emerge soon and were sure to take note of the white guy cooling his heels in a parked car.

Surrendering to a combination of curiosity and impatience, I left the car and approached Hanford's house, taking a legal-sized envelope with me in the hope anyone glancing my way would see a deliveryman or courier. A quick scan confirmed nobody else was on the street, and I swiftly opened the lever latch on the gate and walked up the short sidewalk to his porch.

I mimed knocking on the front door for the benefit of anyone watching, peering through the textured glass of the window in the meantime. The inside was dark, except for what looked like LEDs from various chargers or appliance clocks.

Moving over to the front picture window, I peered in between a crack in the drawn curtains. There was some ambient light from exterior and street lights, but no sign of current habitation.

The curtains suddenly parted and a dog that looked at least two-thirds German shepherd lunged forward, barking furiously at me from the other side of the glass. I stumbled backward, catching myself before I fell off the rail-less porch.

The dog remained on his hind legs, snarling at me even as my fear subsided. Of course the guy had a police dog. I should consider myself lucky he wasn't hanging out on the porch.

I backed off the porch, keeping my eyes on the dog as if I expected him to jump through the glass. He dropped out of sight as I walked down the driveway and closed the gate behind me.

Shipped overseas, but didn't board his dog. Okay.

I was about to pull up stakes when a woman emerged from the house next to Hanford's. She was short and slightly stooped in posture, but moved self-assuredly. She swung the gate open at the head of her driveway, then retrieved her trash can and began wheeling it to the curb.

Conscious of the optics of a six-foot man approaching a diminutive woman on a dark street, I made sure the envelope was in clear view as I came near.

She was busy arranging the can just so — handle facing the street, so the garbage truck clamps could find purchase — so I halted about ten feet away. After admiring her work, she nodded, then turned and saw me. She was Asian and of indeterminate age, though north of 60. If she was frightened, she didn't show it.

"Hello?"

"Howdy, ma'am," I said. "My name's Brett Johnson. I was trying to see if Chet was home."

"Chet … you mean Mr. Hanford?"

"That's right." I didn't dwell on why an elderly person would feel the need to refer to a guy who was still shy of 30 as "mister."

"Doesn't look like it," She glanced at his house as if to confirm her own statement. "Something I can help you with?"

"No, ma'am," I said, holding up the envelope. "I'm a courier and I had a document for him. You don't have any idea when he might be returning, do you?"

She shook her head. "No. Haven't seen his truck in a few days."

Of course. "Well, if you don't mind, could I give you my card so you could let me know when he's in, Miss … ?"

"Nguyen," she said. She took my proffered business card, one of my various fakes, this one confirming my "Brett Johnson" persona. "Why don't you just leave the card for him?"

I sucked air through my teeth in an impressive display of apprehension. "Well, Miss Nguyen, it's kind of an official communication that has to be given to him in person, if you catch my meaning."

"Is that a subpoena or something?" Her eyes narrowed.

I put up my hands. "Oh, no ma'am! It's just some documentation from work. HR can get a little prickly if it isn't put in the right hands."

Looking at my card again, she said, "What's it worth to you?"

A businesswoman. I could respect that. "Twenty now. Twenty after I deliver the document."

"A hundred now."

"Twenty now, a hundred on successful delivery," I said. "A man has to protect his integrity."

I fished the bill out of my wallet and handed it to her, where it disappeared somewhere into the cavernous depths of her robe. Walking away, she held the card aloft. "I'll call you."

It didn't occur to me until I was driving away that my brief conversation with Miss Nguyen was the most I'd talked to a woman I wasn't related to in months.

ELEVEN

The ride back to the office was uneventful. I dared the main
lanes and was treated to the sight of refineries towering in the
night. East Houston sort of reminded one of *Blade Runner*, only
with tractor trailers instead of flying cars.

Charlie's Audi was in the driveway when I pulled up, so
she was still ostensibly "working." Unlike me, she maintained a
residence separate from the office. Also unlike me, she could
afford one. Though given the amount of hours she regularly put in
here, she might as well have her own bed and toiletries. I'd
suggested she could move in at one point in the past and soon
learned that not only was my sister capable of hysterical laughter,
she could also keep it up for quite some time.

Sure enough, she was back at her desk. The only evidence
she'd moved being the presence of a mug of what I deduced to be
ginger-lemon green tea, owing to both the lingering aroma of
ginger as well as the fact it was the only kind of tea she ever drank.

I used to be a hell of a detective.

"What have we got?" I asked from the kitchen as I pulled
out the French press.

"Are you making coffee?" she asked, not looking up. "At
eight o'clock at night?"

I grabbed a bag of roasted Costa Rican, frowning at its lack
of heft, and started spooning beans into the grinder. "I haven't had
any caffeine since this morning; just a beer with Roy."

Charlie said, "You'll never get to sleep."

"I never *go* to sleep," I muttered. Then, to her, "What have you got?"

"Not much," she said. "Just access to Mike's email accounts."

My hand hovered over the coffee grinder. "No shit? Which one?"

"Accounts. Ssss. Plural. DHS and Yahoo!, which he uses for his personal email," she said.

"Hold on a sec," I said, taking a moment to grind the beans to a coarse finish. I lifted the tea kettle, decided there was enough water for my needs, and set it on the burner before turning on the flame.

That accomplished, I walked over and pulled up a chair next to Charlie.

"Show me."

She slugged me in the leg. "Watch it with the orders, Mr. Man."

I rubbed my thigh. "Sorry, I meant, 'Please demonstrate for me how you accomplished this most Herculean of tasks, wise sister.'"

"That's better, but I can't demonstrate it for you, because I'm pretty sure I'd lose you forty-five seconds in. Suffice to say these guys really need to upgrade their OS. I used a known Windows 7 exploit to backdoor DHS's single sign-on mechanism and their own lax password protocols to crack into their client access server." She looked at me. "With me so far?"

"I, uh, think I hear the water boiling." I didn't, but it was close enough, and I hated it when Charlie went full techno-speak.

Her smirk was practically audible behind me as I poured the adequately hot water into the press. As the grounds steeped, I said, "Okay, so you hacked the Internet, how did you figure out Mike's password?"

"Which one?"

I rolled my eyes. "Surprise me."

"His DHS password was the hardest, probably because he had to adhere to agency standards."

"Let me guess, it can't be 'password.'"

Charlie said, "True, but that's about the extent of it. Certain words are off-limits: 'password,' any consecutive series of numbers, 'QWERTY,' 'Astros,' 'Rockets,' but not 'Texans,' curiously."

"Need to make it to a conference championship for that kind of respect," I guessed.

She laughed. "Maybe. Anyway, the only other real restrictions are the requirement for one capital letter and one number. As far as I can tell, he could've inserted as many special characters or wildcards as he'd like, but ..."

"Charlie?"

"Yeah?"

"My coffee's getting cold."

"Asshat," she muttered. "The point is, Mike only used one capital letter in the word, plus two numbers, which is the bare minimum."

I nodded. "Just like Jennifer Aniston's flair in *Office Space*."

Charlie ignored me. "From there I ran a simple Python script to brute force upper and lowercase and digits. Took about six hours."

"You have a snake?" I secretly understood about ten percent of whatever Charlie was talking about when it came to computers, but it helped to let her think I was even more ignorant than that.

"You're such a tool." She breathed in deep. "Man, that coffee smells really good."

"Here, I'll pour you a cup."

She held a hand up. "Forget it. I drink that, I'll be up until four in the morning. You must be some kind of mutant."

"Worst superpower ever," I said, and emptied the rest of the press into our carafe. "Okay, so that covers his DHS email, what about Yahoo!?"

"What a joke," Charlie said. "It was his wife's name and the birthday of his son."

I thought for a moment, "'Kayla0917?'"

"You are the world's worst brother," she said. "Tyler was born on August 5."

"Sorry. I think I have a mental block when it comes to that name."

"Could've been 'Braden.'"

"Give him time." I resumed my seat and looked at the monitor. "Did you find anything in his work email?"

Charlie nodded. "Plenty, but I'm not sure there's anything to use."

She brought up a series of tabs and started scrolling through them rapidly. I didn't bother trying to follow along until she selected one to show me.

"This is pretty indicative of his work email up until last week: weekly reports, meeting reminders, agency-wide bulletins, that sort of thing."

Okay," I said. "What happened last week?"

She said, "I'm getting to that."

Charlie scrolled through another series of tabs, of which there must have been dozens open across multiple browsers. How the hell she kept track of them was beyond me.

"Here we are," she said, pointing to the screen. "What do you see?"

I scanned the text of the Outlook form. "There's an update about suspicious activity at the Port," I said. "Hammond's telling his subordinates to prepare for possible extra-office action." I looked at her. "So?"

"Keep reading."

I did so, then stopped. "What the hell is that?"

At the bottom of the email, below Hammond's email signature, was a line with six characters, then an unbroken string of what appeared to be random text. "Is that PGP encryption?"

Charlie turned to me sharply. "What do you know about that?"

"Hey, I pay attention sometimes," I replied.

"I'm gratified to hear it," she said, "but what you're thinking of is a PGP public key, appended to the end of an email, and that's not what this is."

I said, "Then what is it?"

"It's a cypher," Charlie said, a smile dawning on her face.

"A cypher," I repeated. "Like code? Hammond sent this?"

"Not Hammond," she said. "Mike. Look at the subject line: 'FW' means he forwarded this to himself and added the cypher at the end of it."

"Why?"

"I have no idea."

"Well, what does it say?"

"I have no idea," she said again, "but I bet these initials have something to do with it,"

She pointed to the nine characters above the gibberish. "C2U0J9M7D," I read. "What are they supposed to be? A license plate? Phone number?"

She sat back, her smile fading. "It's a key of some type. The rest of Mike's emails are the same boring office crap, until we get to three days before he disappeared, then they all have this text added to it."

This was getting strange. "Is it the same text each time?"

"The text is the same, but without knowing what the key is, I have no way of deciphering it."

I rubbed my eyes. "Just our luck the disappearing sibling turns out to be an Enigma enthusiast."

"Yeah," Charlie said, and rose from her seat. "I'm out, little brother. I downloaded most of the directory contents in Hammond's secure drive, but there's a lot to sift through, and it's been a long day. I need to recharge if I'm going to crack any of this." She gave my arm a squeeze, which was about as close as we usually got to hugging.

"Try to get some sleep," I said.

"You too. You want to be fresh for family night… ."

I sat up. I'd clean forgotten about going to Mom's tomorrow, and from the shitty look on Charlie's face, she knew it.

"Night," she said, closing the door behind her. I could hear her soulless cackling all the way down the path to her car.

Luckily for me the scary guy called before I had much time to dwell on it.

TWELVE

The phone screen showed UNKNOWN CALLER, meaning I should have known better. But I really liked to give those fake IRS agents shit, so I answered.

"Clarke?" A tentative inquiry, to be sure.

"Speaking."

Breathing now, but more ragged than heavy. This was shaping up to be the worst obscene phone call of all time.

"Still there? I gotta say, if this is the IRS, I don't know anything about those Swiss bank acc —"

"You need to back off."

I'd been reclined in the chair with my feet up on the desk, but sat up. "Do I now?"

"Yes." The person on the other end of the line had an almost comic Russian accent. I decided right then his name was Boris.

"Okay, great. Uh, thanks for calling?"

"This is not a joke."

I went to the window. It was a straight-up noir cliché, I knew: the sinister figure calling from the shadows right outside the house. And besides, there probably wasn't a functioning phone booth within two miles of me.

I looked outside anyway. Nothing there.

"Are you sure? Because this is all pretty funny."

"You won't think so when we're breaking your fingers."

He pronounced the W in "won't" and "when" like a V. I

wondered if his Vs turned into Ws, like "nuclear wessels."

"Look, Boris …"

"My name is not Boris."

"I don't give a shit," I said. "But maybe if you could tell me exactly what I need to back off from, we could come to an agreement."

"You know what —"

"For example," I interrupted, "if this is about the fact I haven't watered the grass in three months, I'd remind you our neighborhood doesn't actually have a binding homeowners association agreement."

"That's not —"

"Also," I continued, "I think it's fairly obnoxious to expect us to deplete our water supply for our yards. Now is the time to rise up against the tyranny of Big Lawn! Wake up —"

"We know where your sister lives."

It was the flat, emotionless way he said it that cut me off, and "wake up, sheeple" was always my favorite part of my anti-lawncare diatribe.

"Is that a fact?"

"It is," said Boris. "And as long as you stop snooping around the Ramirez shooting, she'll be just fine."

"The Ramirez shooting," I repeated.

"Not such the comedian now, are you?"

My mouth was always causing problems. I developed into an incurable smart-ass early on, a condition not helped by the existence of four big brothers who loomed in the imaginations of potential bullies every time I cracked wise at school. Ironically, it was joining the force, and learning to develop relationships with the community and rapport with citizens, that kept it briefly in check.

However, now that I was a civilian again, all bets were off.

"Still there, Clarke?"

"Sorry, I was just trying to imagine how small a penis a man must have in order to threaten a defenseless woman."

"What?"

"You heard me, needle dick." My tone was light, and I had to keep myself from snort laughing when I referred to Charlie as "defenseless," but my non-phone gripping fist was clenched hard enough I heard knuckles crack. "You've got a beef with me, then that's just the way it is. But leave my sister out of it, because if anything happens to her, I will reach down your throat and strangle you with your own fucking intestines."

I hung up on Boris before he had a chance to splutter whatever dime-store threat he'd saved up. Now that I knew he was referring to the Ramirez thing, I didn't need to indulge his bullshit theatrics anymore.

My phone buzzed. UNKNOWN CALLER again. I sent it to voicemail and called Charlie.

"Hey," she said.

"Hey yourself. You home yet?"

"Just got here. Why?"

I gave her the briefest of rundowns on my conversation. "Just thought you should know."

She said, "I appreciate it. You going to be okay there? Maybe you should bunk with me for a bit."

"Nah," I said. "I'll be harder to get to at your place, and I kind of want them to make a move."

"The better to suss out who it is."

"Yeah," I agreed. "Or to put an end to their BS straight away. Make sure you're buttoned up tonight, okay?"

"Will do. What about Mom?"

"They didn't explicitly threaten her," I said. "And unless these guys are even dumber than I think, they had to have noticed the constable car parked across the street."

Charlie said, "And Kayla's staying with her."

"I'll call them in the morning," I replied. "For now, just stay alert."

"Will do. Night."

"Night." I ended the call and looked to see if Boris had left a message. No such luck.

This was an interesting development, I thought as I undertook the laborious task of checking the locks on all the doors and windows. Was Boris's apparent Russian accent a coincidence, or was I dealing with an international issue? Was he also threatening DHS folks like Hammond? Or cops like Roy? Those guys were more likely to have an impact on the case than me. I was just trying to find Mike.

Maybe Boris was, too.

"Jesus, this house has a lot of windows." I worked my way up to second floor and seriously wondered what good it was doing. Any individual could gain ingress to a dwelling if they were determined enough, a lesson I'd learned quickly while on the force. And you didn't have to be especially determined to bust into a house built before central air-conditioning.

Which was one of the things that made Boris's threat against Charlie so hilarious. He was undoubtedly counting on my protective instinct as a sibling, as well as the heightened nature of the implied threat against a helpless female.

The thought made me smile as I drew the curtains on the last upstairs window. Neither she nor I had served in the military, obviously, but neither were we naive. I'd seen enough horror as a detective to tide me over for the rest of my adult life, and I don't care what hippy-dippy impressions of the organization you might have, no one serves in the Peace Corps in Africa, as Charlie did, without seeing some shit. I only knew a few of the details, but even though she'd been posted in the relatively hospitable confines of Zambia and Namibia, that didn't mean conflict hadn't spilled over from neighboring countries. Conflicts which sometimes required Charlie's … direct attention.

Besides, her house was wired for security, with cameras covering every entranceway, the backyard, and her street for a block in either direction. The alarms were loud enough to temporarily paralyze any interloper, which should give Charlie ample time to get to her panic room.

"Panic room" was a misnomer, though. The place was more a combination command center and armory. From there, she could cool her heels while talking to the cops, or grab a weapon and do some hunting. This was Texas, after all, and there wasn't a jury between El Paso and Beaumont that'd convict a person for blowing away someone who'd broken into their house, especially after said someone was stupid enough to make threats on a phone call.

As I turned the lights off and armed my own (relatively meager) security system, I almost found myself hoping Boris *et al.* did try something.

I wouldn't be surprised if Charlie was hoping that too.

THIRTEEN

In spite of all my assurances to Charlie, it actually took me a while to fall asleep, though I chose to think it was more because of the phone call than the caffeine. Once I finally drifted off, it was into restless sleep. If I dreamed, I didn't remember it.

The sun was almost up when I woke, and I had to fumble for my phone to see what the actual time was. I don't keep a clock by the bed because I'm an idiot. Also because I hate waking up in the middle of the night (which often happens) and seeing how many hours remain before I have to get up.

There are medications for this, I assume. For now, the phone works just fine.

The first thing I did upon rising (well, after the obvious stuff) was check the doors and windows. Everything seemed in order, so I fired up the security camera footage. Charlie set up the surveillance and was kind enough to create an icon called SNOOPY on my desktop so I could access it without having to do anything more strenuous than click the mouse.

I fast forwarded through the fairly mundane video. Aside from various cars driving by and another appearance by the big bastard of a possum who I'm pretty sure lives under the porch, the night passed without incident. Guess I'd have to wait a little longer for Boris to make his move.

I checked my email next, scrolling through the usual spam and seeing if there was anything pertaining to current or old cases. I sent a couple of invoices (resending, in one case) for services rendered, and that pretty much covered my clerical duties for the day. Now came the less fun part: talking to people.

Roy was first, as he needed to be informed about the phone call. His phone rang for a while and I had just enough time to wonder how early it actually was when he finally answered.

"Clarke?"

"Hey buddy, did I wake you?"

"What time is it?"

I looked at the clock on the desktop and cringed a little. "It's seven … ish."

He said, "It's 6:40 in the goddamn morning. Who the hell calls that early?"

"I'm genuinely sorry, man," This was mostly true. "But there's been a development in my brother's case."

That seemed to placate him. "Tell me."

I gave him what overpaid consultants like my sister refer to as the "ten-thousand-foot view" of my conversation with Boris, including the threat against Charlie, but leaving out most of my own hilarious contributions.

"Interesting," Roy said. "How did Charlie take it?"

The man was as predictable as the tides. "She's fine. Honestly, I think she's hoping they try something."

"Your family has a weird attitude toward imminent danger."

I said, "I'm not convinced there is any danger. Right now, I think there's just as good a chance it's a red herring as a genuine threat."

"What kind of red herring?"

"If you're trying to be menacing and mysterious, why pick the guy who sounds like he came out of an eighties Chuck Norris movie to make the call?"

"You don't think there's a Russian connection?" Roy asked.

I said, "I mean, I can't discount any possibility. It just seems a little on the nose, is all."

"I know someone you can talk to, if you want to follow up," he said.

"Give me a sec." I fished through the desk, looking for a pen. It was the curse of working with someone who used a keyboard to enter every conceivable piece of information that you couldn't find a writing instrument when you wanted one.

"Any time," Roy said.

"Shut up. You weren't exactly swamped when I called."

I finally found a pen: a promotional item from Minute Maid Park, given out at a past Astros game and festooned with orange and blue fuzz. Beggars can't be choosers.

"Go."

He gave me a name and an address that sounded familiar and off at the same time.

"6000 North Freeway? Is that a car dealership?"

I could almost hear his shit-eating grin over the phone. "Not quite. It's the address for Bottoms Up."

A strip club. I groaned. Of course. "You don't have a home address for this person?"

"Sorry, buddy," Roy said, in a tone that was anything but. "Bring plenty of ones."

"Yeah, screw you too."

"You have a great rest of your day." He hung up.

It looked like I was going to have to squeeze a visit there into my itinerary, presumably before the get-together tonight. That reminded me: I needed to call Mom.

She picked up on the first ring, because of course.

"Hello, Cy."

"Mom, how are you holding up?"

She sighed. "I'm making it, which is all any of us can ask. Have you heard anything more?"

I thought it best not to bring up the phone call. "I have a lead I'm going to check out, and I'm talking regularly with the police working the case," I said. "Charlie's also reading through Mike's email to see if there's anything helpful there. We'll find him, Mom."

"Oh, I know," she said. "I just feel helpless. Kayla's staying here with Tyler, and all we can do is wait for the phone to ring and watch HGTV."

The horror, I thought. Mary Clarke forced to go to ground in her own home was too terrifying to imagine. Maybe she was teaching her grandson some *aikido*.

"How's Tyler doing?" It felt like the right thing to ask,

even though everything I knew about raising kids came from watching reruns of *The Brady Bunch* while hung over in college.

"He's holding up, I suppose. Do you want to talk to him?"

"What? No, that's —" But she was already calling for him. This day was off to a bang-up start.

A child's voice. "Uncle Cy?"

"Hey, slugger." I think Mike called Cousin Oliver that once. "How's it going?"

"Okay, I guess," Tyler said. "Do you know when my dad is coming home?"

Oof. "Tyler, your mom and grandma and me — and all of your aunts and uncles — are doing everything we can to find him. Do you believe me?"

"I guess so," he said.

I bulldozed ahead. "Your aunt Charlie and I are working really hard over here to bring him home, okay?"

A pause. "You promise you'll bring him home?"

Christ. "Yeah buddy, I promise I'll find your dad."

"Thanks, Uncle Cy. Here's Grandma."

"All right, pal. Love you."

"Love you, too."

There was some shuffling as he handed the phone back to Mom. "You did good," she said.

"I promised a little kid I was going to find his missing father. If Mike turns up dead, he's going to hate me for the rest of his life."

"Then you better make sure that doesn't happen," she said. "Do you want to talk to Kayla? I could wake her up —"

Oh god. "No, Mom, I need to get to work. Just tell me what you need me to bring over tonight. If we're still doing this."

"We are. The family needs to be together at a time like this. You're on plates and plasticware duty. Also, I need you to pick up some brisket from Ruzicka's."

"There's always a line at Ruzicka's," I said, conscious of the whine that had crept into my voice. "Bubba's is closer."

"Bubba's is crap, and you know it," she chided. "Are you getting a ride with Charlie?"

"Only if you want me to get there on time instead of pushing my car two miles," I said.

"I think I told her to make the pie, but please remind her. We'll see you at six o'clock."

"Okay. Hey, wait a minute," I said.

"Yes?"

"You always have Charlie cook or bake something, but I either bring plates or drinks or pick up barbecue. Why?"

Her reply was brutal in its matter-of-factness. "Because you're a lousy cook. See you tonight, dear."

"Take care, Mom."

"You too."

And it was on the heels of that heartwarming familial conversation that I made plans to visit a titty bar on a Thursday morning.

FOURTEEN

The history of strip clubs in Houston is as sloppy and confusing as that of the city itself. While they're not as prevalent as in years past, they still occupy a distinct niche in the city's landscape. From higher-end establishments tucked away in the Galleria area to the casino-like freeway places to the occasionally terrifying "all-nude" joints (which are BYOB, thanks to the state's Byzantine liquor laws), there's undoubtedly something for every prurient taste out there.

The city ordinances concerning so-called sexually oriented businesses are similarly all over the place. Dancers have to maintain three feet of distance from patrons, unless you're one of the baker's dozen clubs that sued with the city and won the right to ignore the so-called "three-foot rule," provided they donate a chunk of their proceeds to an anti-trafficking fund.

What else? Your club also has to be at least 1,500 feet from a school, church, public park, or day care. And if that sounds like no big deal, you've clearly underestimated the number of churches and parks in this town.

What shouldn't be glossed over is the role these places play in trafficking. *Beverly Hills Cop* notwithstanding, as someone who's occasionally been tasked with tracking down runaway kids, I know better than to blow off a lead just because it's going to take me to a "gentlemen's club."

The name Roy gave me was "Nevaeh," which is — you guessed it — "heaven" spelled backward. New to me, but a cursory web search showed it growing in popularity in recent years. Beats "Chardonnay," I guess.

Bottoms Up didn't open until 11 a.m., and even that seemed weird. I mean, I've heard of guys who eat meals at strip clubs; I just assumed they were mythical creatures like leprechauns or honest city politicians. I figured the best course of action was to get my dinner errands out of the way and call in the brisket order so I wasn't cooling my heels at Ruzicka's for an hour.

As is often the case when you're not actually in a hurry, both of those things took me less than 45 minutes, and so it came to pass that I found myself parked in the Bottoms Up parking lot at 10:30, looking not at all like a stalker lurking in wait for the ladies.

The club itself was nondescript. "Gentlemen's clubs" in this city either advertise their intent in the most garish way possible or attempt to stay under the radar, and Bottoms Up had evidently decided it was better to try and avoid the notice of ordinary commuters or evangelicals. The stucco facade was the sort of dull brown that could have been intentional or merely the result of proximity to freeway exhaust from I-45.

It was also, as is the case with most such establishments, completely lacking in windows. I don't have a lot of rules I live by, but "avoiding bars without line of sight inside" is one. The other is "never ask a woman if she's pregnant." Trust me on that one.

There were a handful of cars scattered near the rear of the parking lot, and I assume they belonged to kitchen or cleaning staff. I was checking my phone for the weather forecast when I heard footsteps in the gravel approaching the driver's side of the car.

I turned, and only the fact I had left the window down kept me from exclaiming in surprise and/or fear. The man outside my car was almost as wide as he was tall, with a regular tossed salad of a face (cauliflower ears, potato nose, tomato complexion). His hair looked like his mother had skipped the customary bowl and instead stuck his tongue in a light socket and hacked away at the strands as they stood straight up. His arms drooped so low I began to question mankind's inability to find the missing link.

In short, this was not an attractive man.

"Morning!" I offered. It was worth a shot.

"What do you want?" It came out more "whuudyawunt,"

but I got the gist.

I chin-pointed to the front door. "Just waiting for y'all to open up. Got a hankering for some prime rib." I hoped the online flyer I'd seen advertising their lunch specials was current.

Kong Jr. didn't say anything; he just blinked a few times before turning and continuing to the front door of the club. I checked my rearview mirror and looked behind me but didn't see a car. Almost like he'd … materialized out of thin air.

Or gotten off a bus. That seemed more likely.

I watched him trudge up the stairs and knock on the door. It opened after a second and, after a last glance in my direction, he entered. If that guy was floor security, this was going to be a hell of a visit.

Minutes ticked away and some of the dancers started showing up, one or two in cars, the others dropped off by (I assumed) significant others. How does *that* conversation go, I wondered? "Have a nice day at work, try not to let any truckers stick a finger in your ass"?

I didn't see anyone who looked like a "Nevaeh," but then, Roy hadn't bothered with a description. Undoubtedly, he found the idea of me wandering through a dimly lit bar and clumsily asking every girl their name hilarious.

I waited until about ten minutes after eleven to get out of my car, reasoning that no one inside would be especially enthusiastic about the Thursday lunch crowd. And sure enough, I was the only customer in sight as I approached. Screwing my sense of fatalism to the sticking place, I walked up the steps and tried the door. It swung inward.

If you've never been in a strip club, the first thing that's likely to strike you is the darkness. They keep the lights way low in these places, for a variety of reasons. Romantic types would say it's to preserve the mystique of the exotic beauties on the prowl therein. Assholes like me would speculate it's a lot easier to table dance for Jethro and his oilfield buddies if you can't see their acne scars and ingrown hairs.

As my eyes adjusted, I realized the shape in front of me wasn't a chest of drawers, but was in fact my old buddy from outside. He was wearing a name tag that read "Nigel," and my faith in the inherent comedy of the universe was restored.

He looked me up and down. "Ten bucks."

I craned my neck past him and the lady in the cashier booth. It looked like there was a large center stage and at least one side stage in view. Neither were occupied at the moment.

"Ten bucks? You expect me to dance as well?"

Nigel looked over at the girl in the booth who was doing a hell of a job avoiding his gaze, then back at me. "Ten bucks."

I wasn't looking forward to getting in a scrape with this guy, especially before I'd even set foot into the club proper, so I took out a twenty and handed it to the cashier. She placed it in a drawer and asked, "You want the change in ones?"

"Sure," I said. I wouldn't be making it rain. At best my cash would be like spitting off an overpass.

She handed me the bills and stamped the back of my hand in case I wanted to make a day of it, and with that I was turned loose into the bowels of Bottoms Up.

There was literally no one else in sight as I scanned the room. As it turned out, there were two secondary stages, but I didn't want to be near any of them. I found a two-top more or less centrally located and sat down. And I wasn't entirely alone; there was also a skinny young man in a T-shirt I couldn't read past the "Keep Calm" part shuffling around in the DJ booth next to the main stage.

After what felt like an hour, a waitress emerged from the back. She wore a bustier and heels and my arches immediate ached in sympathy.

"Get you a drink?"

I placed another of my twenties onto her tray and said, "Is Nevaeh here?"

"Who?"

Was I pronouncing it wrong? "Nevaeh? Nuh-vay-uh? Nee-vee-yeh?"

Recognition bloomed in her face so brightly I almost didn't notice her pocketing the sawbuck. "Oh, you mean Ne*vaeh*," She pronounced in like "navy," because of course. "She might be in the back."

"Could you check for me, please? I need to talk to her."

"Uh-huh," She gave me Nigel's patented once-over, or maybe it was a Bottoms Up special. "And who are you? You a cop?"

"Not at present." I handed her one of my rapidly dwindling supply of cards. "My name's Clarke, and I'm following up on a missing person case."

She turned the card in her hand like it was written in Mongolian instead of English. "We don't have any missing people here."

I forced a smile. "Well, that's good news. But see, I don't think the person in question is here, but I think your boss might have some information that will help me find them."

I could tell the conversation was already boring her, dashing my fleeting dreams of going home with a waitress, Warren Zevon style. "You want anything to drink?"

"Coffee?"

"I'll have to make it," she sniffed.

"Okay."

That really didn't seem to be the answer she wanted to hear, as she turned and stomped off to the kitchen, if what she was doing in heels could adequately be described as such.

A single spotlight kicked on, illuminating the center stage at the same moment the first chords of "All Right Now" by Free came out of the PA system. I watched as a tall brunette in a bikini walked out with all the enthusiasm of a hung-over high school student entering an SAT prep class, adjusted her bathing suit top, and draped an indifferent leg around the pole.

"Ladies and gentlemen," the DJ intoned, "please welcome Crystal to the center stage. Give it up for Crystal, everybody."

I applauded as enthusiastically as I felt the situation warranted, considering I was still the only person in the place. Trying to win back some of the karma I'd lost on the waitress, I approached the stage, dollar bill in hand. Crystal ignored me for an impressive minute or so, then dropped to the splits in front of me. She tugged out the strap of her bikini bottom and I dutifully slipped the dollar bill in.

"Read any good books lately?"

She smirked. "*The Human Stain*."

I think I'm in love, I thought as she rose to her feet and meandered back to the pole. I watched for what I felt was the appropriate amount of time to not come across any more of a creep than I already did and turned back to my table.

A woman was sitting there.

She seemed a little older than me, but it was hard to say for sure. Her blonde-ish hair flowed like Jane Fonda's in *Barbarella*, and her pantsuit combo was both very businesslike and wholly out of place for her surroundings.

"Nevaeh, I presume?" I sounded like I was introducing the erotic adventures of Stanley Livingston.

FIFTEEN

"Do you need a drink?" Nevaeh asked. She had the faintest trace of an accent, which my linguistic expertise pegged to anywhere between Estonia and Kamchatka. Between impeccably manicured hands, she cradled a mug that read "World's Greatest Grandpa." I had questions.

"I ordered coffee," I said. "I think I annoyed the waitress."

She grimaced. "Brooklynn's always annoyed. Occupational hazard."

"I suppose so." *Especially with a name like Brooklynn*, I thought. "Anyway, thanks for agreeing to talk to me," I began.

She held up a hand, "I'm not entirely sure why you're here, Mr. ...?"

"Clarke." I already had a business card ready and handed it to her. She glanced at it and stowed it in an inner jacket pocket. "A mutual acquaintance gave me your name. They thought you might be able to help me with some information."

"What kind of information?"

Hoping I wasn't overextending myself, I said, "Information about smuggling girls into Houston. Would you know anything about that?"

Her eyes flickered, but if she was angry she wasn't showing it. "Did you say a 'mutual acquaintance'?"

"I did."

"And you're not a cop?"

"No. Used to be, but I've been private for a few years

now," I said. "Brooklynn already asked me that, in case you were wondering."

"Was our mutual acquaintance a cop?"

She wasn't going to let it go, and I was starting to get irritated, especially since my coffee was nowhere in sight.

"Does it matter? If it'll speed things along, then yes: They're a cop. But I'm not here as part of any official investigation." Not entirely a lie, but let's not dwell on that. "I'm looking for a missing person who might be connected to a trafficking raid that went down in Southeast a few days ago."

Her expression hadn't changed, but I thought I detected a thaw in her demeanor. "All my girls are legitimate, Mr. Clarke."

"No doubt."

"If I knowingly dealt with those kinds of people, I'd get even more attention from people like *our mutual acquaintance* than I already do, understand?"

The "knowingly" was a tell, but I let it slide. "Of course, but you know something about the other side of the business, don't you? Or you used to."

She looked away, just for a second. "The past is the past. Keeping my nose clean isn't just for the police's benefit, if you catch my meaning."

I did. And if she'd truly managed to free herself and her business from any ties to the Russian Mafia, she deserved a hell of a lot of credit.

Might as well put my cards on the table. "Nevaeh, or 'Navy' — or whatever your real name is — my brother has gone missing. He worked for Homeland Security and hasn't been heard from since a raid he may have participated in. A fellow agent was killed on that raid, and my brother may know something about it. My family and I just want to find him so we'll know he's safe."

The waitress approached the table and we both sat back, like a couple of boxers at the bell. She set the coffee in front of me, and I was momentarily distressed to discover I wasn't a "World's Greatest" anything.

She left, and Nevaeh regarded me again. "You used to be a cop. Your brother is a cop. ..."

"Well, a kind of cop," I said.

"He works for the government and wears a badge." She

smiled. "That counts in my book."

"That's fair. Except right now I'm private. I don't care what kind of, uh, *shenanigans* go on at your Happy Bottom Riding Club. …"

"Bottoms Up."

"Whatever," I said.

"My place is aboveboard," she said. "Well, as much as any."

"Like I said, I don't care. My only concern is my brother."

She looked around the club. Aside from the DJ and "Crystal," we were still the only people in sight.

"What kind of information do you want?" she asked.

"Nothing too specific." I leaned forward. "I'm not trying to put the finger on you. But if you could give me a nudge, my family and I would really appreciate it."

Nevaeh sat in silence for a bit. Or as much silence as the Def Leppard song now playing in the background allowed.

"Do you know what life is like for those girls, Mr. Clarke?"

"No, I don't."

"Very few of them have any idea what's waiting for them when they come over here. If they do, it's because they were kidnapped from villages in Moldova or Belarus, or sold by their parents or 'boyfriends' for the equivalent of fifty American dollars to the gangs. They might be the lucky ones, because at least there's no illusion about where they're going."

I didn't respond. There really wasn't anything I could say.

"It's the ones who answer the advertisements — legitimate-looking job postings, you understand — in local newspapers or online, that are in for the rudest awakening. They wear whatever clothes they have that can pass for business attire, brush up on their typing, and even learn a little English, all in anticipation of coming to the United States and embarking on a new career."

I knew where she was going with this, but didn't really feel it was my place to interrupt.

"They may even fly business class over here," she continued. "Hell, they might fly alone. Why wouldn't they? There's no reason to keep watch over someone willingly going to their doom."

The song faded and a forbidding silence descended. That

DJ really knew how to read a room.

"It isn't until they're picked up from the airport and driven to a shitty apartment or a rundown house filled with other girls that reality starts to set in. The lucky ones are drugged — it makes what happens next somewhat bearable — others are beaten until whatever resistance they show is gone. After weeks of waiting, and being raped repeatedly by their handlers to 'break them in,' they're shipped out to wherever demand is greatest. Houston's a pretty big hub, as you know, but so are Dallas and New Orleans. And that's only the Gulf Coast."

There was anger in her voice, but her composure never faltered.

"It isn't only the Russians, of course. They're especially big in the Northeast, but the cartels have the lion's share of the market here. On the West Coast, it's the triads. Women are brought from Honduras and Guatemala, China, Ethiopia, and the Ivory Coast. Practically anywhere you can imagine."

"I understand all that," I started.

"You think you do," she said, "but take all that anxiety and fear you have invested in the disappearance of your brother and multiply that tens of thousands of times. That's the scale I'm talking about."

I said, "No one is accusing you of anything."

"Why wouldn't they? Aren't I Russian? Aren't we all criminals?"

"I don't know if you're Russian or not. Your accent is vague enough that your specific country of origin in unclear, though you're clearly educated."

She smiled. "Isn't this the land of opportunity?"

I went on. "And your place is either on the up and up or you pay a pretty penny in bribes to keep out of the papers."

"What's the expression? 'A little from column A ...'?"

"And a little from column B," I finished, "I get it."

"I wonder if you do."

Nevaeh stood up, which I deduced meant our meeting was at an end.

"This place may have an insipid name, and it may cater to the baser urges of certain members of our society, but the women who work here do so of their own free will," she said. "My past is my past, and I don't need to be reminded of it just because you've misplaced a brother."

I stood. "Look, I'm not going to pretend I know what these women — and you, I'm guessing — have gone through, But maybe there's some mutual benefit here."

"Go on."

"Mike, my brother, was trying to shut down a trafficking operation," I said. "Finding him might expose some real operators, not just the street guys babysitting. Surely that's a win for both of us."

She rose. "Perhaps. You've given me much to think about, Mr. Clarke. Maybe you're different than the men who usually come here after all."

"You should probably ask my ex-girlfriends about that."

Nevaeh grinned without much humor and left the room. I looked to the stage and saw Crystal had yet to return. The DJ was also still AWOL from his booth. I needed to consider what I'd just heard and figure out my next move, but it appeared I'd worn my welcome out here.

"Time for you to go."

A hand the size of a dinner plate settled on my shoulder, immediately making my arm go numb. I didn't have to turn around to know who my new friend was.

"Well, hey, Nigel. Good to see you again."

With depressingly little effort, he spun me away from the table and nudged me toward the exit. And by "nudged" I mean propelled me forward with the gentle force of a determined rhino. We frog-marched past the cashier and out into the dazzling noontime sunlight.

He pushed me a few more yards into the parking lot and then abruptly stopped. I saw the Corolla through squinting eyes and fumbled for my keys.

"Hey."

I didn't want to turn around, but figured the odds of getting shot in broad daylight in a strip club parking lot were maybe sixty/forty.

Nigel was extending his hand. I hadn't expected a gesture of camaraderie, but maybe he'd learned something after all.

I clasped his hand and mine was immediately enveloped in

throes of pain I can only compare to sticking your hand into an industrial press. Every bone in my hand screamed out and it was all I could do not to drop to my knees.

"Miss Navy wanted you to have this." And with that, he turned and plodded back to the club.

With effort, I uncurled my fist. Nigel had left a piece of paper within, almost as crumpled as my hand. I smoothed it out and read the one word written thereon.

Steranko.

SIXTEEN

"Steranko."

"That's what it says."

I called Charlie as soon as my hand stopped throbbing and I'd pulled out of the Bottoms Up parking lot, and we were in the midst of rehashing my conversation with Nevaeh.

"I'm impressed you consider a nudity-free visit to a strip club a success," she told me.

I said, "I wish I'd taken a picture of that Nigel guy. You'd be impressed I got out of there with my life."

"Such a drama queen."

"Is there anything on this Steranko guy or not?" I asked.

"Say again?"

I'm pretty sure she was fucking with me, even though my phone was in speaker mode and wedged between the parking brake and the passenger seat as I drove. Hands-free was really the only option when driving a manual car without Bluetooth.

"Is there anything on this Steranko guy?" I yelled, before smiling at the woman staring at me from her Mini Cooper in the next lane.

Charlie said, "Just going by the top web hits, she's either talking about the guy who used to draw for Marvel Comics in the 60s or the Mattress King of King of Prussia, PA."

"Where does the comic guy live?"

"Philadelphia, I think."

"Maybe they're the same dude," I offered.

"Maybe," she replied. "Or maybe he's the local businessman with alleged past ties to the Russian mob."

I said, "That does sound more likely."

I heard the rapid clicking of her keyboard. "The most recent hits are about local investments. He has a piece of the new Galveston entertainment district and is on the board of several local nonprofits."

"That's not exactly the resumé of a gangster," I said.

"It is of one trying to go legit," she replied, "but I'll check HPD's known alias database and the usual deep web sources."

"That's like the Silk Road stuff?"

"Yeah, that's it," Charlie sighed. "It's also where I go to buy all my fentanyl and child porn."

"I'm picking up on your sarcasm," I said.

"For the last time, it's just stuff that can't be accessed through regular search engines," she said.

"Right, right ... so you're on that?"

"I'm on it," she said, muttering something else I didn't catch before hanging up. Sometimes lack of reliable climate control in your car wasn't so bad after all.

I thought about what Nevaeh had said in the club. The Russians weren't the major players in the Houston area, but the raid Mike went on targeted Eastern Europeans, not the cartels. Were the Russians making a move? Did they really have that kind of muscle?

These were questions for the cops to answer, and my bone-crunching encounter with Sir Nigel didn't put me in the mood to talk to Roy again. Until Charlie got more info on this Steranko person, there wasn't much I could do.

Aside from calling my favorite DHS administrative assistant, that is.

"Homeland Security, Director Hammond's office, this is Dot."

"Well hey, Dot. This is Mike's brother, Cy," I ventured.

"Hello, Cy. How are you?"

"I'm good, thanks for asking." For the hell of it, I said, "I don't suppose y'all have heard anything from Mike?"

Her disappointment was palpable. "We sure haven't, Cy. I guess he hasn't gotten in touch with you either?"

"No, ma'am," I said. "Still no word. I was actually hoping to see if there was any word on when Agent Hanford was returning from Brussels?"

"Well, just let me see." I could hear ruffling through papers, which probably would've given Charlie seizures. "I don't have any new information on that. His calendar still shows him out of the office until at least the first of June."

That was roughly two weeks from now. "I see. And there isn't any contact information for him?"

"Now Cy, you know I'm not allowed to give out that kind of information for agents in the field." If I didn't know better, I'd say she was flirting with me.

I laughed. "Well, I just had to check. Thanks for your help, Dot."

"No problem at all."

"And give my best to Mr. Dot. There *is* a Mr. Dot, isn't there?" Please let there be one, I thought.

"Not anymore," she said. "But you never know."

"Well, thank you again," I said as diplomatically as I could and ended the call. I knew private eyes were supposed to use every means at their disposal to solve a case, but I wasn't prepared to go down that particular road just yet.

I exited I-45 and turned east on Cavalcade, heading back to my office/house. The drab, cement landscape gradually opened up to trees and decently kept-up houses as I passed the Anderson YMCA. Like many areas near the Loop, this neighborhood was transitioning from working class to something developers refer to as "professional," which was real estate code for increasingly and punishingly expensive.

Our office isn't a teardown by any stretch, but is still "distressed" enough to earn disapproving looks from the new transplants doing their morning yoga pants power walk or looking for a poorly maintained yard in which to let their Corgis take a shit. If I was home and feeling particularly saucy, I liked to wave at them from the porch, holding a Pabst tallboy and rocking my Korn tank top.

Oh, like your teenage musical tastes were any better.

Anyway, I have nothing against property taxes, but I'll be damned if I'm going to make it easy on the bastards.

The steps creaked under my feet as I walked up to the front door (distressed indeed) and entered. The front door was unlocked, which at this point was more annoying than alarming. I wasn't taking the call from "Boris" all that seriously, but the *Neanderthal* DNA in me (1.2%, according to one of those spit-in-a-tube tests) doesn't like thinking about Charlie sitting in an unlocked house. I resolved to give her a stern talking-to as soon as I'd fortified myself with —

I tripped over an umbrella lying across the foyer and saw the entire stand, in the shape of a tasteful reconstruction of an elephant's foot, was overturned. I let go of the door and stepped over the stand's contents, taking in my surroundings.

Nothing else in the entrance area appeared out of place. Old mail and magazines eventually destined for the recycling bin on the front table, while the picture of Charlie and me in front of the short hallway wall were undisturbed. That didn't keep the hairs on my neck from rising as I peered farther down into the kitchen at what looked like a foot, attached to a leg, presumably attached to a torso lying just out of sight.

I rarely carry a gun. I know: Isn't this Texas? Aren't there people with sidearms walking around day care centers? Well, yes and no. The Lone Star State does have some of the most ludicrously permissive gun laws in the Union, and it's jarring but not unusual to see someone in the checkout line at Kroger open-carrying, just in case the Cubans decide to parachute in while they're buying dog food, I guess.

But even though I carried a service weapon on the job and have a CHL for a .40-caliber Smith & Wesson, the damn thing usually sits in my underwear drawer. Most gigs don't require the use of deadly force, something the presence of a firearm always increases the chances of, and even on those occasions when I've found myself in a fight, I'm generally grateful not to have the gun as a fallback option.

In case you hadn't heard, I have anger issues.

Moving down the hallway as quickly as I dared, I saw more of the leg. It was indeed attached to a body, this one belonging to a Caucasian male, mid-30s, balding, and dressed like he was going to the gym (or returning after doing nothing but calf raises). His gray moisture-wicking exercise shirt was marred by a single entry wound high on the left side of his chest.

He lay on his back, and just beyond the reach of his outstretched left hand was a pistol I didn't recognize fitted with a new modular optic system. Expensive rig, though it didn't look to have done him any good.

I stuck my head in the entranceway for a quick sweep of the kitchen, prepared to duck back until I saw Charlie sitting in one of the breakfast nook chairs. It was an incongruous sight, her calmly swiping through a phone while a dead guy (or one doing a decent corpse impression, at least) was sprawled on our kitchen floor.

"You've had a busy morning," I said.

She looked up sharply, reaching for what I recognized as her .38 until she saw it was me. Never let anyone tell you I can't be stealthy when the need arises.

She put the pistol down and returned to the phone. "Nice of you to show up."

SEVENTEEN

Far be it from me to interrupt someone's electronics-related reverie, but I felt I must. "We gonna talk about the elephant in the room?"

"Hmm?" Charlie was still scrolling as fast as her eyes could register info.

When I didn't respond, she looked up. I met her gaze, looked pointedly at the corpse on the floor, then back to her.

"Oh, that guy," she said. "Self-defense."

"I hope you have more than that when the police get here."

She smiled with what would have passed for innocence if I hadn't known her since we were in the womb. "Are we calling the police?"

Sitting down, I said, "Unless you're planning on burying him in the backyard, then yes." I nodded to her pistol. "Did you use a silencer? Why aren't they here yet?"

"Gunshots aren't that unusual in this neighborhood," Charlie said. "Or maybe the neighbors are getting revenge for having to see you in your tank top all those times."

I tapped my biceps. "Now that you mention it, possession of *these* guns should be considered a capital offense."

"I ought to shoot you for that joke," Charlie said. "Fine, call the cops. I'm almost done going through his phone anyway."

"Anything interesting?" I dug my own phone out, considered calling 911, then just hit the contact for Roy DeSantos. It didn't take my hard-won private investigator skills to figure our "guest" was related to Mike's case.

She said, "I'm downloading his contacts, email, notes, and texts onto an external hard drive. There weren't any photos or videos, and I didn't find a cloud storage account connected to his ID."

Roy wasn't answering. "What about music? Did he have any decent tunes?"

"Like 'Dead Man's Party'?"

"Anything from Dead Can Dance?"

"The Grateful Dead?"

I inclined my head at him. "Think he is?"

Before she could answer, Roy finally answered. "Clarke, what an unpleasant surprise."

"It's not a social call, Roy, sorry to say. We've got a dead guy in our kitchen."

"What have I told you about letting Charlie do the cooking?" When I didn't take the bait, he said, "Wait, are you serious?"

"Afraid so. How far away are you?"

"Ten minutes. Have you called 911?"

I said, "No, but I can."

Roy said, "Don't bother, I'll send for the meat wagon. Emergency responders are for emergencies and … you did say he was dead, right?"

"Yep."

"Then what's the rush?" He hung up.

"Cavalry on the way?" Charlie asked.

"If by 'cavalry' you mean Roy and a couple of bored paramedics, then yes." I pocketed my phone. "Want to tell me what happened?"

She set the phone down. "I heard the door open and thought it was you, but when nobody yelled, 'Wazzup, Sis!' I got suspicious."

It's my calling card. "And the umbrellas?"

"You remember that one umbrella, the one I stole from the country club?"

The story involved a wedding, a typical Houston spring deluge, and a maître d' who made the mistake of questioning Charlie's fashion choices. "Oh yeah."

She went on, "You know how that big ass crook handle sticks out and you always have to walk around it?"

I nodded. "But our intruder didn't."

"Right. As soon as I heard that, I went for my gun."

"Where was it?"

"My backpack." She scanned my belt. "Where's yours?"

"Sock drawer."

"Lucky for you I was the one at home."

There was no argument from me. "Then what? He comes running into the kitchen?"

Charlie said, "Yep. Once the element of surprise was gone, I guess he figured he might as well bum rush the show."

I looked at the body. "Was his gun out when you shot him?"

"What does it look like?"

My silence was probably more accusatory than I intended.

"I didn't plant the gun, Cy." Then, pointedly, "You're the ex-cop, not me."

"That's why I asked," I said. "Have you checked him for ID?"

She held up the iPhone. "I stopped when I found this, but be my guest."

The guy on the floor was big. Not tall, but solid. I'd put his weight at 180 and maybe a few inches shy of six feet. He was white, with hair that might have been blond or gray but was cut so close it was hard to tell. No distinguishing marks or tats that I could see, meaning none on his hands or face.

His outfit was perfect for nighttime shenanigans but seemed a bit out of place in broad daylight: black pants, black sneakers, dark gray hoodie over a gray T-shirt. It was an ensemble that was both nondescript and somewhat attention-grabbing for a neighborhood walk.

There hadn't been any out-of-place cars in view as I drove up, meaning he must have parked a few blocks over and walked past a bunch of household surveillance cameras on the way, or someone dropped him off.

I went through his pockets without much enthusiasm; unless we lucked out and he was as stupid as he was clumsy, then he didn't bring his wallet on a hit. Sure enough, there wasn't anything in the way of identification on him. He had an extra magazine for his pistol and a Zippo with the silhouette of a bat on it. I left the former and pocketed the latter.

"Stealing evidence?" Charlie asked.

"Not many people know this, but the law says anyone who is killed after breaking into your home with the intent of killing you immediately forfeits any personal property on their person to the intended target."

"That sounds more like *post facto* rationalization than actual law." Charlie thought two semesters of Latin in college qualified her for an honorary law degree, apparently.

I said, "It's one of the fringe benefits they don't tell you about, like full pensions, free gas station coffee, and skimming profits from drug dealers."

Charlie shook her head. "Maybe Dad was right about me wasting my potential in the Peace Corps."

"Buck up, sis," I said. "You must have learned something useful from all those government databases you broke into over there."

"I was just scraping financial records. But they do look at a lot of porn."

"That's every government."

If Charlie was going to argue with my well-researched reply, the knock at the front door stole her thunder.

I heard the front door open, followed by Roy saying, "Police! We'd appreciate it if you didn't shoot."

"That was for you, killer," I said.

Charlie held her hands up in mock penitence as I got up to meet Roy.

He was standing in the foyer with two EMTs looking at the umbrellas I hadn't bothered to pick up yet. "How's my girl?"

"Not dead," I said, "which is more than I can say for you if you call her 'my girl' to her face."

Roy's continuous flirtation with my sister was a source of mild amusement to her and low-grade annoyance to me, which of course is why he kept it up. I doubted he harbored any serious feelings for her, and as for Charlie — whatever her other flaws — she had better taste.

I hoped.

"Where's the body?"

"Kitchen," I said, and turned to lead them there. Roy pulled out a pair of nitrile gloves and put them on.

We entered the kitchen. Charlie was standing by the table, the gunman's phone nowhere to be seen — presumably returned to his pocket. She was wearing what she apparently assumed was an expression of contrition but looked more like the face of a person who'd just shot someone and knew she was going to get away with it.

"Charlie," Roy said, his usual sleazy half-smile on his face.

"Detective DeSantos," she replied.

Roy nodded to one of the EMTs, who performed a few necessary formalities like verifying the corpse was deceased. He and his partner then returned to the ambulance to prepare for transporting the body.

Roy knelt down and inspected the corpse. "Recognize him?"

"No," Charlie and I said in unison.

"And he just walked in and started blasting away?"

Charlie gave an abridged version of what she'd told me, leaving out the fact she'd downloaded all the useful info from the guy's phone and also that I'd lifted his lighter. The family that steals together, something something. ...

Roy listened with what I assumed (or hoped) was less attention than he paid to a regular homicide investigation, considering he'd known me for ten years and Charlie for nearly that long, all while going through the body's pockets in the same manner I'd just done. Sure enough, he retrieved the phone.

He picked the pistol up by the barrel. "Nice rig. European?"

"Russian," Charlie said. "Makarov."

We both looked at her. "What?" she said. "The Angolan army used pistols like that. I saw plenty of them in my Peace Corps days."

"I didn't know the Peace Corps operated in Angola," Roy frowned.

"They don't."

Roy wisely abandoned the conversation, and instead dropped the gun in another evidence bag and zipped it up. "Now can I see your weapon?"

Charlie broke open the cylinder and dropped the five remaining shells into her palm, then handed it and the bullets to Roy. He took it, smelled the barrel, and nodded.

"This seems pretty cut-and-dried," he said. "And while I appreciate the convenience, I have concerns about what this means for the investigation into your brother's disappearance."

I said, "It can't be a coincidence, especially after that phone call."

"Unfortunately," Roy said, "this guy can't answer any questions. Might have been useful to see if he had an accent."

Neither Charlie nor I said anything. I had my doubts about any Slavic connections, but nothing more than a gut feeling to back them up.

The EMTs returned with a gurney. Roy took enough pictures of the corpse, the room, and Charlie's .38 to fill two rolls of film, if anybody still used that, and then they zipped him up and loaded him out.

Roy removed his gloves. "I don't see any need to make an arrest for this. Like I said, cut and dried. As long as I've got your assurances you're telling me everything," He glanced at Charlie's now-closed laptop as he said this. She just smiled.

"It happened just like I said," Charlie told him.

Roy said, "Be that as it may, I need to get a statement."

"Uh-huh." He was right, I knew. Even in Texas, and even when it was clearly a "clean shoot," as the cops called it, a formal interview had to be conducted.

Charlie grabbed her phone and her jacket, and the expression on her face told me Roy should probably lay off the flirting for a while.

So *something* good was coming out of this, at least.

They turned to go, then Roy paused. "Something about this doesn't add up. I don't know what it is, but until we find your brother, I want you both to stay close."

"Is that an official directive?" I asked.

He looked at me. "I'm assuming I don't have to make it one."

Roy left, and I exhaled. I don't think I realized how tense we'd been.

"You heard the man," I muttered to myself. "It's time to go

to Dallas."

EIGHTEEN

No, I really had no intention of going against the barely veiled warning of my very good police friend. That's because "Dallas" is the name of one of my former CIs.

The relationship between so-called confidential informants and the police is a perverse form of symbiosis: the former receives compensation or leniency for past (or future) crimes, while the latter receives information that will hopefully help them solve a case.

But the cops hold all the leverage in the relationship, and their satisfaction with the info provided can be the only thing keeping the CI out of the joint. For their part, the danger to the informant if they're tagged as a snitch is very real, and they can often grow to resent the arrangement.

I assume it's the same with most marriages.

Which brings me to "Dallas," real name Irving Phelps, a wannabe concert promoter who ended up on the radar of some unsavory types over mounting gambling debts. When I had just been promoted from patrol to detective, I ended up collaring him at a raid on one of Houston's numerous illegal casinos. Faced with three to five for what was his third arrest at an "illegal gaming establishment" — poker in a private dwelling is legal, in most cases, but poker in the back office of a closed Mexican restaurant is not — he elected instead to give HPD dirt on the folks running the games.

I know what you're thinking: *You're not a cop anymore,*

dude. That is very true, and 999 times out of a thousand, an ex-cop doesn't maintain contact with his old informants. It crosses all kinds of murky ethical territory, and it doesn't make sense from the CI's standpoint, because there's no longer anything for him or her to gain.

But Dallas was that rarest of three-time losers in that he was the kind who improbably straightened up and flew ... well, let's not call it "straight." Suffice to say, he stayed on the good side of the ledger for the most part these days. He was married, with a kid and a job in real estate. I wouldn't say we were friends, necessarily, but I would still shoot him a text from time to time.

I hadn't told Roy about Steranko yet. I still (mostly) trusted him, but Houston's police department is as prone to corruption as any major city's, and I couldn't risk the possibility someone else in his detail might let word slip to the guy, whoever he ended up being.

New-and-improved Dallas wasn't going to have any current information on the Russian mob, but until Charlie could return to run down information on her hapless assailant, I'd take what I could get.

I went out on the porch and sent my text. It was short and sweet: *Call me, C.* I didn't want written evidence of what we were going to talk about, as much for his safety as for my own peace of mind.

I didn't have to wait long. The phone rang. "Clarke," he said, "it's been a while."

"You still going by Dallas, or do I get to call you 'Irving?'"

"My wife doesn't even call me Irving," Irving, er, Dallas replied.

I laughed. "I admire your commitment. Had a question for you, if you've got a minute."

"Anything for the former cop who used to dangle the threat of prison over my head every waking minute."

"Harsh but fair," I said. "I'll make it quick: Have you ever heard the name Steranko in connection with your, let's call it, 'past life'?"

Dallas paused long enough that I momentarily thought we'd been disconnected. "Where did you hear that name?" he finally asked.

"Is that important?"

"It might be," he said. "On second thought, I don't really want to know."

I sat on one of the porch's camping chairs and said, "You're starting to make me think I shouldn't have contacted you."

He exhaled uneasily. "Sorry, it's just … that name brings up a lot of memories. Most of them bad."

"What can you tell me about him?"

"He's Russian mob," Dallas said. "But I assume you knew that. Got his start fighting in the Second Chechen War."

"Oof."

"Yeah, nobody's really sure what his exact role was, but he came out of it with a reputation for brutality, even by the standards of that particular conflict."

"When did he come to Houston?" I asked.

"Not sure. I first remember hearing his name … 2004? 2005? It was before my second bust, I know that."

I thought about it for a second. "That's when I was still in patrol."

He chuckled without much humor. "Right, I hadn't had the pleasure of making your acquaintance yet."

"Do you remember anything specific, or was it mostly boogeyman stories?"

"Let me think," he said. And then, after a bit, "There were rumors he was behind Juan Cortez getting whacked, but neither the Mexicans nor the cops could ever prove it."

I remembered that. "Hard to confirm anything when you can't turn up a body. But the Cortez thing opened the road for the Russians, though. Especially on the south side and the coast."

"It makes the most sense," he said. "And that's when you really started hearing more about him. Us poker guys weren't really caught up in that world, but people talk."

I said, "Y'all had a regular coffee klatch going."

He laughed. "It was easy to fancy ourselves outlaws, sitting around smoky card tables and committing petty crimes, but nobody knew anything that important. Poker is fun, but it's not really worth getting murdered over."

"Can't argue with that."

"Not sure what else I can tell you," Dallas said. "Are you sticking your nose where it doesn't belong again?"

"You know me too well," I said. "Take care of yourself, Irving. And say hi to Jennifer for me."

"I'll consider it, Clarke. Watch your ass."

I put the phone down and watched a few cars roll by. I had about as much info as I did before my phone call, which wasn't exactly jack shit, but wasn't too far off, either.

Meanwhile, Mike was still missing.

Three days into this and I still didn't have any solid leads. Hanford was in the wind, and likely to stay that way as long as his masters at DHS felt he was a risk. Steranko may play a role in all this, but how big or small, nobody could tell me. And the unpleasant suspicion that kept nagging at me said if he was more than peripherally involved in this, Mike wouldn't turn up alive. If he wasn't being digested in a bull shark in Galveston Bay this very minute.

It was easy not to go down these rabbit holes on a regular case. Even the handful of missing kid jobs we'd taken hadn't hit me like this, not coincidentally because we found all of them. And almost all of *those* were in the company of one of their recently separated parents. Want to really freak children out? Tell them that they're less likely to be kidnapped by a guy in a panel van than they are their own mom or dad.

Given my own (admittedly brief) history as a cop and subsequent experience in the PI business, people are often surprised to find I'm not a terribly pessimistic person. Maybe I quit the force before the horrors of the job really had a chance to take up residence in my subconscious, and perhaps my tenure in my current career taking long-range sexy time photos and running down meth dealers who skipped out on their $750 bond hasn't sufficiently awakened me to the depravities of mankind. Whatever the case, I'm generally upbeat, if occasionally (okay, often) too sarcastic for my own good.

Which is why my fatalism regarding Mike's fate wasn't sitting well with me.

It had been three days, but then again, it had *only* been three days. This wasn't some toddler wandering into the woods; Mike was a decorated Marine, accomplished with small arms, hand-to-hand combat, and could generally find his way home with nothing but the sun and a wristwatch. Assuming nobody got the drop on him, he'd be more than capable of handing a wide and varied selection of humanity their asses. Still, like the man said, anybody can get got.

And that left the more intriguing — but no less frustrating — proposition that he went off the grid of his own free will, leaving behind a wife and kid in the process. That seemed almost as implausible as the other alternative, but until I got to the bottom of all of it, I couldn't assume anything.

Charlie returned as morning turned into afternoon, and immediately disappeared into her office to return to the dead guy's phone. Mom, for some reason, still hadn't called off tonight's gathering, and after an hour or so of bookkeeping, I decided I had to get the barbecue and attempt to drag Charlie away from one of her few true loves: forensic data recovery.

As if she'd read my mind, she came out onto the porch with a look I can only describe as incredulous on her face.

"Come in here. You're going to want to see this."

NINETEEN

SportsCenter was on as I came back inside, and even though I didn't think it had anything to do with what Charlie was talking about, I asked, "Did the Astros sign Clayton Kershaw or something?"

"Ha," was more a programmed response than an actual acknowledgement of anything I'd said. Charlie walked into the kitchen and sat back down at the table. Her hard drive was hooked up to her MacBook Pro and she positioned the laptop so I could get a better look at the screen as I entered.

"This the dump from dead guy's phone?" I asked.

She nodded. "Some of it. Looks like it was a burner, so there wasn't a ton there."

"I don't guess there's an email from whoever ordered the hit on here?"

"You never were the lucky twin," Charlie said. "There was a reminder that just had the name 'Clarke' and our address, nothing in contacts, and two calls from unknown callers."

I frowned. "Well, that doesn't sound helpful."

"Ordinarily I'd agree with you," she began.

"No, you wouldn't."

"You know what I mean, and I admit at first glance, it looks like a big fat zero, but look closer."

I leaned in to get a better fix on the screen. "This is a bunch of numbers, which is all Greek to me."

Charlie said, "The numbers were named 'Unknown Caller'

in the contacts, but whoever was calling wasn't doing any concealment. The shooter just created a contact called 'Unknown Caller,' most likely hoping it would get overlooked in a cursory check."

I stood up. "But that's …"

"Stupid," she finished. "You don't need any special tools to figure that out; you just need to check the details of the number."

Shaking the carafe to see if there was still coffee (there was), I thought for a moment. "You said there's nothing else on the phone? No pictures or apps that might give us something?"

She said, "It had the factory-delivered apps, but no media, browsing history, or even basic settings changed."

"How sure are you this was a burner?"

"As sure as I can be without the actual phone," she said with a shrug. "If I could hook it up to my software or desolder the chip I could be certain, but there are precisely two chances of that."

"Slim and fat," I said, completing one of the Clarkes' many family proverbs. "So this is a burner."

It wasn't a question, but she answered, "Out of the box iPhone 9, which looks to have been used for exactly two phone calls and to find our house on the map app. He was probably going to pitch it down a storm drain when he was done."

"Who spends seven hundred dollars on a burner?" I asked, more pissed off than I cared to admit that the dead guy was carrying around a phone that cost more than half my monthly mortgage payment.

"Maybe seven hundred dollars, maybe more," she said. "We don't know if it was a Pro version or not."

"Don't remind me."

"Russians?" Charlie offered.

I shook my head. "Dropping nearly a grand every time they send a guy out for an op? That's bad business."

"Maybe they're just better at maximizing profit than a guy who routinely does *pro bono* work for down-on-their-luck clients."

I didn't feel like arguing her point, mostly because she was right.

"We're not hurting that much," I said, more defensively than I'd intended.

She held her hands up. "I'm not complaining, just pointing

out our line of work doesn't generate the revenues necessary for that kind of overhead."

I still wasn't buying the Russian angle. "The cartels have money, too. And they make a hell of a lot more geographic sense."

"The guy I shot wasn't Mexican."

"Mexicans can't hire *gringos*?"

She turned back to her laptop. "You know as well as I do the cartels don't farm out hits. At least, they don't farm them out to guys Central Casting calls when they're doing a period piece about the Norse conquest of America."

To quote Peter Cushing in *Star Wars*, this bickering was pointless.

"Want to come with me to Ruzicka's?" I asked. "I'm sure Mom wouldn't object to her favorite son and daughter showing up to the house early."

"You mean Jim's actually going to be able to make it?"

I pantomimed laughing while she disconnected her hard drive and stuck it and her laptop in the messenger bag she carried everywhere. Shadows lengthened across the kitchen floor and I paused in the doorway.

"You think this is the first time anyone's died in this house?"

Charlie shouldered her bag and looked around the room, "Oh, I doubt it. This house is almost a hundred years old. People dropped like flies in here all the time, especially before they invented air-conditioning."

For some reason, that response didn't comfort me the way I'd hoped.

"Worried about ghosts?" Charlie asked. "I don't think a guy entering a house with the intention of committing foul play is allowed to haunt it."

"Ghost code?"

"It's in the Bible," she said, "Deuteronomy. Right after the part about how you can't get into heaven if your dick's been cut off."

"Guess you won't be seeing any of your exes up there," I said.

She gave me what amounted to an affectionate kidney punch and we walked out of the house. I made sure to lock the door behind us.

Ruzicka's BBQ was one of the older joints of its kind in north Houston, which was a testament to its quality, given the competition. The owners hadn't done much to sweeten up the facade aside from adding air-conditioning. The corrugated roof always seemed to have the same amount of rust no matter when you visited, which led the conspiracy theorist in me to believe it was painted that way to engender authenticity while the Ruzickas laughed it up on their brisket-financed yacht.

Most of my conspiracy theories involved people making more money than me.

The concept of "rush hour" in Houston is fairly nebulous. Commuters in the city's far-flung suburbs may depart for downtown as early as 4:30 or 5:00 in the morning in order to beat traffic. Meanwhile the evening rush begins at 3:00 PM and goes until 7:00, the next morning, as the joke goes. Whatever the case, the return of workers on any given afternoon meant there'd be a line out the door at Ruzicka's, and today was no different.

I don't normally stand in line for food. Houston simply has too many options to justify wasting the time, especially when the hip joints rotate out every few months. If you didn't care about being "seen" — and I honestly hadn't had a reason to care in that regard for over a decade — you could wait three weeks until the new hotness was no longer desirable.

Just don't wait too long. The average life of a Houston restaurant was only slightly more than that of a mayfly.

I'd violated my own line policy a few times for Ruzicka's brisket and pulled pork before, but Charlie and I sauntered in breezily this particular evening and walked straight to the take-out counter. We were the only ones there because they only took phone orders if you were ordering at least five pounds of meat. I loved brisket, but not enough to gorge on it solo to the point of spontaneous heart attack.

Had to save something for retirement, after all.

After a bit, an improbably large fellow wearing a Cowboys baseball cap and stained tank top approached the counter. This was Clifton, eldest scion of the barbecue clan.

"Help you?"

"Pick up order for Clarke."

He pawed through the slips next to the registers and came up with ours. "$\78.50."

While I was digging through my wallet, he nodded to my sister, "Hey, Charlie."

"Hey, Cliff."

He smiled until I handed him four twenties and he was forced to acknowledge me again.

"Be out in a minute," he said, pocketing the change without asking and disappearing through a door into the back.

"Cliff?" I said, in mock scandalous tones.

"Can I help it if I'm more memorable than you?" Charlie said.

"I'm just grateful I'm not his type."

"Attractive?" she offered.

"Dallas fan."

Clifton ("Cliff" to his friends, apparently) emerged from the back and brought us our order. I hoped eight pounds of brisket and a quart each of potato salad and baked beans would be enough, then realized Mike wouldn't be there to share it and grimly realized it was a good possibility.

I thanked the guy, and Charlie and I returned to her Audi (you didn't think we were taking my POS all the way out to my mother's, did you?), and set off for Mom's.

TWENTY

Houston's a big city. This much is obvious, if you've ever spent time here other than cooling your heels in one of our airports. Thanks to a combination of agreeable terrain, municipal manifest destiny, and an almost pathological aversion to public transit, the metropolitan area sprawls out from a network of endlessly expanding freeways.

A few years back, someone superimposed the area corralled by the 88 miles of Beltway 8 (the second of three highway loops encircling the city) over various other metropolitan and geographical areas. For example, the distance from Mill Valley, CA, to San Mateo, or New Rochelle, NY, to Elizabeth, NJ, is easily contained within Houston's environs. So is most of the Big Island of Hawaii.

You spend a lot of time in your car here, is what I'm saying. And that's just if you're driving around Houston proper. Once you decide to move to the sticks, all bets are off.

The Woodlands is one of Houston's northern suburbs, about a 25-mile drive from my and Charlie's neighborhood, and is where our mother currently resides. Depending on weather, time of day, and whether or not you've sacrificed the requisite number of goats to the transit gods, the subsequent drive time can be anything from 30 minutes to the director's cut of *The Godfather*, Interstate 45 being one of the last remaining local freeways that, for a variety of reasons, hadn't been expanded to 15 lanes.

Fortunately, there is an HOV lane that takes you almost the

whole way, and we sped up I-45 with little delay.

I don't really remember much of the process involved in convincing Mom to move up here, but it happened with what seemed to me surprising swiftness. One day she was still in the same Heights home she'd raised us in and shared with my dad for what seemed like (and actually was) decades, the next she was paying an HOA for the privilege of checking the height of her lawn and making sure she didn't decide to open a backyard alpaca farm.

This all came at the tail end of my detective career, and my mind was clearly on other things. Otherwise I might have more assertively stated my aversion to master-planned communities and white flight evangelicals. Still, she was in a gated community and I did my best to balance the peace of mind that came with my mother being in a safe neighborhood with the hypocrisy of my having railed against such communities for most of my adult life.

Charlie drove us in silence for a good portion of the trip. Unlike me, she enjoyed driving. Having a functioning car was only part of it, since she'd developed the habit when we were teens, borrowing Mom's old pickup and ramming the roads until the wee hours. She said it was to "clear her head," and I had no reason to doubt that. Charlie rarely drank in high school, and I could count the number of boyfriends she had on one hand with three fingers removed. She also suffered from insomnia, which she described as the result of being unable to turn her brain off. Barreling down a highway at 80 miles per hour while blasting Fear or Black Flag was pretty cathartic for a kid as off-the-charts brilliant as my sister.

And despite my gripes about this city's traffic, that scenario isn't as far-fetched as it sounds. Houston may be the quintessential sprawling metropolis, but this was still Texas. A half-hour's drive would put you in rural territory that could just as easily have been plopped down in the middle of Kansas.

It wasn't until the dollar stores, discount furniture stores, and shady vape shops started giving way to more generic strip malls and higher-end vape shops that anyone bothered to speak. I started.

"Whose idea was it for Mom to move way the hell out here, again?"

Charlie sighed. "It was a joint decision. Just because you don't remember giving your approval doesn't mean it didn't happen."

I turned the Audi's air-conditioning down from Charlie's preferred setting of "absolute zero" to "Shackleton Ice Shelf." "I'm not saying it didn't, just that it's weird I don't remember the conversation."

"You were in and out of the hospital a lot. Even for you."

"Yeah, but I wasn't in a coma or anything."

Charlie raised an eyebrow.

"Not for very long, anyway," I said.

"Mom needed to be someplace where people could look in on her," she said.

I replied, "You and I were a mile and a half away."

She said, "Don lives in Spring, Mike and Kayla live in The Woodlands, and Kayla's a stay-at-home mom besides. And you and I don't exactly keep normal hours."

It's true I was just as likely to be staking out a house as home in bed on any given evening. Some of this was starting to come back.

"And the old house was two stories," I said. "She was starting to have trouble getting up and down the stairs."

She nodded. "Now you're remembering. And even then, Mom wanted to try and tough it out. But ultimately she couldn't handle the taxes."

"Yeah," I said. "We could have walled off the top floor," I began.

"Or made it into a museum devoted to your medical injuries," Charlie said. "And she was still going to get priced out of there."

Fun fact: Texas has no state income tax, so the bulk of everything — school, infrastructure, hospitals — is paid for by property taxes. There's a 10% cap on the increase your homestead can be appraised for every year, but when developers are moving into your 90-year-old neighborhood and tearing down two-bedroom bungalows to build 4,000-square-foot McMansions, it adds up.

The end result — whether in Mom's old neighborhood, or in Oak Forest to the north, or in Museum Park and the Third Ward further south — was the same: the steady driving out of those unable to afford a new luxury home, or the attendant taxes that come from owning a house in proximity to them.

Which is what happened to our Mom. Even with Dad's life insurance and her own military pension, it was only a matter of time.

Exit and entrance ramps for the various transit centers are spaced along Houston's HOV lanes, and it's generally a good idea to use caution when navigating them. So of course, as we slowed down on the approach to one of these exits, which would deposit us in the main lanes of the freeway, someone in a Ford pickup who'd been riding Charlie's ass for the last mile or so actually honked. I started rolling my window down.

"Don't," Charlie warned, and hit the window lock button on her Master Control Panel. Or whatever it was called.

"What?"

"Don't flip the guy off," she said. "This is Texas, for Christ's sake. The guy probably has three pistols under the driver's seat alone."

I looked at her. "You're telling me Roy took your only means of personal protection?"

Charlie snorted. "Of course not, but I'm not getting into a rolling gunfight while speeding down a cement cattle run."

"You had me worried for a minute."

She said, "You know, for someone who's already been shot, you're in a big hurry to make another bullet's acquaintance."

Fuming silently at being foiled by a child lock, I sat back, noting with satisfaction she'd slowed somewhat. Through the passenger side side-view mirror, I could see the pickup driver gesticulating angrily.

"What's the minimum speed on the freeway?" she asked innocently.

"You're worse than I am," I said. "Your passive-aggressive deceleration is going to piss this guy off worse than me flipping him the bird."

"We make a good team."

This being an HOV lane, the guy behind us had no way to get around, and we continued up the road, basking in the satisfaction of having annoyed some asshole for a bit.

I watched the northbound traffic alongside us. It was moving at a pretty good clip, all things considered. What looked like a red Ferrari was keeping pace with us, and I idly hoped his brief voyage at highway speeds helped overcome the immense frustration the guy otherwise must have felt owning a high-performance sports car in this city.

"Do you think Mike's okay?" Charlie asked.

"I ... don't know," I said after a pause. I wasn't expecting that.

Charlie checked the mirror for a second and said, "I want to believe he's all right, and if anyone can get out of a jam, it's him, but ..."

"But it's been three days," I finished. "Three days and no word. Have you been able to look at that code he left yet?"

She shook her head. "I had it on my to-do list this morning but was rudely interrupted."

The HOV lane came to an end just south of the Woodlands proper, and Charlie eased the Audi out into regular traffic. Fortunately, we were still moving close to posted speeds.

"We have to assume it's something he'd know you could crack," I said. "He had to believe you'd be the one to get into his email, right?"

"Yeah," Charlie said. "It just doesn't look like any other key I've seen before."

I thought about that. "Mike wasn't a crypto guy, was he?"

"As in, into codebreaking? In the Corps? Not that I was ever aware of."

"Then it has to be something simpler that only you — and maybe I — would be aware of."

"That makes sense. I —" Charlie started. She looked up suddenly at the rearview mirror and said, "Oh shit."

"What?" I said, starting to turn around. "Is it that asshole in the pickup again?"

But all she said was, "Hold on!" and before I had time to face all the way forward, she jerked the wheel to the right. I lurched in the opposite direction with the force of the turn and felt a sickening *crump* in the Audi's rear left corner and we began to spin.

I grabbed the oh shit handle above my door and clenched it so hard I was afraid it would break off. Charlie was trying to steer into the spin while simultaneously avoiding dozens of surrounding cars in three lanes of traffic bordered by cement barriers. All I could do was hold on and curse under my breath.

I saw a flash of red, then something slammed into the Audi on the passenger (my) side, slightly behind me. The force of that impact spun us in the opposite direction. Charlie and I were both using profanity my mother would've been very disappointed to hear when her car came to a sudden stop, the front end just a foot or so from a cement block. The intermittent sound of screeching tires came to us, but soon died away. I let go of the handle and looked at Charlie, who returned it. We both exhaled (I hadn't even realized I'd been holding my breath) and started to laugh. The car was probably totaled, but we were alive.

Then her airbags went off.

TWENTY-ONE

We were both able to get safely out of the car. Charlie had powder burns from the airbag on her face, and I'm sure I did too. I saw a handful of people emerging from their stopped vehicles, and I waved them off. I could see a number of others, still in their cars, on their phones. I hoped they were calling 911, but could just as easily imagine them irritably describing the latest traffic delay to their friend: "*Yeah, I'm gonna be late. There's an accident on 45 and nobody's moving. Idiot was probably texting and didn't check his blind spot before changing lanes. Record* The Bachelor *for me.*"

Just another day on Houston's freeways.

"You okay?" Charlie asked.

"I think so. You?"

She felt cautiously along her torso and winced. "That last hit knocked me into the door; I think I might've dinged a couple ribs."

"How bad did you 'ding' them?"

"Think I might've broken a couple of the sons of bitches," she said, frowning.

I walked her to the barrier separating the north and southbound shoulders and let her sit down. As I turned around, a meaty hand grabbed my upper arm.

"Hey buddy! Are y'all all right?"

I looked up and recognized the face of the pickup driver who'd been trying to sodomize the Audi ever since we passed

Beltway 8. Ordinarily, when someone grabs my upper arm and calls me "buddy" I want to break off a foot in their ass. But when that same person is the redneck POS who just wrecked my sister's car, almost killing us in the process, I decide to go straight to tearing out his larynx.

I ripped my arm out of his grasp, but fortunately for him, Charlie saw or sensed the flat murder in my eyes and said, "Cy, don't."

I'd pivoted my weight to my back foot and clenched my fist already, but I replied, "Why the hell not?"

"Because he didn't do it."

I looked again at the dude. He was 300 pounds if he was a kilogram, most of that in the gut straining over the waist of his jorts. He was wearing a gimme cap with a bald eagle on it and a T-shirt emblazoned with "TERRORIST HUNTING PERMIT" in block letters. The only thing missing from his ensemble was a dip tucked into his lip, though admittedly his beard was so massive it was impossible to tell.

I found myself getting angry again, but for different reasons. Looking to Charlie I said, "Are you sure?"

She held her side with a pained expression, her words coming out in strained bursts. "He was three car lengths back. When we got hit. It was a Ferrari. Red one."

I forgot about Cletus and went over to her. "Son of a bitch, I saw that car too. Are you sure? A *Ferrari*?"

Charlie nodded. "Couldn't believe it. Hundred-thousand-dollar candy-apple sports car, straight up our ass."

I couldn't remember the driver. "I think the windows were tinted. Did you see who was driving?"

She shook her head.

"So y'all are gonna be okay?"

I looked back at Cletus and — bless his heart — he actually looked worried. Two minutes ago he was probably ranting about "foreign-car-driving pinkos," and now he was a concerned neighbor inquiring after our well-being. Heartwarming, really. Maybe if all Americans could get into near-fatal automobile collisions with each other, we might come together as a nation.

"Hey, Cl ... uh, *man*, I think we're all right. What did you say your name was?"

"Stu." He extended the aforementioned ham hock and I shook it. His grip was sweaty, but that understandable considering we all just almost died. I was a little moist myself.

"Thanks for checking, Stu," I said. "Let me ask you: Did you see who was driving that Ferrari?"

He shook his head. "Naw, man. That old boy ran up on you so fast I couldn't believe it. He was like a greased pig out of a chute."

I've heard that expression before, and I suppose it speaks to my urban upbringing that I've never understood the context for applying grease to a pig. And now probably wasn't the time to ask.

"Don't know about that other car, though."

Oh shit, I realized: the second impact. I looked past Stu and saw a white panel van, of the kind you see a dozen times a day on Houston roads. They usually carry day workers to a job laying carpet or painting or installing plumbing.

I walked over and saw a man in the driver's seat wearing white overalls and a T-shirt. There was no one else inside.

"You okay?" I asked.

He smiled and gave me a thumbs-up, then glanced over his shoulder. I followed his gaze and saw three similarly dressed dudes trotting across the access road. He looked back, noticed me watching them as well. He suddenly became nervous, until I grinned and gave a small shrug. He returned it. *What are you gonna do?*

Qué pedes hacer, indeed. The other three guys were probably undocumented, and sticking around for questioning could easily earn them a one-way ticket back south of the border.

The damage to the van was negligible. At least, I couldn't tell which of the existing dents and scrapes were new or old. Insurance could sort it out. I gave the guy a thumb's up and walked back to Charlie, who was on her phone.

Sirens grew louder in the distance, and I saw a fire truck approaching from the south. A police car was heading in from the opposite direction, but both were having difficulty navigating through the ranks of stopped cars (on our side) and gawkers (on the other).

Charlie hung up. "Called Mom."

"I figured. What'd she say?"

110

"Wanted to make sure we were okay. I said we were."

I said, "Did you tell her about your ribs?"

"I did not," she replied. "You and I already know what's going to happen. They're going to take me, by ambulance, to Northwest Medical. I'll get X-rays and be released with a compression wrap that mashes my boobs flat. *Don't* say it."

I grinned. Twin brothers are the only males allowed to make jokes about a woman's breasts, and even then, it's an iffy thing.

"Did she finally agree to call tonight off?" I asked instead.

"Yeah. Still sounded pissed off about it."

"Well, you know, her ungrateful kids never come to visit her," I said.

Charlie chuckled, then hissed. "Shit, don't make me laugh." Then she nodded to the car. "Did the barbecue make it?"

I checked the back seat. "You want the good news or the bad news?"

"Bad."

"It didn't make it."

She nodded, as this is barely a surprise considering what we just went through. "And the good?"

I said, "Your upholstery has a wonderful hickory sauce shine."

Charlie rolled her eyes. "I hope my deductible covers this."

"You're having a hell of a day."

"That's just what Mom said. And she still doesn't know about the dead guy."

My own phone vibrated in my pocket, and I checked the screen. Unknown caller.

I showed it to Charlie. "Should I answer it?"

"Could this day get any worse?" she said.

I honestly didn't know if that was an affirmative answer or not, so I went ahead and hit the Talk button. "This is Clarke."

"Cy Clarke?"

Another accent. "Boris, if this is you, I'm really not in the mood."

"There is no Boris here, friend," the voice replied with a chuckle. "And I don't believe we've ever spoken, but I'm told you have been looking for me."

The sirens were getting louder and I was still coming down off an adrenaline surge, so it took a moment for that last part to filter through. When it did, I clicked the mute button.

"Son of a bitch," I said.

"What is it?" Charlie asked.

I said, "I think it's Steranko."

TWENTY-TWO

It wasn't the time to ask how he got my number, but I knew that was going to bother me. Instead, I said, "I don't know if I'd call it *looking* for you. I just had some questions and you seem like the best person to answer them."

"Why do you think that?" he asked.

"Let's just say we may have some overlapping interests."

There was a pause at the other end of the line. "Are you in some kind of trouble?"

That was a weird question. Then I realized, he was hearing the various emergency vehicles, who were all converging on us. It must have sounded like, well, a traffic accident.

"Not really. We were just in an accident, so this isn't really the best time to talk."

He said, "How unfortunate. How about tonight? Would that be better?"

"What time?" I asked. "I have no idea how long this is going to take."

"How about ten o'clock?"

I checked my watch. It wasn't five yet. "That sounds doable."

"Excellent. I'm having a small get-together in Galveston. We can talk then."

What. "Galveston?" I asked.

"Yes," he said. "On my boat."

"Your boat." I knew I should be arguing for a neutral site

arrangement, but repeating him was the best I could do.

He said, "My boat is called the *Konev*. It's moored at the Galveston Yacht Club and Marina. Do you know it?"

"I'll find it." The ambulance was pulling up. It had mercifully turned off its siren and I waved the EMTs over as I talked.

That chuckle again. "I am looking forward to it."

I hung up. The fire truck was pulling up behind Charlie's car. Between it and the ambulance, all the lanes of northbound 45 were now blocked. This was called "establishing a safe operating area," as I recalled from my police days. It wouldn't do to allow any injured parties to get run over by a guy playing Fruit Ninja while driving.

And now two black-and-whites were arriving as well. Hope nobody was in a hurry to get to Olive Garden.

I waved the EMTs over and pointed to where Charlie was sitting. "My sister thinks she might have broken some ribs."

Two of them broke off to attend to her. "How are you, sir?"

"I'm fine."

He held a finger in front of my face. "Follow with your eyes, please."

I obliged him to assure him I wasn't concussed.

"Were you both wearing your seat belts?"

"Yes," I nodded, not adding that neither of us had a death wish.

He seemed convinced of my relatively sound mind and went over to where the others were attending Charlie. My brief interlude of peace was short-lived, because right about then the police arrived.

The "investigation," if you wanted to call it that, into the accident was short and sweet. Stu, Charlie, and I and about a dozen other witnesses all told the same story: that a red Ferrari barreled up on us and Charlie did her damnedest to recover from it, as well as trying to avoid damaging other cars. The proceedings were probably hastened by the fact none of the cops recognized me.

The EMTs were loading Charlie into their rig. The one I'd spoken with came back over as the cop was finishing his notes.

"We're going to take her to Northwest Medical for X-rays, but it definitely looks like she was right about the ribs," he said.

I just nodded. Not much point in bringing up the fact she had her own EMT certification.

"Do you have a way to get to the hospital?" he asked.

I was about to say yes, but then I remembered Charlie's car. A wrecker was backing up to it and lowering its ramp as it prepared to haul off the Audi's carcass. The rear passenger side was crumpled in from where the van hit it, and the left rear corner was completely sheared off. The mirror on the driver's side had been sheared off, while there were huge gouges all down the side from where she'd scraped the retaining wall. The rear right tire was leaning in at an angle that indicated — at the very least — a bent rim. Worst case: bent rear axle.

Maybe not a total loss, but definitely out of commission for a while. Charlie was going to be pissed.

"Hey man, you need a ride?"

I turned. It was Stu. He'd been talking with the police but they appeared to have finished with him.

"I couldn't impose."

He shook his head vigorously. "No, it's no problem. I already told the wife what was going on. If they're taking your sister to the hospital, you need to be there."

In the end, I accepted his offer. Sheepishly, because I'd harbored murderous thoughts toward the fellow not thirty minutes earlier.

Excusing myself for a second, I walked over to the wrecked car. The firefighters were satisfied there was no fuel leak and the police had moved the rest of their interviewees to the access road. The wrecker driver handed me his card as I was starting to walk over to the ambulance. I made a mental note to call our insurance company to send an assessor out to police impound, though he'd have to wait until the cops were done looking at it.

"Do you need to get anything out of the car?"

I was about to tell him he could keep the barbecue when I remembered Charlie's gun. I retrieved it from the glove compartment, along with a few personal items I had no idea if she needed or not; were three mascaras too much? Mankind may never know.

The cops had already told me they'd be in touch if they had any more questions. I didn't envy the report that was going to come out of this. A hit and run that shut the entire North Freeway down for almost an hour? Oof.

Satisfied things were wrapping up, I finally made my way to the ambulance and leaned against the back door next to where Charlie half sat, half lay.

"How are you feeling?" I asked.

"Sore. You okay?"

I said, "Think so. Tired after the adrenaline rush."

"How's the car?"

I shook my head, like a doctor in the movies letting the hero know his faithful sidekick didn't make it.

She punched the gurney, then flinched in pain. "God *damn* it! And I guess the Ferrari got away." It wasn't a question.

I nodded. "Guy must have been a hell of a driver to disappear in rush hour traffic. The police have alerts out for it. He's most likely gone to ground at this point, but if he hasn't, a red Testarossa is going to stick out like, well, a red Testarossa."

The EMT came up and said they were ready to go. I gave him a thumbs-up like a doofus, and he shut the rear doors. The driver started the engine, and they were off.

I could visualize the wrecker driving off with the ruins of the Audi and the fire truck pulling away as the police prepared to reopen the freeway. The backup was probably all the way to the Loop by now and likely the top story on local news, judging by the number of helicopters buzzing overhead.

Happy Thursday. Hopefully nobody got shot.

I walked back to Stu's truck and clambered into the passenger seat. The vehicle was high enough off the ground that I had to use the step, but I kept my mouth shut. The guy was doing me a huge favor.

"All squared away?" he asked.

I nodded. "Yep. They're going to Northwest Medical."

"I know that place. My cousin had to get her finger amputated there."

I silently cursed the TABC for not allowing passengers to drink in cars anymore.

If there's one good thing about arriving right behind the EMTs, it's that you immediately get taken into the emergency room. Coming in on a gurney is like a VIP laminate at a concert, and while I felt a little bad for walking in with Charlie past all the mopes in the waiting room, none of them were going to be haggling with their insurance company about covering the cost of an ambulance ride later.

They took the X-rays. Sure enough, fractures of the seventh and eighth ribs on her left side with a bonus chest contusion. The doctor wanted to keep her overnight to make sure there were no complications involving her heart and lungs. Charlie wasn't happy about it, and while I wasn't going to say it, I'd be a lot happier with her under observation in the hospital than alone at the house while I was meeting with Steranko.

My brother Don arrived as they were moving Charlie to her room, having been dispatched by our mother to both check on her only daughter and to keep her apprised of the situation. I gave him the rundown (poor choice of words) on what happened and explained my concerns about leaving her alone.

"Have you talked to the cops about posting a guard?" he asked.

I said, "I did, but they're waiting on approval."

He raised an eyebrow. "A guy with a gun breaks into your house this morning and now this, and they're still not convinced?"

"This is Montgomery County," I said. "Their sheriff's department has to talk to HPD. I have no doubt they'll get it straightened out eventually, but in the meantime ..."

"In the meantime, you need someone to babysit," he said.

Apologetic, I said, "If that's not too much trouble."

He gave me a funny look. "She's our sister, you idiot. Besides, your little excursion already canceled the only real plans I had tonight. Carlos and I were talking about going to the movies, but I'm pretty sure he'll understand."

"Thank him for me."

"I will," Don said. Then, "Can I ask what you're going to be doing?"

I told him about our Russian suspicions and that I was meeting someone to discuss them. I didn't mention Steranko's name — no need to drag another family member into this — or anything else about the case.

He said, "Anything to help find Mike. We'll be fine."

I didn't doubt him. Don was in the Green Berets before he was discharged under circumstances he refused to discuss. From what Charlie had pieced together, it involved him reacting negatively to a superior's homophobia.

Said superior spend several weeks in traction as a result.

"I have another favor to ask," I said.

"Shoot."

"Can I borrow your car?"

He looked at me. "Finally gave up on that heap of yours?"

"No," I said. "But it's still back at the house. And even if I didn't have a bit of a drive ahead of me, I don't trust it outside of AAA's rapid response radius."

He fished in the pocket of his jeans, removed a key from a ring of several, and handed it to me. "You know my old Range Rover. I parked near the ambulance bay."

"Thanks," I said. "I could be wrong, but I think this is Charlie's first time in a hospital since she had her tonsils out. She's not going to show it, but I bet she's nervous."

"I got it covered."

I made sure no one was looking and handed him Charlie's gun, a Browning 9mm. He looked around for a second, then took it and slipped it into his back waistband.

We both went to Charlie's room. She brightened considerably when she saw Don, which I didn't take personally. He was much nicer than me.

"Don!" she exclaimed. "Cy didn't tell me you were coming."

"Cy didn't know," I said. "He's going to hang out with you while I check out a lead on Mike."

We exchanged a look Don didn't notice. She understood: keep Steranko close to the chest until we know more.

"I appreciate it," she said. "But I'm afraid there's not much to do besides watch TV."

"*Au contraire*," he said, and he produced a deck of cards from his inner jacket pocket. "As I recall, you're into me for about a thou. Time to see if you can erase some of that debt."

I smiled in spite of myself. Gin was the closest thing to a combat sport the Clarkes indulged in when they weren't actually participating in combat sports.

Don started dealing cards onto the bedspread and I backed out of the room, shutting the door behind me. Family time was over. Now I had to go see about a Russian.

TWENTY-THREE

Traffic going north was still jacked up from our crash. Luckily, I was heading in the opposite direction.

The island of Galveston is about 50 miles from Houston as the crow flies. As with any place in the greater metro area, of course, it's generally best to allow a good hour to 90 minutes travel time.

Just in case, I don't know, some asshole in a Ferrari decides to run two perfectly nice people off the road.

I elected to avoid taking the freeway straight through downtown and hopped on the East Beltway. It was two hours before I was scheduled to meet Steranko, so there was no hurry. While I cruised through Houston's less-than-picturesque eastern reaches, I called DeSantos.

"You've had a busy day," he said by way of greeting.

"You heard."

He laughed. "Kind of hard not to when every channel is showing aerial footage of Charlie's car holding up ten miles of freeway traffic. Is she okay?"

I said, "Couple of busted ribs and a bruised chest. They're keeping her in the hospital overnight for observation."

"That's good news," he said.

"I'm fine, by the way."

"I figured, or you wouldn't be able to make annoying phone calls."

Asshole. "Roy, I'm about to meet a guy who might be

involved in Mike's disappearance."

I could almost hear him straighten up over the phone. "Really? Who?"

"The only name I have is Steranko," I started.

"Steranko?" He mulled for a bit. "The casino guy?"

Part of the plan for the island entertainment district Charlie had looked up included plans for a casino, though gambling hadn't been legalized in Texas yet. "So you've heard of him?"

"Sure," Roy said. "He's an up-and-comer, and then there's the Russian Mafia rumors."

Steering away from that, I said, "He seems to keep a pretty low profile."

"Well, yeah," he said. "He mostly keeps to himself. Doesn't do the club thing and doesn't come into town much. He prefers to hang out on his boat."

I thought for a second. "The *Konev*?"

"Is that what it's called?" he asked, then, "Wait, how do you know that?"

"Because that's where I'm going to meet him."

Roy said, "Is that a good idea?"

I said, "I don't think I have any choice. And anyway, this is all your fault."

"How the hell is it *my* fault?" Indignant now.

"Because your contact gave me his name."

"Really?"

"Really."

"Well, hell," he said. "Then I guess you really don't have a choice."

I rolled my eyes. "How have they not promoted you yet?"

"When did he contact you?" He was back to being all business now.

"Right after a goddamned Ferrari Testarossa ran Charlie and me off the road."

He whistled. "A Testarossa, you say."

"Yeah," I said. "Why, does that mean something to you?"

"Steranko is known to have quite the sports car collection," he said.

"Ferraris?"

"Don't know specifics," Roy replied. "But I can check."

Something was nagging at me. "Does this seem all terribly convenient to you?"

"What do you mean?"

"I mean: mysterious caller with Russian accent; your contact drops Steranko's name; a sports car runs me and Charlie off the road, and Steranko just happens to have a sports car collection?" I paused. "Doesn't seem a little convenient to you?"

"You're not thinking like a cop anymore," he replied.

"I'm *not* a cop anymore," I said, and hung up.

He'd meant it as an insult, but he was more right than he realized. Cops, especially detectives, are interested in one thing above all: the clearance rate. If a solution to a crime gifted itself to them, as appeared to be the case with Steranko and the now multiple attempts on my and Charlie's lives, so much the better.

Thinking like a cop would mean going along with Steranko as the person responsible for Mike's disappearance. If I was still a detective, at the very least I probably would've paid him a visit with a few uniforms and asked some "friendly" questions.

So, in effect, exactly what I was about to do. Only without backup, or legal sanction, or any force of law behind me. What could possibly go wrong?

My meandering drive to Galveston — including stops at Whataburger and to refuel the Range Rover (the least I could do after eating in Don's car) — took about an hour and a half. I had looked up the Galveston Yacht Club and Marina while in the Whataburger drive-through. It was on the east end of the island, past the end of the famed Seawall and near the cruise terminal, where tourists willingly imprisoned themselves on floating sardine cans for the privilege of getting blackout drunk on "booze cruises" out of Cozumel.

I'm not a cruise fan, in case you were wondering.

The marina was big enough to employ golf carts for those unwilling to walk half a mile or so to their boat's berth. I parked in what I hoped was a public lot (getting Don's car towed would be the perfect cap on a shitty day) and set off on foot.

It was full dark, but several other people were visible walking to and from the dock. A couple men in those ridiculous shirts with the flaps on the back lugged a cooler that one assumed was full of redfish and speckled trout out to the parking lot, while an older couple walked up to a large sailboat, presumably for a twilight cruise. If security had any problem with my roaming, they didn't make their presence known.

The boats ranged in size from Sunfish-style sailboats to catamarans on up to yachts that by rights should have led to the reinstatement of the guillotine. I assumed Steranko's would be one of these.

I was more right than I could have hoped. The *Konev* was the very last boat. It occupied its own dock, far enough from those of the *lumpenproletariat* to ensure it couldn't be missed.

The fact it was also the biggest one around didn't hurt.

It was over a hundred feet long, with three decks and a communications array that wouldn't have looked out of place on an AWACS. I could see people moving back and forth and inside the brightly lit main cabin. There were a number of limos and town cars lining the drive leading to the pier, and two men who were big enough to moonlight as Bigfoot impersonators flanking the ramp leading up to the boat.

It was early yet, so I kept walking.

I wandered past the pier and looked out across the water to Pelican Island. I was shielded from the sea breeze on this side of the island, but the wind never really died down. From my vantage point, I watched as the Bolivar Ferry took another load of cars and people to the peninsula. Ten years after Hurricane Ike had essentially razed the entire place, and there was almost no trace remaining to show it had happened.

People would keep building there. The beach life really must be something else if it was worth potentially having your house leveled to the foundations every summer.

It occurred to me that Roy might be right: This was an extraordinarily bad idea.

I didn't like boats to begin with, and a big reason for that was an inability to leave. It was the cruise issue writ small. Sure, it wasn't like I'd be out in the middle of the ocean, but the problem remained: The only way off if someone didn't want you to leave was over the side.

The presence of other people was somewhat comforting, at least. Not that any of them would lift a well-manicured nail to help me if shit went sideways, but I could at least be reasonably sure Steranko wouldn't straight-up murder me in front of them. Even the rich had limits.

Or so I hoped.

I heard footsteps approaching and turned around warily. One of the sasquatches had detached from the pier and was approaching. I kept my hands at my side and tried to calm the latter part of my fight or flight instinct.

"Mr. Clarke?" He was surprisingly articulate for a missing link.

"That's me."

He turned so his side was facing me and held his arm out in the direction of the *Konev*. "Mr. Steranko would like a word."

TWENTY-FOUR

The interior of Steranko's boat was right out of *Casino Royale*. It was furnished with a degree of opulence I'd never experienced in the flesh, and just standing in the main cabin made me feel shabby.

And that was before I even looked at the crowd. There was quite the soirée going on. People (mostly couples) drifted through the various rooms, murmuring in what I assumed was appreciation for the furnishings.

The bodyguard, or whoever he was, had ushered me in and left me to my own devices. Eager as I was to explore the *Konev*, I felt the more prudent course of action was staying put. Steranko would find me when he was ready.

In the meantime, I got to enjoy some really high-quality stink-eye. Let me tell you, if you've never gotten a contemptuous once-over from a rich person, you're missing out. The dress code was apparently evening formal, and my chosen combination of Costco jeans, sneakers, and Men's Wearhouse sports coat clearly wasn't cutting it with these folks.

I returned a few looks with a smile accompanied by an upraised middle finger. That got boring quick, so I looked around for a drink. There were at least two servers circling with trays of champagne, but I was in the mood for harder stuff. Chancing a look into the next room, I saw an ornate bar staffed by an attractive, yet bored-looking black woman. Nobody named Steranko had approached me yet, so I hurried over.

"Evening," I said.

She assumed a more professional demeanor. "What can I get for you, sir?"

"This an open bar?"

Her raised eyebrow was the only indication I had that I was possibly the dumbest person on the boat.

"Excellent," I said, scanning the racks of booze. "Is that Macallan the eighteen year?"

"The twenty-five year," she said.

"Make it a double," I said.

"Neat?"

"Is that a trick question? Who puts ice in twenty-five-year-old scotch?"

She glanced around the room by way of an answer, and I couldn't tell if she was smiling at my cheek or grimacing at my lack of couth. I took out my wallet as she retrieved the bottle. There was a pint glass on the bar sitting in the usual location for a tip jar, but it was empty.

"Are you allowed to accept tips?" I asked.

"In theory," she said, handing me the tumbler. "Enjoy your drink."

I dropped a five into the pint glass. Big spender. "Thanks. I hope your evening's not too shitty."

She gave me a Cub Scout salute and returned the bottle to the shelf. I turned, raising the glass to my lips. There was a short-ish fellow in a gray suit standing in front of me.

"Mr. Clarke?" The accent was distinctly Slavic, but not overpowering in a "moose and squirrel" sense.

I swallowed my drink (holy hell, was it good). "Mr. Steranko, I presume?"

He offered his hand and I took it. I don't know why, but handshakes have always bugged the hell out of me. Nothing like an outdated mode of greeting to help transfer cold germs and bacteria from guys who didn't wash after taking a leak. And that's not counting the guys who view each shake as a personal challenge to see how many of your metacarpals they can try to grind into dust.

Still, it beat cheek-kissing.

Steranko's handshake was firm, but not desperately so, and he didn't pull me toward him for the one-arm bro hug, for which I was grateful. His hair was close-cropped, the dim lights picking up gray streaks along the sides. He was fit and his suit looked like it cost only slightly less than his shoes.

I tried to remember the last time I'd washed my jeans.

"What is that you're drinking?" He looked at my glass.

"The Macallan," I said, then added "Twenty-five."

He nodded. "An excellent choice." He looked at the bartender. "I'll have the same."

She didn't roll her eyes this time. Smart girl.

When Steranko had his drink, he turned and started walking. I followed.

"Have you had a chance to explore the boat?" he asked.

"Uh, no."

"Please, come with me."

He led me toward the front of the boat, or what you call the "bow," I guess. I was never in the Navy.

"You seem to have done well for yourself," I said, looking around me and acting like I knew anything about boats.

He smiled. "That's not really why you want to talk to me, is it?"

If nothing else, I respected his desire to get to the point, "I'm just trying to find out what happened to my brother," I said. "I don't really give a shit how you make your money."

Steranko opened a sliding door that led to a deck. We were on the middle level of the *Konev*, and, as he closed the door behind us, I couldn't help noticing we were the only people there.

"Why do you assume I had anything to do with his disappearance?"

"I don't assume anything," I replied. "Someone gave me your name and I'm just doing my job by following the lead."

He walked to the railing and leaned on it. We could see tankers and container ships moving through the Houston Ship Channel a short distance away.

"Do you know who I named my boat after?" Steranko asked.

"I'm afraid I don't." *But you're going to tell me, aren't you?*

He took another drink. "Ivan Konev was one of the greatest generals in Soviet history. He helped the USSR win the great

Battle of Kursk in World War II and defended Moscow when the Germans invaded."

"Impressive."

He said, "Very impressive. He was twice named Hero of the Soviet Union and also awarded the Order of Victory, which was the highest decoration given by the USSR and only given to sixteen individuals."

"My uncle has a star on the Hollywood Walk of Fame," I said.

Ignoring me, Steranko continued, "The great Zhukov won it twice, and it was also given to Eisenhower and Montgomery, in thanks for their ... eventual service."

What was I supposed to say? I'd studied the Second World War enough to know the Russians bled by the millions while the western Allies readied the eventual invasion of Europe.

"I've heard of Zhukov, but I'm guessing there's a reason you didn't name your boat after him."

"Konev's military prowess can't be denied," he said, "but I am possibly more of a fan of his survivability in the post-war years."

I said, "He never ended up on Stalin's bad side?"

He shook his head. "He kept his head down. Where Zhukov became embroiled in scandal and ran afoul of Stalin's security forces, Konev emerged from that era even more popular, allying with Krushchev and eventually becoming Commander in Chief of all Warsaw Pact forces during the Cold War."

"You'll forgive my saying this," I said, "but he seems like an odd person for a man of your, let's say, free market tendencies to idolize."

"I am a poor Communist." He chuckled. "And I wouldn't say I 'idolize' Konev, but I very much admire both his prowess as a tactician and his survival skills."

I said, "Sounds like a fitting role model for someone in your line of work."

"What do you know of my 'line of work'?"

Easy now. "Just rumors, mostly. I used to be a cop, but I don't have access to that kind of information anymore." Not official access, anyway, I didn't add.

Steranko turned to face me. "You wouldn't be so stupid as

to come onto my boat wearing a wire, would you?"

"You think this is a sting?" I raised my shirt to show my electronically unadorned torso. "Your boys already frisked me before I came aboard."

"For guns," he said. "And probably not very well. They were hired for the party. I thought it best to leave my regular detail out of sight."

"Too ugly?"

"Too unlikely to show restraint," he said. "I'm the one who maintains a civilized façade, throwing charity cruises and opening restaurants and whatnot."

"But they're the ones breaking kneecaps and feeding guys to pigs," I finished for him.

He sighed. "I *wish* we had pigs. So efficient. The Brazilians, now; you want to disappear, piss off the Mob in São Paolo."

The dull hum of the engines grew louder, and I felt the deck shift under my feet.

"What's going on?" I tried to sound nonchalant. The talk of flesh-eating pigs made that difficult.

Steranko said, "Did you miss the part about this being a charity *cruise*? We're going out into the bay for a bit. Let the rich folks feel like they're getting something for their donation."

This was exactly what I was worried about, and I could practically hear Roy saying "I told you so" all the way from Houston. If things went south while we were still docked, at worst I'd be looking at a short swim back to shore. Heading out the open sea (or the bay, whatever) changed things considerably.

As I was contemplating the sudden shift in my immediate future prospects, the door behind us slid open. Steranko and I both turned to watch the figure who was emerging.

The bulky dude coming through the door must be one of the "regular detail" he mentioned. I took little comfort in noting he was just as ugly as I'd assumed.

TWENTY-FIVE

"What's this about, Ster … " I looked at him. "Is 'Steranko' your first name?"

"No," he said, with a faint smile on his face.

"Do you have a first name?"

He was looking over my shoulder. "Yes, but you should probably attend to the matter at hand."

I turned to see the large fellow had covered the distance between us with surprising swiftness and I barely had time to duck his punch, a hard right that grazed the top of my head.

Throwing an elbow that connected solidly but otherwise appeared to have no effect, I rolled to my right and mostly avoided a knee that bounced off my shoulder and sounded like it cracked the railing behind me.

I came to my feet a little less gracefully than I'd have liked, and shed my sports coat. If I'd known Steranko was inviting me to the *Kumite*, I'd have worn a cup.

Speaking of my host, he'd retreated to a corner and was watching us with interest. *Sell some tickets next time, prick.*

Tiny — we hadn't been properly introduced so I was obliged to come up with a nickname for the guy — closed in again. Large as he was, his style was compact: slight crouch, arms in, moving with purpose and confidence. He had some training, which wasn't good for me. Unlike the guy whose clock I'd cleaned at the bar the other night, this guy wasn't relying on his bulk. It was a potentially unpleasant combination.

I feinted with my left and probed his defenses with a right jab. He blocked that easily, but not the shot to the solar plexus I immediately followed up with, again with the left. He grunted, but if I did any real damage, it wasn't apparent.

He went in low to grab me and I dodged left, dropping an elbow on his right shoulder blade. He swung out with his own elbow and caught me in the thigh. It wasn't a clean hit, but it hurt like a son of a bitch.

We separated and Tiny assumed his defensive posture a trifle more slowly than before. As for me, my shoulder was throbbing from the one knee that didn't even fully connect and I was going to be walking with a limp for the next week or so.

The guy wasn't scoring any solid shots, but he could keep wearing me down with glancing blows and eventually I'd be too slow to get out of the way or too tired to keep my guard up. I needed to end this now.

Dropping my guard a little on purpose had the desired effect as he swooped in with a right cross that would've taken my head off if I hadn't been prepared for it. Instead, I lowered my head and as his fist passed harmlessly over me, I rushed forward and shoved him into the cabin wall.

If his feet were set, he might have been able to stop us, but coming up off his back foot like he did meant I pushed him a good 15 feet with almost no resistance. I applied the same philosophy of aiming your punch behind your opponent's head and tried to knock him through the wall.

I didn't succeed, but we put a hell of a dent in it.

His arms dropped, but he wasn't out yet. I did my best to rectify that, working his body with my fists and his face with my elbows. Finally, after my arms had started screaming in pain and I was nearly out of breath, he slumped to the deck.

I had a brief urge to throw him overboard, but gassed as I was, I doubt I could've followed through with it (and I've never killed anyone, that I'm aware of). I rubbed the sweat off my face. Now that I'd already ruined my clothes, I might as well pound on Steranko until he told me what I wanted to know. I turned around.

The mobster hadn't moved from his observation post. He had, however, been joined by two more dudes. Each bigger than the guy I'd just put down.

"Son of a bitch," I muttered.

Steranko laughed. "How stupid do you think I am?"

I raised my arms into defensive posture and waited. Maybe if I was lucky I could catch one of them with a kick to the nuts. Though given the way my night was turning out, they were both wearing cast iron codpieces.

He put his hands up, palms out, and said, "Please, enough. It is not my intention to make you fight any more. These gentlemen are just here as a precaution."

I kept my arms up, but my heart rate decreased. Poking Tiny with my foot, I said, "And this gentleman?"

"I had to see how serious you were." Steranko said. "If you allowed Ignatius to beat you, then clearly you had more treacherous reasons for being here than simply trying to find your brother."

Ignatius? Nigel? Where the hell were these names coming from?

"You have an interesting way of establishing motive," I said, finally dropping my hands. "You're better than those psychics the cops sometimes use."

He tapped his head. "A criminal I may, ah, allegedly once have been, but I am still a keen judge of character."

At this point, I didn't care if the guy's compass was missing a few points, it was just a relief not to worry about getting my nose broken again.

I straightened my collar in a futile attempt to make it look like I hadn't just been in a brawl and bent over to retrieve my sports coat. "So now what?"

Steranko beamed and walked over to me, his bodyguards keeping a few paces behind him. "Now we have another drink and talk about your brother."

You had to hand it to the guy, he didn't always make you feel welcome, but he was a hell of a host when he put his mind to it.

We were seated in what I assumed was his private receiving cabin, and my mind reeled momentarily when considering how much money it took to have such a thing on a goddamned boat. The chairs were leather and extremely comfortable, and pieces of art I guessed cost more than my entire house were hung at tasteful intervals on the walls.

The rest of the reception was a dull murmur through the walls, except for the brief moment of noise when the door opened to admit a young woman in a black top and what I think Charlie refers to as a "midi" skirt. She brought two more tumblers of what I hoped was delicious Macallan.

It was. Unfortunately, the booze stung the various cuts on the inside of my lips, and the signature sherry cask sweetness was tempered by the taste of blood. Still, Macallan 25, man.

The woman left, and it was just Steranko and me in the cabin. Well, and his goons. They'd retreated to the shadows but were about as easy to ignore as a couple of rhinos in turtlenecks.

He began, "It seems you've been led to believe I had something to do with your brother ... what was his name again?"

"Mike."

"Something to do with Mike's disappearance. Is that correct?"

I said, "Your name came up. I'm just doing what a private investigator does: following leads."

"And what has your investigation turned up?" he asked.

"Honestly? Not much," I said. "I agreed to meet you out here," I waved the tumbler around, careful not to spill any, "on the high seas, to try and figure out if you had anything to do with it."

"And what do you think?"

"Did you send someone to my house to kill me?" I countered.

Steranko frowned. "When was this?"

"This morning," I said.

"I am not in the habit of sending assassins in broad daylight," he said, and I didn't follow up by asking when the optimal time of day for murder was. "Do you have a reason to think I'm involved?"

"He was carrying a Russian pistol."

He asked, "A Makarov?"

I nodded.

"These are not so difficult to obtain. They've been produced for decades, the world over. Still, it would not be my first choice."

I said, "A Glock or SIG makes more sense. The fact it happened to be a Russian gun can't be a coincidence, and has the possibly unintended effect of making me think you actually had nothing to do with it."

Steranko seemed gratified, though not overly so. "Is there any other reason to think him connected to me?"

"Not that I know of." Then I remembered something. I retrieved the lighter from my pocket and tossed it to him. "He was carrying this, but unless you're a big Batman fan I don't see what it has to do with anything."

He caught it and turned it over in his hand. The look on his face didn't fill me with confidence.

"What?" I asked.

He held it up to me. "You don't recognize this?"

I shook my head. "I thought it was some promo thing to go with the old Tim Burton movie. Maybe along with that Prince album."

His smile was without humor. "Mr. Clarke, this is a *Spetsnatz* lighter. It was carried by Russian special forces."

"You sure?"

"Quite sure."

I took another sip of scotch and tried not to appear agitated. The *Spetsnatz* were no joke, and had a well-earned reputation for being utterly ruthless. My gut feeling has been telling me this was all a diversion, but maybe my guts were full of crap after all.

Finally, I said, "Not buying it."

"No?" He'd put the lighter down and was watching me carefully.

"If you were behind it, why tell me where the lighter came from?"

"You could have been bluffing."

I said, "If I was, you had nothing to gain by telling me the truth. No, the more I think about it, the more I think this is a red herring."

Steranko sat back in his chair and contemplated his scotch. "How can you be sure?"

I shrugged. "I'm not. For all I know, you're going to go out in the Gulf, cut my throat, and dump me over the side."

Without being too overt about it, I glanced at the goons, but neither of them acted like they'd heard me.

"Too many people saw you come aboard." He smiled, shark-like. "Why, I would have to sink the entire boat, ha ha!"

"Good one," I said. "Yakov Smirnoff better watch out."

He said, "Seriously, bringing the sort of merchandise your brother was investigating into the United States in this political climate is more trouble than it's worth. The price has increased a hundredfold, the distances covered strain logistics, and local concerns have a much more robust infrastructure to deal with supply issues."

"That's amazing," I said. "You sound like a regular businessman. From what you just said, I'd never know you were talking about enslaving women and children."

He clucked his tongue. "You're arguing semantics."

I said, "Nah, that's always how y'all try to defend yourselves; by throwing out bullshit equivalency arguments about how banks ruin more lives than drugs, or the oil companies cause more lasting damage, but you kill people and force them into prostitution. Or worse. So spare me the evils of capitalism speech."

Steranko was silent and for a minute I was sure my earlier prediction of getting pitched overboard with a Colombian necktie were about to come true.

"I'm not used to being spoken to like that," he finally said.

"I'm not used to mouthing off to … guys like you. Do you have any brothers or sisters?" I asked.

"One brother."

"Is he older or younger than you?"

"Older," he said.

"Are the two of you close?"

He smiled. "We haven't spoken in fifteen years. I think. Perhaps, this is the reason I wanted to clear the air. You are obviously keenly interested in finding your Mike, which is why I wanted to bring you out here and tell you you're barking up the wrong tree. As they say."

"It's all very convenient," I agreed. "The caller with the Russian accent, the car. Do you own any Ferraris?"

He snorted. "Italian trash. I prefer British and German manufacturers. McLaren makes very good vehicles."

"I'm not much of a car guy," I muttered.

"I'll say." Steranko laughed. He turned to his bodyguards and said something in Russian that had them both laughing. Evidently the Corolla's reputation preceded it.

"My point is," I said, "someone is obviously trying to point me at you, but I'm reasonably sure you're not involved."

"That's good to hear."

I rose, finishing my scotch. "Just know that if I find out you actually are involved, you're going to learn how it feels to get a McLaren parked on your chest."

TWENTY-SIX

There were a couple reasons I believed Steranko.

First, he didn't have to meet with me. Hell, he didn't even have to acknowledge me. You might think a guilty person would be only too eager to protest their innocence, except Steranko hadn't protested so much as matter-of-factly explained why he wasn't involved. True, his explanation was almost bone-chilling in its indifference, meaning there was just as good a chance he was a sociopath as he was innocent, but call it a gut feeling: I believed him.

Second — and as I'd already pointed out — it was too much. "Boris," the Testarossa, the would-be assassin with the Makarov … it made me wonder why Nevaeh gave me his name in the first place.

Maybe another trip to Bottoms Up was in order. I could chat some more with my good buddy Nigel.

The cruise lasted another hour after I left Steranko, and I did my best to remain invisible until we docked. My host had helpfully allowed me to wash up in a bathroom that was roughly the size of the first floor of my house, but my clothes were still rumpled and I doubt I smelled all that great.

I went back to the bar to see if there was any Macallan left and was told by a very contrite bartender that I was cut off. Apparently there were reports that I'd been behaving aggressively. I laughed hysterically at that, which I'm sure only served as confirmation of same.

I spent the rest of the cruise on the stern deck, close enough to the engine and the propeller-thing that the volume discouraged conversation seekers. We returned to the marina and I easily beat everyone else off the boat. Don's Range Rover was still in the lot. Looking around at the sea of luxury vehicles, I was happy with my decision to borrow his car, as the Corolla likely would've been towed as an eyesore.

It wasn't especially warm, but I felt grimy from the sweat of my fight with Tiny and the sea air. I cranked the air-conditioning to max and steered the Range Rover onto Broadway, which ran for a few miles along the island then turned into the southern terminus of I-45.

I needed to call Charlie, and probably Roy, and let them know I wasn't sleeping with the fishes, or whatever the euphemism's Russian equivalent was, but I was still mulling over the evening's events.

If Steranko wasn't involved, and I was increasingly convinced he wasn't, then I was back at square one. Mike was missing and whoever was responsible was sending me red herrings to try and implicate Steranko.

But why? What benefit was there to putting me and Steranko together? If someone wanted to get rid of me, there were less complicated ways than engineering a meeting with a gangster and hoping I'd piss him off enough to kill me.

Though I had to say, intentional or not, it had almost worked.

Conversely, calling in a hit on Steranko should be less half-assed then sending an ex-cop to his boat. It'd be some kind of *Splinter Cell* level shit to infiltrate his boat, make my way past multiple bodyguards, kill the guy, and then escape undetected.

Unless whoever was behind this wanted me dead. But that led me back to my first point. No matter how I looked at it, I couldn't see the angle.

Broadway became I-45 and before long I was on the causeway to the mainland. Traffic was light at this hour, though some people getting the jump on a three-day weekend were apparent on the other side.

Steranko's reference to "local interests" was aimed at the cartels, and he was right about the infrastructure. Houston was just one port of entry for anyone they wanted to traffic from Mexico or Central/South America. They could embark from dozens of spots on the Mexico coast or along the Rio Grande, arriving at dozens of others on American soil.

And they would come by boat, train, truck, plane, SUV, or on foot. A steady stream of humanity doomed to monstrous cruelty just to fatten the pockets of cruel monsters.

The Russian, on the other hand, would have markedly fewer options. Steranko would have to use large ships and planes, unless he tried to funnel them through Canada (the cartels wouldn't let any Russian cargo disembark on their territory, after all). And recent crackdowns on immigration, both legal and otherwise, meant more palms to grease. The higher costs he'd referred to.

If the safe house DHS raided wasn't one of Steranko's, then it stood to reason it belonged to the cartels. Ron said most of the women were Central American, and I made a note to ask him about the last time the task force had run across any Russian or Eastern European women. Maybe Steranko was telling the truth about being out of the business.

I wasn't taking anything for granted, and even if that revenue stream was done, Steranko was still rumored to be bringing in heroin, guns, and god knew what else. He was still a scumbag, in other words.

I was missing something, I knew, but I was too tired from car crashes and boat brawls to figure it out right now.

I called Charlie, but it went straight to voicemail. She'd be asleep, seeing as it was almost 2:00 a.m., but recent events made me worry nonetheless. I left a message telling her I was okay and not to wait up.

My phone rang. It was Roy.

"Hello?" I said, holding the phone to my ear. "Hello?"

Nothing. I glanced at the screen. *Dumbass.* The phone had paired to the Range Rover's Bluetooth, so I hit the hands-free option and Roy's voice filled the car.

"Cy? You sound like you're at the bottom of a well."

"Sorry," I said. "Technical difficulties."

"How'd the meeting go?" he asked.

I replied, "About as pleasant as could be expected."

"He didn't throw you over the side, at least."

"No," I agreed. "And he let me drink some of his twenty-five-year-old scotch."

Roy whistled in appreciation, except I hated whistling and he knew it. "So y'all are friends now, I take it?"

"I'm not going to marry his daughter or anything, but at least he didn't try to kill me." *Directly*, I didn't add.

"He has a daughter?" Roy suddenly sounded interested.

I wasn't in the mood to deal with his libido. "Why are you calling me?"

"Have you seen the news this evening?" he asked.

I rubbed my temples with my non-steering hand. "Uh, no, Roy. Steranko's boat only gets QVC and Telemundo."

Roy said, "I wanted to call you before you heard anything, but the story leaked tonight. They've officially linked Mike's gun to the Ramirez killing."

I sat up straight, all fatigue leaving me. "What?"

"Easy," he began.

"Shut up," I said. "They have a ballistics match?"

Roy said, "Yep, someone leaked the report from the DHS testing facility this evening. Two shots fired from a SIG P229 that matched the weapon taken from the scene. It's registered as the service weapon for DHS Technical Enforcement Officer Mike Clarke."

I couldn't believe it. I *wouldn't* believe it. Could Mike really have killed a fellow agent in cold blood? It would explain why he ran; after all, if it was a clean shoot, the subsequent investigation would clear him.

"No," I said.

"No what?"

"This is bullshit, Roy. There's no way Mike would shoot one of his guys, I don't care what the report says."

"Cy." Roy's tone was gentle. "When was the last time you talked to Mike?"

"A few weeks ago, so what?"

"And when was the last time you talked to him about anything of substance?"

I didn't have an answer for that.

Roy continued, "I know you two weren't that close. Isn't it possible there was something going on, something at work, that might have gone south?"

"No," I said.

"Cy —"

I cut him off. "No, Roy! I don't care if we didn't get along or if he was an asshole sometimes, he's my brother and he didn't fucking do this!"

"Our hands are tied, Cy. Mike is officially going to be charged with Hector Ramirez's murder," Roy said. "I just wanted to let you know before you saw it on the news. I owe you that much."

He hung up before I could tell him to get fucked.

TWENTY-SEVEN

Mom's phone was ringing but she wasn't answering.

I thought about just driving straight on to The Woodlands, but I wanted to get out ahead of the news, if she hadn't seen it yet. She usually went to bed by 10:00, so chances were pretty good she was unaware.

My own phone rang. It was Charlie.

"Hello?"

"Hey."

"Why the hell are you up?" I asked.

I heard Don. "She won't take her painkillers." He sounded annoyed.

She said, "I slept when they brought me in. Don found Settlers of Catan in the pediatric lounge, so we're playing that."

"She's cheating, as usual," he interjected.

"He thinks I rigged the dice to get sevens, and won't even let me explain how stupid that sounds," her voice faded, and I realized she was directing her next remarks at Don. "If the dice are rigged, how come you're not rolling sevens, too? They're the same dice!"

"You probably hacked them."

"Dice don't have chips in them," she scoffed. To me, "Sorry, what's happening?"

I was glad to hear she was in good spirits, even if I was about to dash them. "They're charging Mike with Ramirez's murder."

"Goddamn it!" she said. I could hear Don asking what was going on. "Hold on, Cy. I'm putting you on speaker. Go."

I told Charlie and Don what Roy relayed to me a few minutes prior. They were silent for a moment.

"I'm not sure how to process this," Charlie said.

Don said, "What a crock of shit."

"I don't disagree," I said, "but there's nothing we can do about it now."

Charlie asked, "Has anybody talked to Mom?"

"I tried calling, but no answer. She's probably asleep."

"I'll try Kayla," Don said. "I need to get some air anyway." I heard him get up and, a second later, a door close.

"He's not taking this well," I said.

"Can you blame him?"

"No," I admitted. "And it feels like we're banging our heads against a wall, especially after the Steranko meeting."

"How did that go?"

I gave her a high-level version of my boat trip, right down to my near brawl with the Russian's prodigious pair of bodyguards.

"Nice." She chuckled. "He probably could've goaded you into it if you hadn't already tired yourself out on the first guy."

"It wouldn't have been a fair fight," I agreed, "but I bet I could've taken them."

"Two to one?" she asked, her incredulity apparent even over a 4G connection. "Boy, they would've beaten you like a drum. Holy shit."

"What?"

I heard her rustling around. "Where's my laptop?" It didn't sound like she was asking anyone in particular.

"Charlie?" I said. "Charlie, what's going on?"

"Where's my goddamned laptop? Nurse? Nurse!"

I was close to yelling now. "Charlie, pick up the phone!"

"Cy? I'm sorry," she said. She'd picked the phone up again. "I think I can crack Mike's code."

"What? How?"

She said, "I won't know until I can find my laptop, but I think it's a lot simpler than we initially thought."

"Didn't we get your backpack out of the car?" I asked after

a second.

"I thought so, but everything was so hazy when we — wait a minute." She dropped off again, which was starting to get annoying.

There was another voice in the room now, a female one that I assumed was the nurse. Really, I'm not sexist.

Charlie came back on. "Okay, that was the nurse." Told you I wasn't sexist. "She said the backpack was with my clothes and is going to get it for me."

I said, "Can you clue me in? What's the code?"

"I don't know for sure." She was lying, because her voice had the excited lilt to it that always appeared when she was about to solve a technical puzzle. "But visualizing you getting beaten up by two guys clicked for me."

"That's not entirely reassuring —"

She said, "No, listen! Two to one, beaten like a drum, beats, pulses ... I think I know how Mike encrypted his message."

That didn't make sense, to me anyway. "Charlie, I read those emails. Are you telling me you can read them now?"

"Not until I decode it," she said. "He ran it through an encryption cipher to garble it. I don't know what the key is, but once I have a copy of the emails I can start running them through some basic sets and see if there are any patterns."

This was all Greek — or Ultra, or Enigma — to me, but if Charlie was confident, that would be a huge boost.

"Now if I could just get my *goddamned laptop,*" she yelled. Evidently the nurse wasn't moving quickly enough for Charlie's purposes.

Not that any of us ever did.

I heard another voice, then Don came on the phone. "What the ever-loving hell is going on? Our sister looks like she's about to pop a blood vessel."

"She thinks she's figured out Mike's code," I told him.

Momentary silence, then, "Sounds like we'd better find that goddamned laptop."

In the movies, when hackers are shown breaking into secure government systems, it's to the accompaniment of techno/house or indie rock music while lines of code scroll across their face, cast by some mysterious projector bulb only found in movie laptops. In more extreme scenarios, it's depicted as a battle against formidable security apparatus poised to terminate the user's connection or — more terrifyingly — trace back the interloper's location, resulting in imminent arrival of squads of police in riot gear.

The reality, as is often the case, is depressingly tedious.

I was trying to doze in the hospital waiting room, because I knew Charlie would be incommunicado for a while, as she tends to get absorbed in even the most mundane of tasks. And trying to decrypt what might very well be her older brother's last words was another matter entirely.

Don't be so pessimistic, I kept telling myself, but professional experience and life in general worked against that approach. Most people who went missing in similar circumstances didn't turn up alive, and even if Mike wasn't "most people," he'd participated in a raid in which one of his fellow agents was dead and another was MIA.

That reminded me: I needed to check on Hanford again.

Things were moving too fast. It had barely been two days since we learned of Mike's disappearance. Time was a luxury we most assuredly did *not* have, and all I could do was sit on my thumbs and wait for Charlie to (hopefully) succeed. Mike's emails were literally the only real leads we had.

That wasn't entirely true, I guess. Someone had seen fit to put me on Steranko's scent, and my meeting with the Russian wasn't sitting well with me for that reason. I resented being used, and I wasn't getting back those hours wasted farting around on a boat.

I'd ruled Steranko out, but could I be sure? What real proof did I have besides his word that he wasn't involved? Forcing my mind to slow down, I tried to piece everything together.

Nevaeh had given me the name, and Bottoms Up was already on my agenda for tomorrow. But Roy was the one who tipped me off to look her up in the first place. Was the detective trying to throw me off the scent? For what reason? We went a ways back, but I'd been off the force for a while, and rumors always followed him, like seagulls behind a shrimp boat.

Shelving my suspicions about Roy for the moment, there

were other considerations. The lack of geographically appropriate women at the raid site, for starters. I'd never known a Russian operation to traffic in non-Eastern hemisphere "merchandise," for lack of a better term. The exception being Cubans, but the fall of the Soviet Union and the growing influence of regional cartels put an end to that.

Really, the only Russian link was the "Boris" guy who called and threatened us. And as someone who thought the guy who played Stringer Bell on *The Wire* was American for about 15 years, I couldn't really comment on the veracity of his accent.

The waiting room was mostly empty. Northwest Medical wasn't a trauma center, so your usual Friday night ER traffic was going elsewhere. I also wasn't sitting near the maternity ward, and since elective surgeries weren't generally scheduled on weekends (wouldn't want to interrupt your surgeon's tee time), I had the place mostly to myself.

The TV was playing a rerun of *Law & Order*, where Jack McCoy was berating someone wearing an Army uniform on the witness stand, but since the sound was off, it was easy to ignore.

Watching their silent courtroom theatrics, I suddenly remembered a comment Charlie made earlier that day about *pro bono* work. It was in relation to the phone the guy she shot was carrying. I remembered arguing with her that the phone's excessive price wasn't necessarily proof the guy was bankrolled by the Russians, but hadn't really known why.

Idly, I looked at the TV again. McCoy was really letting this Army guy have it, and as I wondered what he was charged with (and why he wasn't up before a military court), it struck me who else just might be able to afford to shell out for a constant supply of iPhones.

My own phone rang. It was Don.

"Talk to me, Goose."

"Get up here. Charlie figured it out."

TWENTY-EIGHT

The uniform they'd assigned to watch the room barely gave me the once-over as I walked by. Hopefully this was because his keen eyes had already recorded my comings and goings and not due to his looking forward to the Hooters waitress he was going to hit on when his shift was over. I glanced at him as I entered and got a barely perceptible shrug in response.

Charlie sat in bed, the annoying glow of self-satisfaction on her face. Her laptop was open but she wasn't working on it. Instead, she was staring at her apparent handiwork and nodding to herself.

"Well," I said. "Don't keep me in suspense."

Don said, "Don't look at me. Lisbeth Salander over there wanted to wait to spill the beans until you got here."

"A literary reference?" I said to Don. "I'm impressed."

"He saw the movie," Charlie said. "Have a seat." I did so.

She continued, "I didn't bother to ask for a projector, since it would probably be next week before they could track one down, so just lean forward and look at my screen."

She turned her laptop around on the bed and Don and I both awkwardly scooted our chairs forward.

To me, she said, "Do you remember the characters at the top of the encrypted portion of Mike's emails?"

"Yes, and I remember there being a lot of garbage text after them."

"Do you remember what those characters were?"

147

I shook my head. "Come on, sis. I can't remember my own Gmail password."

She pressed a key and the screen displayed the characters I now remembered as "C2U0J9M7D."

I glanced at Don, who was starting to look annoyed. "Okay, I remember now. So?"

She smiled, clearly having more fun than either of her brothers. "Look familiar?"

"I think I guessed it was a license plate earlier, but I suppose that's still not right," I said.

"Nope."

Don spoke up, "Excuse me, I know you assholes are big Sudoku fans and what not, but some of us would rather not spend the rest of the night jerking off in a hospital room. Figuratively."

"Literally is okay, I guess," I offered.

"Don't tempt me."

"Boys," Charlie interrupted. "The answer was right there all along, and it didn't even take … *crackerjack* timing to figure it out."

Don and I looked at each other. Maybe Charlie had sustained a head injury in the crash.

"Okay, I give," I said. "What the hell are you going on about?"

"I'll answer a question with a question," she said. "Are you crazy? Is that your problem?"

Don said, "Funny, we could ask you the same question."

She sighed. "Guys, you're going about this all wrong. Put it this way: What are some Clarke family traditions?"

"Bottling up our rage," I said.

"Disappointing our parents," Don offered.

"Passive aggression."

"Not picking up checks."

"Passive aggressively not picking up checks," I said.

"I didn't intend for this to turn into an airing of grievances," Charlie said. "What do we do every holiday season when we get together?"

Don and I both opened our mouths to reply and Charlie said, "Throttle back the sarcasm for a second and think."

"We … watch movies?" Don said. It was funny watching a

dude who had killed people with his bare hands answering questions with the timidity of a second grader.

Charlie nodded. "Very good. But what movies, or should I say, what *movie* in particular?"

I groaned. "Is that why you were quoting *Big Trouble in Little China* to us?"

"Finally," she said, "Yes, we watch *Big Trouble in Little China* every holiday season."

Don said, "Ugh, I hate that movie."

"We can argue about Kurt Russell's charms or John Carpenter's skills as a director another time," she said. "The point is, Mike loved the movie, and knew there was a good chance one of us would pick up on the hint."

"I still don't get it," Don said. "What do those letters have to do with anything?

Charlie looked at me. I rolled my eyes and peered even closer at her screen.

"Any time now," she said.

"Kiss my ass." I looked at the characters again. "Shit, now I see it: Mike just shifted the initials in the title and the year of release up one. "B1T9I8L6C' becomes 'C2U0J9M7D.'"

"You got it."

Don said, "And?"

Charlie said, "What you have here is a classic running key cipher. It's polyalphabetic, and uses text from a book or something to create the substitution key. In this case, the movie provided the text, I just had to figure out what quote to use to backward translate the ciphertext."

Don stared at me and I held my hands up. "I generally only comprehend about a quarter of what she's telling me, but if I'm understanding this correctly, Mike used a quote from *Big Trouble* to encrypt the message he wanted us to see."

"That's right," Charlie said.

"How did you figure out the quote?" Don asked.

"You never paid attention at Christmas," Charlie admonished him.

"Don't you remember?" I asked. "He was always quoting the opening scene, when Jack Burton is talking on the CB."

"And one line in particular," She began.

"'It's all in the reflexes,'" Don and I both finished.

"Son of a bitch," he said, "Was that really it?"

Charlie nodded. "Sure was."

"And running the ciphertext whatsis through that key gave you the message?" I said, vaguely proud of myself that I'd followed along to this point.

"Oh, no," Charlie said. "The decrypted text is actually Morse code"

Don said, "You're shitting me."

She smiled. "I shit you not. And it was actually Cy's phone call that gave me the clue I needed to solve it."

I frowned. "I did what in the what now?"

"You were talking about Steranko's two guys, whining about two on one and all that."

"That was hardly 'whining,'" I said. "I just remember you losing your shit when I told you that."

"It's called inspiration, you meathead. Archimedes? 'Eureka'? Any of that ring a bell?"

It did, but never give your opponent the upper hand. "That's why you were talking about beats and pulses," I said instead.

Charlie said, "The ciphertext had too many repeat characters to be anything but a series of dual characters."

"Dots and dashes," Don said.

"Exactly," she said. "Once I decrypted the Morse code, the rest was easy."

"So what does it say?" All this technical gobbledygook was giving me a headache, to go with all the other aches I'd earned this evening.

"That's the weird thing," she said. "It isn't really a straight message so much as it's a series of — I think — movie titles."

I perked up. This was my bag, baby. "Are you sure?"

She turned her laptop back around and started typing. "Not one hundred percent, but I figured you'd be the one to ask."

Charlie typed some more, hit Enter with authority, then turned the laptop back around so Don and I could once again look at the monitor.

"What do you think?"

I looked at the screen, where the same four coded phrases

were repeated over and over:

> WHEN A STRANGER CALLS
> 48 HRS
> MY BLUE HEAVEN
> ENEMY AT THE GATES

They were all movie titles all right. And they were sending a lot of mixed messages.

Charlie looked at me. "Well, can you make anything out of this?"

"I think so," I said, ticking off salient plot points to each of them in my head.

Don looked like he wanted to gnaw through my forehead. "And?"

"And I think Mike is alive."

TWENTY-NINE

"How the hell can you possibly know that?" Don asked.

I said, "Call it an early hunch, based solely on what I know about these particular movies."

He coughed in a way that told me he was having difficulty believing me. The truth of the matter was, Mike and I were the movie fans in the family, so the contents of the email made a certain amount of sense. And if he didn't get that, tough shit.

Charlie whistled low.

"What?" I said.

"He knew," she said. "He knew you'd start sniffing around into this. That's why he used titles of movies instead of just leaving a regular message."

"Like a sane person," Don added.

"But he encrypted it," I pointed out. "Because he knew you and I would be working together on the case."

Don snickered again. "He sure as hell knew *you* wouldn't be able to figure that shit out, Cy. Hell, we trained on field encryption in the Rangers and I don't think I could've picked up on this."

I said, "If he wanted to send the message to you, he would've wrapped it in a meat loaf," I said.

Don flipped me the bird. It was good to know the stress wasn't getting to him.

"If we can set aside this meeting of the mutual admiration society," he said, "what is it about these movies that makes you think Mike's alive?"

I looked at the list again, letting the images play out in my head. I'd seen all of them, multiple times in the case of all but the last one.

"He's trying to give us clues based on various plot points is my guess," I said.

Charlie said, "Fine, let's start with the first one."

"*When a Stranger Calls*." I nodded. "Classic 1979 horror movie starring Carol Kane."

"Where do I know that name?" Don asked.

"*Scrooged, The Princess Bride,*" I said absently. "*Annie Hall, Addams Family Values*, uh, *Joe vs the Volcano*, but only in a bit part ..."

Don raised his hands in defeat. "Enough, I bow to your movie nerd superiority. Jesus."

"*When a Stranger Calls* is the one about a babysitter who starts getting threatening phone calls while she's watching some kids. She calls the cops, who trace the calls and ..."

"Oh, I remember!" Charlie said. "They're coming from inside the house!"

I nodded. "Right, that's pretty much the whole thing that movie's known for."

Don said, "So what's the point?"

"It was an inside job," Charlie said.

I said, "There's no way to know for sure, but given the choice of movie, it'd be a safe bet there's something rotten in the DHS. Maybe Mike was onto it."

"*Hamlet*," Don said.

Charlie and I simultaneously: "What?"

"Something rotten in Denmark. *Hamlet*."

"Okay."

Don tapped his head. "I know stuff."

Charlie ignored him. "Okay, we think Mike was onto something dirty going on at DHS. What else?"

"I can't be sure," I said, "but I think the news about his gun is bullshit."

"Why's that?"

"The second movie on the list," I said. "*48 Hrs.*"

Don said, "I think I remember that one. Eddie Murphy,

right?"

"And Nick Nolte," I replied. "Probably the first 'buddy cop' movie. Murphy's a convicted bank robber Nolte's cop springs from prison to help him track down Murphy's old partner."

Charlie looked at me. "I'm not seeing the connection."

"One of the reasons Nolte's character is after Murphy's partner is because he stole his gun."

Charlie and Don looked at each other.

"That's a hell of a stretch," Don said.

I shook my head. "I don't think so. Mike could've used any movie in that genre. *Lethal Weapon, Tango and Cash, Beverly Hills Cop.* There are dozens. I think he picked this one precisely because of the missing gun subplot."

"So what we've extrapolated," Charlie said, "is that dirty deeds are afoot at the DHS, and somebody has Mike's gun?"

"Maybe," I said. "One thing I'd bet on: Mike's gun isn't the one that shot Ramirez."

"Is this what private detectives really do all day?" Don asked. "Because I'm thinking y'all charge way too much if that's the case."

"Relax, bro," Charlie said. "When we need somebody to punch a hole in a wall, we'll call you."

"That was one time."

"Only if we're limiting the definition of 'wall' to interior partition," she said. "I can throw in a few car doors, a couple of fences, and at least one live oak."

"Live oak?" I said. "You punched a tree? Let me guess: it barked at you one too many times?"

"It wouldn't leaf him alone," Charlie offered.

"I think we've found the root of his personality problem," I said.

"Stop!" Don said. "Jesus, this is why I don't visit you assholes."

"Where the hell was I when this happened?"

"You were still in the Academy," Charlie said. "Mom didn't want to embarrass him."

Don sat up. "And you're both going to hell for going against a mother's wishes." To me: "Can we get on with it?"

Charlie said, "The next one is *My Blue Heaven.*"

"Anyone?" I said.

Charlie shook her head. Don raised an eyebrow. "You serious?"

"Film from 1990. Steve Martin plays a mobster in witness protection. Rick Moranis plays the cop assigned to monitor him."

"And?" Don asked.

"And that's it. It's a comedy, in case you hadn't guessed from the cast. One interesting thing: both it and *Goodfellas* are based on the life of Henry Hill, and both came out the same year."

"That's fascinating," Don said, though the tone of his voice indicated it was anything but.

Charlie said, "There's nothing in the official raid reports or Mike's emails about WITSEC."

"Yeah," I said. "I don't know exactly where he's going with this one."

"That leaves *Enemy at the Gates*," Don said.

"Came out in 2001," I said. "Takes place during the Battle of Stalingrad in World War II."

"Sounds cheerful," Don said.

"Jude Law plays a Soviet sniper named Vasily Zaitsev, based on a real guy, who racked up over two hundred kills during the Nazi siege."

Now it was Don's turn to whistle. "Holy shit."

"Yeah," I said. "And Zaitsev wasn't even one of the top twenty Soviet snipers of the war."

Charlie said, "I don't get it. Those other movies at least were somewhat contemporary. A World War II flick? How does that relate?"

"Maybe Mike was trying to tell us Nazis are bad," Don said.

"He didn't need to send an encrypted email for that," I said.

Charlie snapped her fingers. "Maybe there really is a Russian gunning for us."

"I was just on a Russian's boat, in the middle of Galveston Bay." I shook my head. "No, we've been over this. Whatever Steranko is, he's not our enemy. Not directly."

"Maybe that's it," Don said.

"What?"

"Maybe Mike knew whoever was behind all this would try

to finger the Russians, and he chose this movie because it has the Russians as good guys."

"I don't know," I began.

Charlie said, "It fits. Mike would be guessing the future based on our expected reaction to events, without knowing who'd contact us, and only a vague idea of how things would play out."

Don said, "And he was always a good chess player."

"I guess it makes sense," I said. "But that still leaves the big problem."

"Where's Mike?" Don said.

"And where's Hanford?" Charlie added.

As if in answer, my phone rang. I didn't recognize the number, but it was a local area code. And at least it didn't say "unknown caller."

"Hello?"

A pause. "Is this Mr. Johnson?"

It took me a minute, and then I remembered. "It is indeed. Is this Mrs. Nguyen?"

"He's back," she said.

"Who's back? Mr. Hanford?"

Don and Charlie looked at each like I was losing my mind.

"He must have gotten in last night," she said. "Because when I came out to get my paper, his car was in the driveway."

I thought about telling Charlie I had a fellow paper reader but decided an elderly person wasn't really helping my case.

"Thank you very much, ma'am. I'll be along directly."

She said, "Don't forget my money." And hung up.

"Who was that?" Charlie asked.

I stood up, looking for my keys. "Someone I owe a hundred bucks."

THIRTY

It was while I was driving back to DHS agent Chet Hanford's house Friday morning that the old feeling returned.

In previous cases — not all, but some — you'd sometimes be overtaken by the sensation events were leading you along, not the other way around. Many investigations, be they murders or robberies or whatever, moved glacially. You could follow leads as diligently as possible, but many times the outcome hinged on a witness coming forward, or a piece of previously undiscovered evidence turning up.

Mike's case didn't feel like that. It was the investigative equivalent of sensory overload, with information coming in almost faster than we could process it. Charlie's decryption of Mike's email confirmed some of what we'd thought, but other questions remained. One of which I was trying to get answered after snatching a few hours' sleep on a hospital waiting room couch.

Charlie talked to Mom about the news linking Mike to Ramirez's murder before I left. She'd reacted about like the rest of us, which was surprising considering how rarely she used profanity.

I'd convinced Don to let me take his Range Rover again, as he was staying with Charlie for the time being, and I didn't fancy getting stranded in East Houston if/when the Corolla decided to give up the ghost again. For all his bluster, Don was still a good dude, though I tried not to consider what he'd demand from in me in payback as I once again entered Hanford's neighborhood. I took stock of the scene as I pulled closer to his address and came to an abrupt stop three houses down.

There was a truck in the driveway.

I climbed out of the Range Rover and left the door ajar, though not enough to leave the interior light on. The street was quiet, though you couldn't get away from the sounds of the freeway, which was simply a reality if you lived inside or near the Loop. The faint roar provided a kind of white noise that in rural areas would be supplied by crickets or something.

Or howler monkeys, for all I knew. I grew up in the city.

There wasn't much activity on the street. I heard lawnmowers in the distance, the sound of which might as well be the official anthem for the city, but it looked like most of Hanford's neighbors were at work.

I wanted to check out Hanford's house before I completed my business transaction with Mrs. Nguyen, so I moved past her driveway and walked up the sidewalk to Chet Hanford's place.

My Smith & Wesson .40, which I'd elected not to bring onto Steranko's boat, was back in its holster, snug against my hip. I didn't know the extent of Hanford's involvement with Mike's disappearance, but DHS had him out of the country (and incommunicado) until the end of June. If he *was* here — and I had no way of knowing if this was his truck, if he was letting a buddy crash at his place, or if one of his neighbors was squatting in his driveway — then I had a few questions for him.

I paused at his gate, remembering the dog. I didn't want to hurt the animal, but I also couldn't have him alerting the whole neighborhood to my presence. There was gravel at the end of Hanford's driveway, so I picked up a rock about the size of my thumb and tossed it onto the porch.

Nothing.

Taking a deep breath, I opened the gate and entered the yard. Walking like I had a legitimate reason to be there, I crossed the lawn quickly and climbed the three steps to his porch.

The house was quiet, and I peered inside house as I knocked. The big TV in the living room was off, and no movement inside caught my eye. I glanced at the closed blinds in the other windows, but if someone was watching me from behind them, they were keeping still.

Satisfied I wasn't about to be surprised by the dog, and uncomfortable standing in full view on the porch any longer, I hopped down and crept swiftly around the side of the house. Looking into a window was one thing; if I was going to break into the guy's house, I needed to do it from the back.

Hanford's fence was chain link and only rose about three feet, which was suboptimal from a breaking and entering perspective. The backyard was a little better. He or someone else had half-assed a full wooden fence, and that gave me a little cover as I put on a pair of gloves and started working on the back door.

It took me all of 30 seconds to jimmy the door, which looked like original 1950s issue. Hanford either didn't have anything anyone would want to steal, or he really didn't care about security. Kind of weird for a DHS agent.

Looking around one more time to make sure I wasn't being watched, I drew my .40, opened the door slowly, and entered Hanford's house.

Two steps in and I found out what happened to his dog as I almost tripped over its inert form on the kitchen floor.

In the dark, I couldn't see exactly what caused it to shuffle off its mortal coil, but the blood pooled around the dog's body pointed to shooting or stabbing. Given its previous aggression, I doubted anyone would get close to it on purpose, so the former seemed likely.

The interior of the house was dim, so I pulled out the small Maglite I carried and shone it around the dog. I didn't have the means or motive to try and more accurately determine time of death, but the congealed blood hopefully indicated the perpetrator had already hit the road.

I turned the light off and moved to the kitchen doorway, careful not to track through the dog's blood.

The house was small, and moving through it took little time. Hanford was apparently the unsentimental type, as there were no family photos or real personal touches. A few bookshelves held typical bestsellers of the John Grisham and *Chicken Soup for the Bureaucratic Automaton's Soul* variety. If Charlie hadn't confirmed the address via property databases, you'd never know this was Chet Hanford's home.

I cleared rooms as I went through — old habits and all that

— which didn't take long. Finally, I reached a closed door. Judging by the room I'd already seen, this would be the second bedroom of a 2–1. There were few options for what lay beyond, and given the dead guard dog in the kitchen, none of them were good.

I grasped the doorknob and turned. It wasn't locked. Slowly, keeping low, I pushed the door open.

My eyes flickered across, attempting to pick up any movement in the darkness. Gradually, what little light there was filtering through the drawn blinds and coming in through the opened door started revealing details, but by then I was already pretty sure what was in the room.

My tenure as a detective was, by most accounts, brief and unremarkable. I cleared a fair share of cases, but by no means all of them.

Even allowing that, there were some things that would never leave me: the sight of a dead child, the thrill — not wholly fear and not wholly anticipation — one felt before kicking down a door, and the smell of blood. It was metallic and earthy and even in Houston's often musty atmosphere, it was something you recognized as soon as you scented it.

There was blood in this room. A lot of it.

Closing the door behind me to minimize visibility, I chanced the Maglite again. I was indeed standing in a bedroom, or at least a room with all the requisite associated furniture. A dresser stood in a corner, topped with pictures and an assortment of personal items, while a full-sized bed occupied the center of the room. It was made, while the source of all the blood lay slumped next to it.

Holstering my weapon, I knelt beside the body. It was a male of what appeared to be average height and weight. He was dressed in street clothes, and a quick pat down produced a wallet. The driver's license within confirmed the body was that of Chet Hanford.

I was grateful for the ID, because the close-cropped hair was the only thing recognizable from his DHS photo. The exit wound had completely obliterated his face, and the forensic techs would likely be picking up teeth for hours. I checked the entry wound at the back of the skull, and noted he'd been shot from enough of a distance there were no powder burns.

Somebody lying in wait? I flashed the Maglite back on and swept the room, confirming I was alone. Since Hanford looked like he'd been greased the same time as his dog, the killer was most likely long gone.

He had come home, and judging by the monsterish truck in the driveway, he didn't really care who knew it. Had he come home early from Brussels? Did Hammond know he was back? Had he ever *been* in Brussels?

I had to call the police. Anonymously. The better to avoid creating an official connection between Mike's disappearance and his snoop little brother. First, I'd check out Hanford's truck and see if that yielded anything.

Hanford's keys weren't in his pocket, but a quick check of the front hallway turned them up. I figured now that I could do it without knocking it down or picking the lock, I'd go ahead and leave through the front door.

I'd just had enough time to step across the threshold onto the porch when my legs were kicked out from under me. I went down hard, and thought about reaching for my weapon when I noticed the lights. Red and blue was strobing everywhere and I could hear bellows of "Hold him!" and "Watch him! Watch him!" My arms were wrenched behind my back and I felt high-tensile steel bite into my wrists and the cuffs were slapped on. Someone removed my .40 from its holster, possibly the same person who had their knee in my back, driving the side of my face into the wood floor of the porch.

Several hands hoisted me from the ground. There were four squad cars I could see, as well as a van I initially took for SWAT issue, except for the "Homeland Security" stenciled on its side. As if I needed any more proof this was a setup.

A guy in a Kevlar vest and a black baseball cap stood before me. "Cy Clarke?"

"Like you didn't know."

"You're under arrest for the murder of Chet Hanford."

Looks like Mrs. Nguyen wasn't getting her money after all.

THIRTY-ONE

None of the dudes who bundled me into the van read me my Miranda rights, which either meant this whole thing was headed for a mistrial, or these particular gentlemen weren't overly concerned with due process.

The interrogation room was familiar enough: a long table made of wood substitute with a ring bolted into it (the same ring my right hand was currently handcuffed to), molded plastic chairs, and a two-way mirror running the length of one wall. I had no idea who was observing me from the other side, and didn't feel like giving them the satisfaction of seeing me react, so I sat relatively motionless.

There are a couple schools of thought regarding how one should act when accused of a crime. Some psychological studies believe the truly innocent will loudly — even violently — protest their arrest, while no less an authority on incarceration than *The Usual Suspects* presented the hypothesis that only the guilty sleep their first night in jail.

Anyone who's spent the night in jail knows how difficult sleep is. We'd usually check on the ones who appeared to be snoozing to make sure they were still breathing.

By those metrics, I should've been yelling my head off. Maybe banging on the table to boot. Truth was, I didn't have the energy. After too little sleep, the previous day's events were taking their toll, but as tempting as the proposition of putting my head down and catching a few Zs might have been, the specter of Chazz

Palminteri's words kept me from doing so.

Basic furnishings aside, Homeland Security's interrogation room was pretty nice and new. It clearly hadn't been used all that often, or at least not enough to acquire the usual wear and tear such chambers eventually suffered, such as cigarette burns, nicks from handcuffs, or bloodstains.

Hopefully my being here wouldn't result in any changes to the decor.

I heard a bolt slide back and the only door in the place opened and a man entered. He was in his mid-40s, balding, carrying a manila folder, and looking about as tired as I felt. He might even have been the guy who arrested me at Hanford's, though it was hard to tell without the flak jacket and cap. Those had been replaced with a button-down shirt rolled up at the sleeves, necktie, and slacks.

He sat down without saying anything and started going through the contents of the folder. I watched him with what I hoped was a bored expression.

"Your name's Cy Clarke, is it not?" He asked this without looking up.

"Lawyer."

He didn't say anything, just kept turning pages. I was mildly curious as to the contents of his dossier but didn't want to look overeager.

After another half minute or so of riffling through the pages, he produced an 8x10 black-and-white photo and slid it in front of me. I already knew what it was and so didn't look down.

"This is the man back in the house in Denver Harbor. Or rather, what's left of him after somebody shot him in the back of his head," my unnamed interrogator said.

I glanced down. It was indeed a better lit shot of the dead man I'd found in the bedroom. I was more interested in the way he'd said 'somebody' instead of implicating me directly.

Figuring I had nothing to lose, I feigned surprise at the photo. "Heavens! What a shocking turn of events!" I raised my un-handcuffed hand to my forehead in mock consternation. Hell, if I'd had a forelock I would've tugged it.

"Clarke ..."

"Lawyer," I said again, glancing at the mirror, "or don't

y'all hear so good?"

He leaned back, regarding me with all the curiosity he might've spared for a cicada on his screen door. "You don't appear to appreciate the seriousness of this situation," he began.

I leaned forward. "I appreciate that I'm an American citizen and the Department of Homeland Security has no jurisdiction over murders committed in the city of Houston. You don't want to Mirandize me, fine, but slapping a crime scene photo down in front of me and expecting me to collapse in tormented guilt is shit that would've gotten you laughed off the set of *Perry Mason*." I sat back again. "Lawyer."

He pulled the folder toward himself, opened it, and withdrew a single sheet of paper. Smiling slightly, he slid it over to me so that it half obscured the photo of Hanford.

"What's this?" I didn't look down.

"You might want to read it," he said. "It's an executive order from the President of the United States, cosigned by the governor of the State of Texas, giving Homeland Security full jurisdiction over crimes committed against their agents." His smile widened. "Whether those crimes were committed on federal property or not."

"You're bluffing."

He shrugged. "Read it, I've got all night."

I looked at the paper, which had the Presidential seal and was printed on heavy bond paper. Hell, the signatures looked authentic enough. That still didn't mean I was trusting baldy's word on the matter.

"So what?" I said, sliding the paper back to him. "You can find this paper at any Staples store. And while I'm not the most technical person around, I know there are graphics programs out there that can produce passable copies of birth certificates and passports," I nodded at his so-called executive order, "much less mock-ups featuring the official letterhead of POTUS."

I was pretty sure I still had the mock Presidential citation Charlie had whipped up to show to one prospective client, come to think of it.

"Not going to talk, eh Clarke?"

"And another thing, you could at least tell me your name," I said. "I mean, you've got all the cool paperwork and I'm the one in handcuffs."

He smiled again. "Name's Chet Hanford."

That got me. "Say again?"

"Come on, I know you've heard the name before."

He was trying to draw me in, and I had to admit it was tempting. "How was Brussels?" Was the best I could come up with.

He laughed. "Oh, Dot. You know, you really should've given her more credit. She went straight to Hammond when you told her you were supposed to be kept in the loop."

"I figured," I said, knowing my charms were strictly hit or miss and I'd whiffed early on with the secretary. "Still doesn't explain the dead guy in your house. That was your house, wasn't it?"

"Registered in my name, but I never lived there," the agent currently known as Hanford said. "Not my kind of neighborhood."

Why was I not surprised?

"What is this about, Hanford? Why the full court press back there?" I raised my shackled arm. "And why am I cuffed to this table like a common perp?"

"Are you waiving your right to a lawyer?"

"Are you saying I have a right to one now?"

He grinned. "No, just hoping to get it on the record."

I sat back. "I don't get you Feds, I really don't. HPD would kill for a tenth of the budget you've got, and you can't keep from screwing up."

"How have we screwed up?"

"Where's my brother?"

Hanford frowned and I was dismayed to see a flicker of sincerity on his face. "We don't know."

"Bullshit," I said. "You covered up the fact that you were never out of the country and now you're trying to frame my brother for the murder of another agent."

"Ballistics don't lie."

"Not generally, no," I said, "but it's hard to know for sure when the results aren't released to other agencies. And since when does DHS run its own lab? I thought all your shit got farmed out to the FBI."

Hanford couldn't help glancing at the mirror. "That's a, uh, new directive."

I folded my hands in front of me. "Sure, Jan."

"I think a better question" — he was trying to get the ball back in his court — "would be how you came by some of this information."

"You mean besides the information your own boss's secretary told me?"

He gave good glare, you had to credit him for that.

"The dead guy's address was on the county appraisal district website," I said. "Contact info for your people is publicly available, if you know where to look."

"I was thinking more about how you learned about certain … operational details," he said.

Hanford either suspected we'd hacked their files and couldn't prove it or was on a fishing expedition. Either way, he could pound sand.

"We all have our sources," I said. "Are y'all going to charge me with something? Or are we going to keep going around in circles?" I nodded to the mirror. "Somehow I don't think your people are getting all the material they want."

Hanford scooped all the papers (except the photo of the anonymous dead guy, of course) back into his folder and walked to the door, knocking once. It opened enough to let him out then closed. I heard the bolt latch again.

Sighing, I rubbed my eyes. This was shaping up to be another long day in what was already a very long week, and instead of being any closer to finding Mike, I was cooling my heels in what I was increasingly sure was a black site. Hanford hadn't used the word "terrorism," but accusing me of that seemed like the next logical step in justifying my detention.

I must have dozed, because I jerked awake at the sound of the bolt on the door being thrown again. It wasn't Hanford who came in this time, though I did recognize the man. His expression wasn't as friendly as it'd been the first time I'd made his acquaintance.

"Dave   Hammond,"   I   said.   "How's   Dot   doing?"

THIRTY-TWO

Though I have no proof, this is how I imagine events played out this morning.

First, I'm arrested. Pretty straightforward.

Next, after a brief interval (call it 90 minutes or an hour) Charlie and/or Don would have grown worried and tried to call me. My phone was taken away when I was arrested, so their calls would've gone straight to voicemail, probably alarming them further.

One of them (Don, probably) would have fired up his police scanner to see if there was any chatter. DHS traffic wouldn't have shown up on this, but a raid in an East Houston neighborhood would likely generate some conversation.

Depending on how much detail they were able to dig up, Charlie could check the booking databases to see if they had any information. No, I don't know what databases, my only superpowers are taking punches and movie quotes.

If DHS was careless, my real name would be on the booking sheet. Not that it mattered, because "Caucasian male, mid-30s" would stand out just as starkly.

The only wild card at that point would be who they decided to contact to get me out. I was fairly sure Don wasn't careless enough to leave Charlie alone at the hospital, and he had to know it wouldn't do any good to show up *solamente* at … wherever I was.

I didn't even know if this place had a front desk.

That's assuming Charlie didn't fake an email ordering my

release. If she spoofed it from the President's address, I'd buy her a new pair of Chucks.

Anyway, these were my thoughts as Hammond started talking to me in the interrogation room. Forgive me for not being especially interested in what he had to say.

"Mr. Clarke?"

"Hmm?"

"Did you hear what I just said?" The earnestness of his expression was precious.

"Sorry, I must have zoned out," I said. "It happens when I've been wrongfully arrested for murder."

An expression of annoyance crossed his features, but he composed himself. "I was saying, while we at the DHS understand your family's concern over Mike Clarke's disappearance, we condemn in the strongest possible terms your insistence on interfering in our investigation."

"Wow, what a heartfelt expression of sympathy. I'd give a round of applause if you hadn't chained me to a table," I said. "Was that a version of the official statement you were going to release if I got shot at fake Hanford's house?"

"I'm not sure what you're talking about," he said. "We're trying as hard as we can to find out what happened to Mike."

"By telling everyone he shot Ramirez."

"We didn't leak that." He was visibly angry now.

"Bullshit. It couldn't have come from anyone else," I said. "HPD doesn't even have the weapon to do their own testing, so either you ordered it or you're incompetent."

Hammond stood up. "Now listen to me, you son of a bitch …"

I remained seated. "Or what? You're gonna bounce my head off the table a few times? Might want to turn the cameras off before you do. Lawyers have a field day with that kind of thing."

Like Hanford, he couldn't resist sneaking a look at the two-way mirror. It comes with time, I thought; spend enough time in the interrogation room and you don't even think about who else is watching. It can cause problems.

Hammond sat down, looking ruddy as ever.

"You and Hanford really need to work on your good cop/bad cop thing," I offered. "By which I mean, you can't both be the bad cop ..."

"Clarke ..." He began.

"... it's right there in the name."

"Enough!" Then, "You know what? It doesn't even matter if you stop snooping around the Ramirez investigation," he said.

"Is that a fact?"

He nodded. "We have you cold on murder, which ought to put a stop to your —" he made the "air quotes" symbol with his fingers " — investigation."

"You have exactly jack shit," I said. "That guy was dead half a day by the time I got there."

"Won't matter if the ballistics match your weapon."

I said, "Oh right, ballistics. Would this be the same lab that so expertly tied my brother's gun to Ramirez? The lab HPD has never heard of? Is the Department of Justice aware you're operating your own shop for that now?"

Hammond didn't answer, so I kept going, "In fact, I bet all concerned law enforcement agencies would be very interested in this little fiefdom you've set up out here. Does this have official sanction from the Secretary?"

"You don't know what you're talking about," he said.

"Maybe not," I said. "Tell you what, y'all see if you can get the U.S. Attorney to bring charges based on the garbage you've got, and I'll see how quickly I can get my lawyer to sue your asses. All this?" I waved to the mirror. "Inadmissible the second I asked for my attorney."

He opened his mouth as the door opened behind him. It was an agent I didn't recognize. Hammond turned. "What?"

"Need to talk to you," the agent said.

Hammond got up for the second time and walked over to the door. An intense, albeit quiet, discussion ensued. At the end of it I saw Hammond's shoulders slump somewhat and he returned to the table. He didn't sit down.

Instead, he produced a key and unlocked my handcuff. "You're free to go."

I stood, rubbing my wrist, but didn't say anything. Truth be told, I was about as surprised as he was. Not waiting for someone to change their mind, I stepped past him. The agent glared at me, but didn't shut the door in my face.

"Where to?"

"Follow me," he muttered.

He led me down a long, brightly lit hallway with a disconcertingly large number of doors that appeared identical to the one I'd emerged from. After a couple turns, a door marked "Exit" appeared, though without the usual prominent red neon sign accompanying it.

He stopped, and so did I, until he held his arm out. "That way."

"Thanks," I said. "Do I want to know?"

"I don't know how it happened," he said, then shook his head. "Your lawyer's here."

Hoping my poker face hid the fact I was just as surprised as they were, I nodded like my lawyer popping in was something that happened all the time and walked through the exit.

And then stopped, unable to keep the surprise to myself this time.

Son of a bitch, I thought. *Twelve thousand lawyers in this city and my ex-girlfriend has to be the one to bail me out.*

Emma McKenzie and I broke up a little over a year ago. Nothing sinister: no screwing around, no domestic violence, no fundamental disagreement on principles (she wasn't a Yankees fan or anything), we just sort of … drifted.

She was an attorney with a fairly well-known downtown firm. We'd dated for almost three years, and at one point I (and everyone in my immediate family) thought we were going to get married.

After a while, her partner track lifestyle and my own increasing workload caused us to start drifting apart. I don't remember what the final straw was, but I'm sure my own petulance at her success had nothing to do with it. Nope.

I knew she's already made junior partner, because we both kept up to date on each other through mutual friends.

At least, I kept up to date on her. I assumed she did the same, because otherwise it made me a bit of a creep.

"You're looking … fit," Emma said. "Still like throwing hands, I take it."

I touched my swollen eye self-consciously and was

immediately annoyed with myself for doing so. "What are you doing here?"

"Getting you out of government custody. You're welcome." She smiled, and for a moment it felt like old times again. I let the moment pass.

"I just meant I'm surprised you showed up is all."

She said, "I'm a little surprised myself. This place is like the Black Hole of Calcutta with better toilet facilities."

It finally clicked. "I assume Charlie had something to do with that."

"Yes, *something*," she said. "She was practically frantic when she called me, after what I assume was some time spent doing things on her computer to uncover your whereabouts that I as her attorney advised her not to tell me about."

"Did you talk to Don, too?" I was trying to get us out of there without as fast as possible without looking like we were doing so.

"I did," she said. "He asked how I was, then convinced Charlie to take a sedative so she could get some sleep."

"I didn't ask to get arrested," I said, defensive.

She stopped and turned to face me. "No, just like you didn't ask your family if you should go breaking and entering into a federal agent's house without a warrant and put yourself and them in danger."

"The back door was unlocked," I said, trying to ignore her usual correctness. "I think that's just called 'entering.'"

"Hasn't your mother been through enough? She already lost Lee, then Mike goes missing, and you want to add to that by getting thrown in Supermax?"

"I don't think I'm sexy enough of a criminal for Supermax," I said.

Her eye roll was still on point, as the kids say. "Let's just get out of here. I'll give you a ride to the hospital."

I said, "Who says I need a ride?"

For the first time in over a year, I heard her laugh, and it was … great.

"I say." She chuckled. "Because either the car you drove is in impound, or you're still in that shit-ass Corolla, and I wouldn't trust that thing to roll downhill if the dump was at the base of

Mount Everest."

THIRTY-THREE

"This is a nice ride," I said.

We'd settled into Emma's 2018 Lexus RX, a car I might be able to afford if I stopped eating for 10 years. Or if I ever decided to sell my soul and become a lawyer.

"Shystering does have its perks," she said, starting the car and easing us out of the parking labyrinth nestled beneath the DHS complex. Apparently we'd been in Pasadena this whole time, so I was even more eager to get going.

On any other week when I'd been up for almost 24 hours, involved in a near-fatal traffic accident, beaten by Russian thugs, and illegally interrogated by the government, my first inclination would've been to recline the passenger seat and pass out. I hadn't seen Emma in a year, though.

And naturally, she wasn't done talking.

"I think you need to back off," she said.

"Nice to see you, too."

"I'm not kidding," she said, "I know you. I know how you latch onto something like a pit bull until you find the answer you're looking for. The problem is, you always do this without thinking about how it affects anyone else."

"Mike's my brother," I began.

"And I get that, but Cy," her tone softened, "you're practically on a suicide mission to find him. Meanwhile it sounds like Charlie is basically working herself to death. And I don't have to be at your mother's house to know it's tearing her apart."

I kept my mouth shut, not sure if it was out of agreement or aggravation.

"I'm not family," she said, "and I gave up my right to my opinion a year ago, but if you're not careful, this is going to tear you guys apart."

"'You guys,'" I snickered. "You've been lawyering too long."

"You know I'm right."

"And what do you suggest?" I snapped. "Everybody take a week off? Maybe a spa day? I'm not trying to cause collateral damage, but this is the only way I know how to find him. All of us are doing the best we can. Except maybe Jim."

"You're wrong about that," Emma said.

"Am I?"

"He may not be the one to call when you want to kick a door down, or hack into the NSA, but I know for a fact he's been calling in favors from everyone he can think of, including local lawyers."

"He called you?"

She nodded. "He's playing to his strengths, just like the rest of you."

Great, now I had guilt to go along with my exhaustion and internal injuries.

"I don't want to argue with you, Emma," I said, "but this whole thing is bigger than I think you realize."

"How do you mean?"

I said, "This isn't just a case of Mike being accused of a crime he didn't commit. At the very least, his superiors are trying to railroad him, and it looks like they're even actively covering up illegal activity in the DHS."

She stared straight ahead. "That's a pretty serious charge. What are you basing it on?"

"A little from column 'hunch,' a little from column 'stuff I can't tell you about because of your chosen profession.'"

She scoffed. "You sound like one of those YouTube psychos ranting about chemtrails or the NSA putting acid in the water supply."

I shrugged. "I'm not ranting, and I don't believe 9/11 was an inside job, but if you honestly think the Department of

Homeland Security is incapable of this sort of fuckery, you've been spending too much time in your penthouse office."

"My office isn't in the penthouse," Emma said.

"Does it have a window?"

"Lots of windows."

I said, "The defense rests."

She shook her head as she steered the Lexus onto the I-45 north onramp. "Always have to be the superhero. You haven't changed one bit."

"As opposed to all the other thirty-six-year-olds who can completely reverse personality in twelve months' time." This was all sounding familiar. "Look, I've had a bitch of a day. If you don't mind, I'm going to catch some sleep on the drive back to the hospital."

"Okay," she said.

"And Emma?"

She looked at me. "Yeah?"

"Thanks."

The hum of the Lexus's engine lulled me into slumber almost before my head hit the seat. It wasn't much as far as naps go, maybe 25 minutes, but every little bit helped.

I dreamed about Mike.

Sometimes the dreams we have are full-blown epics, dredging up stories from our pasts or subconscious and shaping them into exciting new narratives. I have one recurring one that's been going on since I was a teenager, involving the stable, long-lasting relationship I've built (in my head) with Beyoncé. In my dream narrative, she and I have been married nearly 15 years, possibly with kids (children filter in and out, but are never the focus), and are living on a ranch in Montana.

[That last part may be a result of my love for *The Hunt for Red October*. Something to do with an inadvertent crossing of pop culture streams, or whatever. I'm not a neurologist.]

Dreams can also be influenced by events taking place in our lives. They can be as ephemeral as dreaming about doing laundry because you passed a laundromat that morning. Others are a result of events so traumatic they've left lasting psychic impressions, which is why I assume everyone has the same one about showing up for a class final having done none of the reading on the syllabus.

This wasn't like any of those.

My Mike dream was a pastiche of vignettes, inelegantly edited (if I may offer critical commentary), not all of which were based on actual events. Here was a memory of the time we'd ridden our bikes to White Oak Bayou and gotten chased by older skateboarders; next, that evening I caught him coming home drunk after Reagan High School's baseball team won the district playoffs.

I made him give me his 1986 Mike Scott Topps baseball card for that.

But then we are both at Lee's funeral, which wasn't right. Mike hadn't attended that because he was in Iraq. And he didn't come to my graduation from the Academy, but in my dream he's sitting next to Mom and Charlie.

And Beyoncé, who looked especially proud.

The images fade, and in their place comes a room, plain except for two chairs. Mike is sitting slightly across from me, but at an angle, like we're on an old talk show, only instead of a TV camera, we're both facing what looks like a two-way mirror.

We converse, but I can't hear what's being said. My frustration grows until I'm mercifully jerked awake as Emma pulls to a stop in the hospital parking lot. A glowing "EMERGENCY" sign greets me, and I rub my eyes in annoyance.

"Did you have a nice nap?" she asked as she turned off the ignition.

"I dreamed about Mike," I said.

"Really?" she asked with seemingly genuine interest. "Any insights?"

"Apparently I'm still in love with Beyoncé."

"This is news?"

We exited the Lexus and walked through the sliding glass doors into the Waterway Hospital lobby while I thought about my unintelligible dream conversation with my brother.

"I don't know what's going on," I said. "It's possible I'm losing my mind. Also, I think I need to talk to Charlie."

"That's not happening." Don was waiting for us in the lobby and being his usual pleasant self.

"Don," I said, "How's she doing?"

He embraced me in the bro hug style of our time and said, "Sleeping. Looks like you could use some yourself."

"I was telling him the same thing," Emma said.

Don smiled widely at her. "Emma!" She got the full bear hug, which is terrifying to watch if you don't know him and understand he's not actually trying to snap your spine.

Releasing her, Don said, "Y'all missed all the fun."

"Oh?"

He smiled. "It took Charlie and me both to convince Mom to stay with Kayla instead of coming here."

"How did you manage that?" I asked.

"We ... may have downplayed the extent of her injuries. If Mom calls you, Charlie's just having some routine tests."

We walked to the elevator bank and Don hit the button for Charlie's floor.

I said, "I think there's something we overlooked about Mike's disappearance, and I need Charlie to help me check it out."

"I appreciate that, but even if I was inclined to let you annoy her with this, the dose of temazepam they gave her will keep her knocked out for another six hours, at least."

"Shit," I said.

Emma said, "Is there something I can do?"

Don raised an eyebrow and I ignored him. He'd clearly been surprised by Emma's appearance and, after he'd given her a hug, couldn't keep the shit-eating grin off his face.

I shook my head. "Not unless you can get the DHS report on the raid where Ramirez was killed."

When she didn't immediately say no, I looked in her direction. "Em?"

"I'm technically your lawyer now," she said. "I could request it as evidence pertinent to your case, but that won't work if it's classified."

"That'd be great if you'd check," I said, hoping my gratitude wasn't that obvious.

"What's the point?" Don asked.

We exited the elevator and started down the hallway to Charlie's room.

"What's the point?" Don asked.

"I need to see if the report's been updated to say what kind of gun was used."

"What difference could that make? They've already said it was Mike's service weapon," Don said.

"They're not going to release this to the public," I said. "At least, not before someone has a chance to alter it. If we can see it before that ..." I trailed off.

"Where's the guard?"

Don and I both looked around. The chair was across from Charlie's door, but the deputy who'd been sitting in it was gone.

"He was there when Emma called to say you were on your way," Don said, "So ... twenty minutes ago?"

"Maybe he went to the bathroom," Emma said.

Before I could comment on whether that was possible or not, movement at the end of the hallway caught my eye. Fluorescent lights glinted off gunmetal and I barely had time to yell, "Down!" before shots rang out. I hit the floor, pulling Emma down with me as bullets thudded into the wall where we'd just been standing.

THIRTY-FOUR

Don already had Charlie's 9mm out and was returning fire as he rolled to find some cover against the wall. His shots drove the gunman back behind the corner, and I grabbed Emma's arm and pulled her up with me.

"Come on!" I yelled, but she was up almost as fast as me and we ran for Charlie's room.

I held the door open, unsure if it would stop our assailant's rounds. Still, any cover's better than none, and I said, "Don! Get your ass in here!"

He was in a crouch, his off leg pointed straight in front of him to minimize his silhouette. He glanced at me, squeezed off two more shots, then sprinted across the hallway. Bullets cracked in his wake, but he lunged through the doorway unscathed.

Charlie was still asleep. Gotta give it up for temazepam.

"Sitrep?" Don said. He fished Charlie's extra magazines out of her backpack, then moved to cover the door, which had a small window about three-quarters of the way up. Thankfully, this room wasn't one of those maternity ward types with walls made of glass.

"Single shooter, automatic rifle," I said. To Emma, "Did you see anyone else?"

She shook her head. She was perhaps a little shaken, but no worse for wear. "I didn't, but it doesn't mean he's the only one."

I went to draw my own weapon, then remembered it was still in a DHS evidence locker. "Shit!"

"What?" she asked.

I nodded to my brother. "That's the only weapon we have."

"No, it isn't." She reached into her purse, a black Chanel job I'd studiously been trying to ignore, and withdrew a pistol.

I stared. "Are you shitting me?"

"What?"

"How many arguments did we have about me bringing my gun on dates?" I said.

She shrugged. "There were some … nonspecific threats made against my firm several months ago. The partners paid for concealed carry permits for any associates who wanted to get one."

I laughed. "This must be the End Times."

"Enough with the foreplay," Don hissed. "I think he's moving."

Emma looked like she was about to join him at the door, then sighed and handed the gun to me. It was an H&K .380. Nice.

"I mean, I am the better shot," I offered.

"I'm in heels, asshole."

She went to Charlie's bed and picked up the phone to the nurse's station. "Nothing."

I nodded, taking position next to the door. "If they're not dead, they're getting patients to cover under the active shooter protocol. This whole wing will be locked down until SWAT shows up."

"Meaning we're on our own," Don growled.

"Yup."

He muttered something that Mom certainly wouldn't have approved of and put his hand on the doorknob.

"What's your plan?" I said.

"Shoot this prick," he said, "find out if there are any other pricks with him, and shoot them too."

I nodded. "I like it."

He pulled the door open and fired without looking. We heard someone who was a lot closer than they needed to be scrambling for cover, and I looked through the doorway to see a figure in a familiar jeans and hoodie combo moving into a crouch behind an abandoned gurney.

Fuck it, I thought, and stepped into the gap, taking aim as I did.

He saw me a fraction of a second too late, and I shot him twice as he raised his weapon. The first shot hit him in the shoulder, rotating his torso to his left, and the second bullet entered his right side. He toppled noisily to the floor and lay still.

Don peered around the door and gave me an expression I read as a grudging "not bad."

"What do you think?" he asked.

"I think that was too easy."

He said, "I agree." Dropping to one knee, he risked a look down the hallway in the opposite direction. He ducked back with a curse as more gunfire followed from that direction.

"They were trying to pincer move us," he said.

"How many?" I asked.

"Two on that end. You sure the guy you capped was the only one coming from the north end?"

"I wouldn't swear on a Bible," I said, "but I didn't see anyone else."

"You wouldn't swear on a Bible because you're an atheist," Emma chimed in.

"Does this count as a foxhole?" I replied.

Don ignored us. "We can't make the north exit; we'd be exposed for too long to both shooters before we got there."

I agreed. "And my trick isn't going to work again. The rear guy can just plink away at whoever sticks his head out."

Don looked around. "I'd give anything for a sniper right now."

Something clicked in my head, but I couldn't coalesce it into anything before Emma said, "Do these windows open?"

"Why?" Don asked.

"You already said the hallway's a shooting gallery," she said. "You need to flank them."

I hated when she was right.

"She's right," I said, and went to the windows. Don dragged the mutant bed-chair over and jammed it up against the door.

Unsurprisingly, the windows wouldn't open. Guess they didn't want anyone jumping after they got their bills.

Looking down, there was something that resembled a ledge running the length of the building. It looked about eight inches wide. Not ideal, but serviceable.

"What do you think?" Don said.

"I'm going to break the window with this cart," I said. "When I do, I want you to squeeze off a couple of shots their way to mask the sound."

Emma said, "But you won't be able to get back in. Or are you planning to carry the cart outside with you?"

I thought for a second. "Give me the nine," I said to Don.

"I was afraid you'd say that." Nevertheless, he traded me the Browning for Emma's .380.

"Why do you need his gun?" she asked.

"Better penetration," Don said. "He ought to be able to punch through the glass, unless it's bulletproof."

"If it's bulletproof, I won't be able to break it with the cart either," I said. "There should be thirteen left in the mag. Will that be enough?"

"Go to hell," Don said, then moved to the door. "Ready when you are, bro."

I nodded and picked up the dining cart. "On three."

On the count, I swung the cart with all my might at the window as Don wrenched the door open and fired down the hallway. The blasts were like cannon fire in the room, and I was pretty sure the glass breaking hadn't been heard.

Don shouldered the door shut again. "The rearguard shooter is about twenty yards north. Going by the dimensions of this room, that means he's three windows down."

"When you hear me shoot, come out the door and unleash hell," I said.

He said, "Just be sure to haul ass across that room. Thirteen rounds aren't going to last very long."

"You got it."

Using the heavy curtain to protect my hand, I grasped the sill and eased my way out onto the ledge. It wasn't much but supported most of my feet. I stuck the Browning in my waistband and hesitated.

I looked at Emma, and my throat felt tight. In spite of the way things ended, it was good to see her. I needed to come up with a good farewell, something meaningful and profound that would resonate with her through the years in the very likely event I died as a result of this stupid stunt.

"Uh, see you around, I guess."

Oh bravo, I thought, *You're an asshole, Clarke.*

Fortunately, Emma had better command of the scene and walked over to me, pausing a moment as I dangled (metaphorically) over the hospital parking lot.

She kissed me. Didn't see that coming.

"Don't die, moron."

She always was the romantic one.

There are thoughts that go through your mind as you're inching along a precarious ledge to what is quite possibly your doom. I expected my life to flash before me, or regrets of paths not taken, all that philosophical shit. Instead, what I was left with was: *enough.*

This was, by my account, the third attempt on my and/or Charlie's life in the last *two days*. I didn't need a much clearer indication that we were on the right path to whoever was behind Mike's disappearance, and I was ready to take the fight to those bastards.

First, however, there was the immediate threat to deal with.

Progress along the ledge was maddeningly slow, and I could see red and blue lights blinking frantically in the parking lot. SWAT was probably on the way, if not on site already, and the shooters should have known that. So why weren't they pressing their advantage?

Maybe they were idiots. Maybe — and this was an interesting thought — maybe they didn't do this all the time.

It would explain the guy at the house who couldn't get past the entranceway without being detected. Even the guy driving the car hadn't executed the spinout maneuver correctly.

This was all food for later thought, because I was at the third window.

The curtains were open, and the room looked mercifully empty. Bracing myself as well as I could on less than a foot of space, I put a hand in front of my face to shield it from broken glass and fired six shots in a rough circle about a foot in diameter.

Sounds of Don shooting followed immediately, and I elbowed the glass as hard as I could, throwing my weight behind it in the hope the blow and my weight would carry me through the bullet-weakened window instead of bouncing me off and onto the asphalt 60 feet below. My luck held, and I crashed noisily into the room.

I was barely up on my feet when the door opened and the muzzle of an automatic rifle poked through, firing on full auto. I dropped behind the bed as the window behind me shattered completely.

Should've brought one of those, I thought.

From my vantage under the bed, I saw the man enter, sweeping the room with his rifle as he did. I shot him twice in the knee/shin area, and when he dropped howling to the tile floor, I put two more rounds into his head.

I crossed the room as quickly as possible and peered into the hallway. Don was standing over another man, who was in the process of bleeding out on the shiny hallway floor.

"Clear?" I called out.

"Clear," he said.

Emma emerged from Charlie's room a second later. "Is it over?"

"Yes," Don and I said in unison.

I walked over to where Don was impassively regarding the corpse at his feet. "Any problems?"

"Nah," he said. "He had his back to me. Must have thought we were both shimmying around the building."

"One of them should have come forward," I said. "These dudes weren't very smart."

Don shrugged. "They're dead now. Who gives a shit?"

I touched one of the rifles with my toe. "These are M-16s, not converted ARs, right?"

He nodded, giving me a look. "This is military-issue hardware."

I turned to Emma. "Government conspiracies, you say?"

THIRTY-FIVE

In what was becoming a familiar scene, Don, Emma, and I were rounded up by the police and held in separate rooms for questioning. Since these were Harris County Sheriff deputies and not DHS, we were actually treated with a modicum of respect.

But not too much.

Having shot two of the three assailants, and also being one of the two assumed targets, I received the bulk of the attention. Charlie woke eventually and was hilariously befuddled as to why there were six cops in assault gear in her room

Unfortunately, I didn't have any new information to give them. Don and I had searched the bodies and the only thing we learned was that whoever sent them had figured out not to send phones or IDs. The guys were generic white dudes. Only dead.

I was cooling my heels in a conference room while the HCSO checked my CHL when who should walk in but my old friend Roy DeSantos.

"I've got nothing to say to you," was my greeting.

He feigned offense. "That's no way to talk to your only remaining friend in law enforcement."

"Seems like a friend would have known I was in DHS custody earlier tonight. A *friend* would've tried to get me out, even."

He said, "There wasn't anything I could do about that. City cops can't override federal authority, even if they want to."

"The hell does that mean?"

"It means I can't give you cover anymore," he said. "You broke into a civilian's house and they think you killed the guy."

I leaned back, bored. "The guy was long dead when I got there and Dr. Nick from *The Simpsons* could tell them that."

He said, "And what about tonight?"

"What about it?" I asked.

He scoffed, "You're leaving a trail of bodies behind you a serial killer would envy. Enough is enough. Leave the rest of the investigation to *professional* police and let us do our jobs."

"I agree with you," I said.

"Dammit, Cy, I'm not … what?"

"You're right," I continued, "enough is enough. I'm clearly doing more harm than good and I need to knock it off before innocent people are hurt."

Roy looked at me with frank distrust, which would've been insulting if he wasn't exactly right.

"That's … good news," he said finally.

"Anything else?" I asked, smiling.

He looked around the room, as if expecting the guy from *Candid Camera* to walk out. Would've been a neat trick, considering he died almost 20 years ago.

"No," he said. "Try to take care of your family and leave it up to us. We'll find Mike."

No you won't, I thought but didn't say. I'd made up my mind what to do while having my ledge epiphany, but letting Roy know that would only complicate matters.

Roy left and I was once again alone with my thoughts. There was planning to do and a tough road before we got Mike back, but all of that faded with exhaustion and I nodded off.

I had no idea how long I'd slept, but when the deputy returned to the room, the sun was well past midday. I'd like to say my nap was refreshing, but I only felt slightly less like hammered shit. My abdominal muscles ached and my right shoulder made a disconcerting grinding sound whenever I tried to rotate it. I decided to stop rotating it.

"Your concealed carry permit checks out," he said, sliding the paper across the table.

I retrieved it and stuck it back in my wallet. "Took you that long, huh?"

He left the room without replying and I belatedly realized baiting a cop after being involved in a fatal shooting was in the top tier of dumb things I'd done today. He also hadn't told me whether or not I could leave.

As I debated walking out, the door opened again. It was Emma.

"Hey," she said.

"Hey yourself." *Smooth.* "Are they letting us go?"

"I talked to the commander on scene and he says eyewitnesses and everything else bears out that you and Don acted in self-defense," she replied. "I think they know something hinky's going on, but they aren't planning on formally charging you with anything."

I said, "Finally, some good news. How are you holding up?"

She ran a hand through her dark hair and I felt my breath catch in my throat. *Goddamn it.*

"Pretty tired," she said. "You sure know how to show a lady a good time."

"We should get a meal first next time. Firefights go much better on a full stomach."

My lame attempt at asking her out hung between us for a moment, then she said, "Also, I wanted to apologize."

"For what?"

"For not believing you." She sat down. "I don't know why I thought you were making it all up. You never were much for paranoia."

I smiled. "I have many negative personality traits, but that's never been one of them."

She said, "What are you going to do now?"

"Oh, I have a few ideas," I said.

"Cy ..."

I waved her off. "Don't worry. I shouldn't require your services anymore, counselor."

"That's not what I mean," she said, leaning forward. "These people are trying to kill you, Charlie, and now Don, too. Where does it stop?"

"It doesn't. Don't you get it?" I leaned forward as well, and our faces were mere inches apart, it was ... exhilarating. "I have to *make* it stop, otherwise they're just going to keep coming." I sat back. "Thank you, sincerely, for your help. But I can't ask you to do any more."

"So that's it." A statement, not a question.

I sighed. "I'm not going to lie, it's been great seeing you again. But believe it or not, things might get worse before they get better. I don't know if I could live with myself if something happened to you."

She smiled. "That might be the nicest thing you ever said to me."

"Oh, I'm sure I complimented your butt once or twice."

Laughter at that, which hopefully meant she'd accepted my dismissal. I wasn't lying, exactly; I did care for her still, more than I'd realized until this very night, and knowledge aforethought of what I was planning might jeopardize her career.

Emma stood up, and I did the same. We walked around the table and hugged awkwardly. She smelled faintly of the lavender shampoo she'd always used. She definitely got the short end of this embrace, as I was pretty sure I reeked of gunpowder and stale sweat.

I held the embrace as long as I dared, then eventually withdrew.

"Take care of yourself, Cy," she said.

"You too, Em."

She turned and left the room before I could do something stupid like ask her to take me back, which I might have done anyway if Don hadn't walked in at that moment.

"Hey," he said. Popular greeting.

"Are we sprung?" I said.

He nodded. "Looks that way. The sheriff's department is talking with HPD to see if there's anything they need to hold us for, but as far as they're concerned, it's a clean shoot."

"Nothing from DHS?" I asked.

"Nope," Don said. "Somehow I doubt they want any more publicity on this."

"I'm counting on that."

"Huh?"

I ignored him. "Is Charlie still up?"

He said, "Still up and still pissed off."

I chuckled. "She's just mad she didn't get to shoot anybody."

"That's exactly it. Why are you in such a good mood?"

"Because I think I've come up with a way to go after these bastards," I said, "but we're going to need Charlie's help."

He said, "She'll be so grateful to finally be useful."

"I wouldn't put it that way when we talk to her."

We walked out of the conference room. I stretched and tried to get my bearings. It was a new day, but there was still lots to do and not a lot of time to do it. Mike was still out there — alive — and we'd wasted enough time.

"Did Emma come and see you?" Don asked.

"Yeah, why?"

He favored me with a shitty smile he knew would get a rise out of me. "No reason. It was nice to see her again."

I grunted, not willing to give him an iota of satisfaction.

"Why did the two of you break up again?"

"She didn't like my family."

"Ha! You're the only member of the family she didn't like."

THIRTY-SIX

"Y'all had a busy night. Assholes."

Charlie was up and much more well-rested than I was. She was leveraging that for maximum annoyance.

"Please," I said, "in your condition you would've shot yourself in the foot."

She laughed. "On the best day of your life, you couldn't outshoot me." She nodded to Don. "Him, maybe."

"Damn right," Don said.

I said, "Anyway, nobody's filing charges." I had a thought. "Has anybody talked to Mom?"

Don said, "They kept our names out of the news reports, and I already talked to Kayla and she's making sure everybody watches Netflix."

"Good deal," I said.

"Jim called, though."

Charlie said, "What did he want?"

"To make sure we were all okay," Don said. "*Somehow* he'd already heard about the shooting. And your arrest," he said to me.

"Curious," I said sarcastically. Jim instantly knowing about something taking place 3,000 miles away was actually the least curious thing that had happened in the last 24 hours.

"Don said you had a plan," Charlie said. "Let's hear it."

"It's not really a plan," I said. "More like switching from passive to active mode. I want to take the fight to these ass-clowns instead of waiting around for them to try and kill us again."

Charlie said, "That sounds fine, but we aren't even a hundred percent sure who's behind this."

"You ruled the Russian guy out?" Don asked.

"The only thing linking him is the Ferrari that ran us off the road," I said. "He said he doesn't have any, which is easy to check. You know what else is easy to check? DHS seizure manifests."

"I'm going to need my regular setup if we're breaking into those servers," Charlie said. "Are we free to go?"

Don nodded. "With the usual 'don't leave town' condition attached, of course."

"Okay," I said, "let's beat it before the hospital decides to sue us for damages."

I didn't feel particularly safe returning to our attempted murder house, but if our enemies didn't mind coming at us on a freeway or a hospital, anything short of Branch Davidian compound levels of protection wouldn't make a difference.

And it hadn't really turned out all that well for the Davidians, anyway.

Don dropped us off and left to check on Mom. I wouldn't have minded having his skillset at the house, but it made more sense for him to keep an eye on her.

Charlie went to her lair, more slowly than usual, and I hoped she wasn't going to end up with a permanent limp. She emerged about a half hour later with her first batch of results.

"Steranko isn't listed as the legal owner of any Ferraris," she said. "That doesn't really mean anything, so I checked manifests for shipments received by his holding companies and nothing on those either, not even for sale to other entities."

I said, "Anything on the DHS side?"

Charlie shook her head. "Their publicly available list of seizures didn't turn up anything, so I've got a script running to crack their internal server. Shouldn't be too long now."

I appreciated the casual way she referred to procedures it would take hours to walk me through using small words.

"Feeling okay?" I asked.

She shrugged. "A little stiff. My neck still hurts. Maybe if we ever find out who wrecked my car, I can sue him for whiplash."

"If he skates on the attempted murder charge, you mean?"

"Civil versus criminal cases," Charlie said. "I gotta get paid, yo."

"Did you ever look at the rest of those reports you downloaded from Hammond's secure drive?"

She snapped her fingers. "Shit! I was going to do that after we got back from Mom's, and of course we never made it."

She went back to her room and returned with a laptop. She had five or six and I was never sure which one was for what purpose. It wasn't her personal one, which I only knew because this one wasn't covered in 80s punk rock stickers.

After typing for a few seconds, she scrolled through several screens before slowing and finally stopping to read something in its entirety.

"Well, this is interesting."

"What?" I said.

Charlie said, "There's a report here from Ramirez, dated two weeks before his death."

"No shit? Wait, was that on the original list of reports?"

"No," she said, "and it's not in Hammond's sent files, meaning he received it but never passed it to his superiors."

"What does it say?" I asked.

She gave a low whistle. "Ramirez talks about irregularities in the numbers of individuals intercepted in their trafficking searches."

I looked over her shoulder (it couldn't be helped). "What kind of irregularities?"

"There's quite a list," Charlie said. "Leads not followed up, failure to notify relevant local agencies, but he mostly talks about failure to report. Ramirez says he's concerned the numbers going out are — and this is a direct quote — 'underrepresented by the hundreds.'"

I sat back. "DHS is taking women being brought in by human traffickers into custody and not reporting them?"

"That's right."

"And Ramirez noticed, then reported it to his boss, who did nothing."

She nodded. "Looks that way."

I said, "Do you think Mike knew?"

She hit a button and her screen's magnification increased. "See for yourself."

I looked at the report. Sure enough, there at the bottom, under Ramirez's signature, it read "Cosigned, Technical Officer Mike Clarke."

"In other words," I said, "Mike signed a report detailing — if we're being charitable — DHS incompetence, and shortly thereafter he murdered the guy who filed the report and went AWOL."

"Yeah."

"Are you sure Hammond sat on this?" I asked. "Do we have examples of other reports that he passed up the chain?"

She said, "He has a whole directory in his work drive of reports he sent along to his boss, a Director Morris. Morris reports directly to the Area Port Director, who oversees all Houston and Galveston entry points for Customs."

I'd already known Dave Hammond had lied to me about some things, but now it looked like he was covering up even more. A lot more.

"Do you think you can access the manifests now?" I asked.

She said, "Let me check," and returned to her room. A minute later, she emerged with yet another laptop. "Here we go."

After a moment, "Jesus."

"Now what?"

She said, "Hammond or whoever has been sitting on an unbelievable number of seizures. I'd say they're maybe reporting half of what they're taking."

I said, "Any cars?"

"Cars, cash, drugs — you name it," Charlie said.

"You know what I'm looking for," I said.

She said, "Give me a sec." She searched for a moment, "Looks like DHS seized three Ferraris in the last year. One was a red Testarossa."

Son of a bitch. "The last year? How long has this been going on?"

"There's no way to tell," she said. "It looks like they use some sort of auto-archiving program that clears files out after a set period. Looks like eighteen months, but they probably have a separate repository for e-discovery if there's litigation pending."

I said, "Can you download these manifests? Without them finding out, I mean?"

"Not a problem," she said. "I'm mirroring the contents to my own secure server."

I said, "Good deal. Get screenshots too, and anything else you think would help from a forensics standpoint. We'll need the evidence when we go after these assholes."

"Already on it," Charlie said, then she looked at me. "Cy, the value of these unreported seizures is more than the GDP of most countries. Are we sure Hammond is the only one involved?"

"No way to know," I said. "But first things first: we know Ramirez's report was suppressed. Let's dig a little more into Mr. Hammond's business and see if there's something we can use for leverage."

"And if there isn't?"

I said, "I guess we'll burn that bridge when we get to it."

THIRTY-SEVEN

"You want the good news or the bad news?" Charlie said.

"I always want the bad news," I said.

It was late afternoon, and our efforts at digging up dirt on Dave Hammond had borne little fruit. Everything Charlie had unearthed from behind DHS firewalls was indeed damning, but the guy's public profile was squeaky clean.

She said, "Ramirez's report is the only one I can find evidence of Hammond suppressing. It looks like he manually deletes everything he receives after a certain period."

"Like that auto-archiving thing you were talking about?" I asked.

"No," she said. "I bet he just has a reminder set to go clean out his inbox. We're lucky we found this one."

I cursed under my breath. It wasn't enough. There was no direct link from the suppressed contraband seizures to Hammond, and without evidence, I had no leverage to use to find Mike.

"What's the good news?"

"I backed up all the DHS material," she said.

"That's great," I replied. "Maybe we can print it all out and threaten to bury Hammond alive in it if he doesn't tell us where Mike is."

"You didn't find anything online?" she asked.

"I found plenty," I said. "He coaches Little League, he's a member of the local Jaycees, and he's on the board of the Fraternal Order of Police. He may or may not be running the biggest black market on the Gulf Coast out of a Ship Channel office, but publicly he's a pillar of the community."

"I guess blackmail is out," Charlie said.

"It was always a long shot," I admitted. "By itself, the report might be enough to go to the authorities with, but if we try moving forward with it, it's just going to get bogged down in internal investigations."

"Meanwhile, they can keep taking shots at us."

I nodded. "Yup. And since we'll have officially shown our hand, they won't hold back. Forget a lone driver on I-45 or a handful of dipshits with M-16s, they'll send a strike team to take us out, then plant drugs or kiddie porn in the house."

Charlie said, "Kind of makes you wonder why they haven't already."

"Like I said, they don't know what we know," I said. "Right now, I'm just a guy poking around to find his brother. They tried to scare us off and probably think they've succeeded."

"That's why you told Roy you were backing off."

I said, "Yeah. I don't know who he's in contact with, but if he is compromised, he'll report that we're standing down. That should buy us time."

"Time for what?" she asked.

I ran my fingers through my hair. "For leaning on Hammond, or so I'd hoped. Now ..." I spread my hands.

"There must be another way," Charlie said, "something we haven't found yet. I can keep digging ..."

"Oh, there's another way," I said, "but I'm really not looking forward to it."

"Tell me," she said.

I told her. She was, to put it mildly, less than enthusiastic.

"You're out of your fucking mind," Charlie said.

"That's entirely possible," I agreed.

She was pacing in front of me now, always a good indicator of when she was pissed off. "How is this supposed to work again?"

I said, "I thought I was pretty clear."

"Yeah, I guess I just thought you were pulling my leg," she said. "You're going to break into Hammond's house to find proof of his heinous crimes."

"With your help, but yeah."

She said, "You're that ready to lose our investigator license?"

"I'm that ready to find Mike," I said. "Hammond would have to be an idiot to keep any evidence on DHS computers, and you've confirmed there isn't any."

"That I can find," Charlie pointed out.

I said, "Well, not to blow smoke up your ass, but if you can't find it, it ain't there."

She chewed on that for a second. "Proceed."

"And I'm willing to bet he's not stupid enough to keep anything incriminating on site, like in an office safe," I continued. "That only leaves one place."

"Technically, it could be any number of places," she said. "He may have a storage container or a boat or a fucking treehouse for all you know."

I pointed to her laptop. "Off the books, maybe. But you looked at his records and there's no indication of any of that: no rental payments, no leases or fees."

She frowned. "I'm not convinced."

"Well, no shit," I said. "Neither am I. Not one hundred percent. Time's running out, sis. If you've got a better idea, I'm game to hear it."

"Do you even know where he lives?" she asked.

"No." I smiled. "But I'm sure you do."

She muttered, "Asshole," and turned to one of her laptops. "But yeah, I pulled it from some of his City of Houston emails. Can you remember it, or do I need to text it to you?"

"Text. I recently suffered a head injury, after all."

My phone buzzed a second later and I took it out. "Zip code 77079. Is that Katy?"

"Memorial," she said.

That was even worse. Katy was more or less the Western Hinterlands to Inner Loop denizens like us, but real money resided in Memorial. There would be actual police — not just rent-a-cops — actively patrolling the area.

Charlie was apparently thinking the same thing. "I shudder to think how many cameras will be pointing at you on that street, or in Hammond's house itself."

"Are you saying you can't do anything about that?" I asked.

"I can disable them," she said. "But only the ones inside the house won't raise an immediate alarm, unless he's watching them at that exact moment. Shutting down every camera on the street and in the neighboring houses is bound to get noticed."

I thought about that. "Maybe I don't go in the front."

She started typing and said, "Hang on a sec." After another minute, "You lucky bastard."

"I hope you're not being sarcastic."

She turned the laptop to me. The screen displayed a satellite photo. "His house backs up to Buffalo Bayou."

I smiled in spite of myself. Buffalo Bayou was the main west-to-east drainage canal, running from the Katy Prairie through downtown Houston and into the Ship Channel. Unless there was a storm, the water level and current would be manageable. Theoretically, it wouldn't be that difficult to paddle upstream and insert from the rear of his house. Best of all, it would avoid prying eyes on the street side.

She said, "People might have motion sensor lights for their backyards, but they shouldn't reach the bayou itself. Same with any security cameras. You can paddle up behind the house, but you'll have to cross about a hundred feet of park and a jogging trail before you get to his yard."

"Is there a fence?" I asked.

"I can't be a hundred percent certain at this resolution, but I'd count on it."

"Now I just need to know what I'm looking for."

"Deposit slips, for starters," Charlie said. "Obvious shit like large amounts of cash or obvious contraband ..."

"What counts as 'obvious contraband'?" I asked.

She shrugged. "Jade monkey?"

"Maltese Falcon?" I suggested.

"I doubt it's something with too much bulk, unless he's holding it somewhere offsite we don't know about yet," Charlie said. "But you'll need to be quick; there's no telling how long it'll take the security system to notice."

"We'll stick with the cash theory, then," I said. "How soon can you get into his system?"

She said, "I know his address and his wireless carrier from his home email account. Shouldn't take more than a few hours, assuming he has a standard DNS and IP setup."

I stared.

"As long as he hasn't changed the default settings on his router, it's not too hard to get in." She sighed. "Otherwise, it might take me longer."

"How much longer?"

"Another thirty minutes." She grinned.

"Okay," I said, "I'm going to call Don and see if he wants to be my backup."

"He going to go up the creek with you?"

"Ha. He's ex-Army. I don't even think he knows how to swim," I said. Which was bullshit. Mom and Dad made sure all the Clarke kids could swim before they started kindergarten. It does wonders for parental peace of mind at pool parties. Or so I've heard.

"You're going in alone?" she asked. "Is that really a good idea?"

I said, "You said I need to be quick. I love Don," mostly true, "but he's built for damage, not speed. If the objective is getting in and out fast, without leaving a trace, this is a one-person job."

"I guess he can stand by in his car."

I said, "I don't want him too close. If you're right about all the surveillance in the area, he shouldn't be anywhere near Hammond's house."

She said, "We should talk to him about it, but I'd think having him cool his heels at a Dunkin' Donuts or something until he's needed — *if* he's needed — is the better plan."

"I better go call him." I rose with some difficulty and limped over to the counter where I'd left my phone.

"You gonna be okay?" Charlie asked.

I nodded, though I was gritting my teeth as I did so. "Let's just nail this son of a bitch and I'll sleep for a week."

THIRTY-EIGHT

The plan moved quickly, which was gratifying. Don was in (because of course he was) and even promised to bring lots of black and digital camouflage clothing for us to wear. The items in his inventory were so numerous and detailed that I was afraid to ask what else he'd squirreled away after his time in the military.

We decided on the next night, partly to give Charlie time to get the technical details she needed to get into Hammond's systems, but mostly to let me get some sleep and insufficiently heal my bodily trauma.

I slept approximately ten hours Friday night, waking with a clear head and stiffness in just about every joint that prefaced what I imagine most days would feel like when I turned 60.

Assuming I lasted that long, of course.

Reflecting on mortality wasn't my style, but as I lay in my bed just then, sunlight streaming in through my window as I tried to will my knees to bend enough so I could stand up without having to roll off the mattress, I had to admit I was running low on lives. Just in the last few days alone I'd cheated death no less than three times. Any of those encounters could have gone sideways, and I still had to see this thing with Mike through.

Perhaps a day was coming when I wouldn't be able to keep this up. A day when my reflexes would be too slow, or my instincts would fail me, and that'd be it. Nothing left but a sparsely attended funeral and interment alongside Dad and Lee at the family plot in Washington Cemetery.

Mom would be pissed. I got out of the dangerous police career at her behest, after all. I can just see her yelling at my open grave about my being a selfish asshole while my surviving siblings nod solemnly.

Would she be right? Was I taking too many risks trying to find Mike? Was I losing my mind debating whether my actions might lead my mother to curse me at my hypothetical funeral?

I pulled myself into a sitting position and tested my legs: sore but functional. Standing up didn't result in any new pain, so I shuffled to the bathroom to perform my morning rituals. I skipped shaving because I hated it and also skipped flossing. I hated doing that as well, but considering the very real possibility I'd be dying in the next 12–18 hours, it also seemed like a waste of time.

I threw on a T-shirt and picked my way carefully down the stairs. Some flexibility was returning to my knees and ankles, and I was reasonably confident in their reliability for the evening's planned shenanigans. Charlie wasn't so charitable.

"Jesus Christ in a sidecar," she said, "who let the Crypt Keeper in here?"

"Hilarious."

She said, "I guess you'll be safe in the zombie apocalypse; they'll just take a look at you and figure you're one of them."

I walked over to the counter. "Please, go on."

"Eh, I'm already bored," she said, turning back to her laptop. "You do look like shit, though."

"You game for a sit-up contest?" I asked, rinsing out the French press. "I'm sure the ribs won't bother you a bit."

She winced at that. "Fair point."

I put the kettle on and turned on the gas. "So where are we?"

"Got into the router last night, while you were unsuccessfully catching up on your beauty sleep," she said. "I've got access to his home network, but there's one problem."

"What's that?"

"Nothing's on."

I paused the process of pouring grounds into the press. "Come again?"

She shrugged with her hands. "His computer's not on, so I can't access it. He must be one of those weirdos who shuts it down every time he stops working on it."

"Didn't you tell me that was good security practice?" I asked.

"Well yeah, but hardly anybody actually does it. It's surprising," she said. "And annoying."

I resumed my coffee preparation. "Can you still get to the cameras?"

She said, "That's what I was trying, but it's controlled from his computer, and I believe we've been over that problem."

"We're screwed," I stated.

"You don't know me very well, I guess," she said, that annoying look back on her face.

"Sis," I said, with as much indignant weariness as I could muster, "you may not have noticed, but I've spent a good chunk of the last week getting the shit kicked out of me. Could you just cut to the chase so I can bask in your brilliance?"

Charlie frowned. "You take the fun out of everything. Look, Hammond's setup, like most webcams, can be controlled either via the web — which he accesses through his computer — or an app —"

"Which he accesses through his phone," I finished.

She nodded. "And we know his phone number. I've been monitoring his calls and texts all morning."

I said, "I sense a 'but' coming."

"But," she obliged, "I can't operate the webcam app remotely. For the last hour or so, I've been trying to get into his password settings to see what his login is."

The water was coming to a boil. I took the kettle off the burner before the whistle could annoy me. "What good is that going to do if his computer's off?"

"I don't have to log into the web app from his computer. I have his home IP address and the IP address of the cameras. I can log in from here and disable everything."

I was impressed, but refused to let on out of general principles. "Sounds good to me."

She smirked. "Don't you want to know about the street cameras?"

"*I* want to know about the street cameras." Don walked into the kitchen unannounced.

"Didn't we get the locks fixed?" I muttered, pouring the water into the press.

Don threw a black duffel bag on a chair. "All right, coffee! Oh, and locks aren't very useful if they aren't, you know, locked."

Charlie said, "My bad. I went out to get his paper and forgot about the door."

Don grabbed a mug from the cabinet and stuck it out to me, knowing I was loath to share my coffee.

"It has to steep, you Philistine," I said.

He rolled his eyes and sat down opposite Charlie. "What's up with the street cams? Are we dark and silent?"

"All these houses are set back from the street far enough that I don't believe they have coverage into any backyards," she said. "But the bend in the bayou as you're approaching four houses down is a little close for comfort. How long do you think it'll take you to get there from that point?"

She directed that one to Don, who said, "He has to make it upstream, cross the open ground, and hop a fence? Cy's not a total pansy, so he should be able to do it in under three minutes."

"Thanks," I said.

"I mean, you're still mostly pansy," he said.

"In that case," Charlie interrupted, "I'll cut them out a minute before you reach that spot and leave them off for five minutes total."

I said, "How long before the neighborhood watch or whoever investigates?"

"No way to be sure," she said. "Centurion Security is the contractor for the neighborhood, and I dug around some in their Twitter DMs and online message boards to see what their response times for outages are."

"And?" Don asked.

Charlie said, "It varies. Anywhere from twenty minutes to a couple hours. I'm hoping because it's the weekend they'll only have a skeleton office staff and have to bring in somebody from on call."

Don nodded. "Saturday night should work to our advantage. What about Hammond? Any word on what he'll be doing?"

"He doesn't have anything on his calendar," she said, "and

there's nothing in his texts or emails. You aren't planning on going in if he's there, I assume."

Don and I looked at each other, and from the look in his eyes I realized it was up to me to be the guiding hand of patience and restraint for once.

"No, we'd have to abort," I said. Don opened his mouth to object but I cut him off "This isn't reacting to an attempt on our lives, this is breaking and entering. Worse, he's a government official. If we got caught and the Feds were so inclined, they could have us up on terrorism charges." I looked at Charlie. "Especially if any of your cyber-shenanigans come to light."

She placed a hand on her chest in, perhaps, mock indignation. "You wound me."

"Wimps," Don growled.

Charlie said, "Hold up." More typing, which I was half convinced she did purely for dramatic effect. "Okay, I cracked his webcam password. I'm in."

"That's it, I guess," I said.

"That's it."

Don looked from me to Charlie and back to me. "So are we going or what?"

I said, with a resolution I only sort of felt, "We're going."

Don rubbed his hands together in a way that was both reassuring and disconcerting. "Hot damn."

THIRTY-NINE

We were going into this with either substantially less or significantly more planning than your usual burglary.

Because let's be clear: My plan that evening was no less than breaking into a man's home with the intention of stealing something. That the "something" in question was digital information I could download onto a hard drive no bigger than a tater tot didn't make what we were about to do any less of a crime.

Thoughts like that really made me feel warm and fuzzy about this wonderful technological age we lived in.

We tied my kayak to the roof rack on Don's Range Rover. It was a sea kayak that I'd made woefully inadequate use of over the last several years. It used to have a twin, but that one moved away with its owner when Emma and I split. In deference to the importance and secrecy of the mission, I'd spray painted it flat black. It wasn't the most aesthetically pleasing result, but it'd get the job done. And it would make for a good conversation starter if I ever invited Emma to go kayaking again.

The plan was to put in the water off the trail near Kirkwood, on the west side of town, about three-quarters of a mile downstream from Hammond's place. Don would park at a Starbucks on the I-10 access road, half a mile away. If things went according to plan, he'd spend the entire time in his car without needing to come to my aid. Because if I had to call Don, then that meant shit had really hit the fan.

Unfortunately, years of experience had taught me to

assume feces would come into contact with blades eventually.

It was go time. I rechecked my bag: wire cutters, duct tape, Phillips and flathead screwdrivers, pliers, tape measure, and my .40. I carried no ID — no point in making it easy to identify my body if things went tits up — which shouldn't pose a problem, as HPD's Marine Unit didn't make a habit of patrolling bodies of water you could throw a baseball across.

I was wearing all black, down to a ski mask that rolled up to a cap. The forecast for the evening was cloudy and lows in the 60s. I'd work up a sweat rowing upstream, but with any luck joggers or casual bystanders wouldn't give me a second look.

"You good to go?" It was Don. I took a second to eye his getup, which made him look like he was deploying to a forward area, right down to his freaking combat boots, and chuckled.

"Someone's going to see you lurking in the parking lot and think you're a mass shooter."

He shrugged. "I mean, they wouldn't be totally wrong."

"Do I need to remind you the whole point of this is to get in and out without attracting attention?"

"I work best when I'm in familiar surroundings." He spread his arms. "Wearing the old kit makes me comfortable."

"Some woman taking her kids into the coffee place isn't going to be when she sees your Son of Sam looking ass."

"The Range Rover has tinted windows."

"Wonderful," I said, zipping up my bag.

"And I'm in much better shape than Berkowitz."

The only way you could tell Charlie was nervous was if she was chewing her nails. Everything else about her was nigh unflappable, as anyone who'd walked in on her as she was going through the phone of a guy she'd just shot dead in her kitchen could attest, but if her teeth were working on her nails, she was nervous.

Judging by the whittled ends of her fingers as she talked to me and Don, she was very nervous indeed.

"Let's go over the timeline again," she said.

"Don drops me off at twenty-thirty hours," I said. Sunset was about eight o'clock. "The drop-off point is about a klick from Hammond's, so it should take me half an hour to get there."

She nodded. "You hold position four houses down until twenty-one hundred regardless, because that's when I cut the feed to the street cams."

"Got it."

"You?" She turned to Don.

He said, "I drop him off, then proceed to the Starbucks on I-10 and Dairy Ashford. Where I hold position unless he requests assistance." He paused. "I still think I should come along."

"We've been over this," I said.

Don replied, "I haven't. You made the call without consulting me."

"Mom's already lost Lee and maybe Mike," I said. "Now isn't the time to go all-in on her kids."

Charlie piped up, "Besides, Cy needs to be fast and sneaky. You may be 'strong like bull,' but you're about as stealthy as one, too."

He sniffed in a supremely petulant manner but otherwise said nothing else.

She added, "Under no circumstances are you to leave the vehicle while in the parking lot, so take a leak now if you need to."

"I have bottles in the car," he said.

"Ew," she said.

I said, "Spoken like someone who's never been on stakeout."

"Look," she said, "I don't care if you drink it, just stay in the damn car."

"Affirmative," Don said.

"Also," she said, "park in the middle of the lot, away from the entrances, and stay off the Wi-Fi. We don't know how this is going to shake out, or if Hammond and his goons are even going to know we were there, but any subsequent investigation might take note of who logged into Google Starbucks while the nearby home of a senior DHS agent was being pilfered."

"Maybe he should park farther away," I suggested.

Don shook his head, and Charlie said, "This is the best compromise between avoiding surveillance and achieving reasonable response time."

"If I have to make an appearance," Don said, "we're probably already screwed, so I might as well get there in a hurry."

I wasn't entirely convinced, but I also didn't want to end up dead because Don was stuck in traffic on I-10.

"Now," Charlie continued, "if things go well, you'll exfil the same way you came in, contacting Don once you're past the bend. Cy, maintain radio silence from twenty-one hundred hours on unless you have no other choice."

"I'm not an idiot."

She ignored the bait, meaning she really was nervous. "Comm check."

Don and I put in our earpieces as she spoke into hers. "Check," she said and we both acknowledged ours were working.

Charlie nodded. "Cy, you have the thumb drive?"

"Check."

"Your first order of business is turning on the computer," she said. "I downloaded his floor plan from the homebuilder's website." She placed a blueprint on the table and we leaned over it.

"Hammond's router shows regular connections to two computers. One we know is his work laptop, so the other must be his home PC."

"Desktop or laptop?" I asked.

"The MAC address of the unknown computer matches to a network interface controller used in HP desktop models," Charlie said.

"There she goes again," Don said.

"You could have just said desktop," I pointed out.

She said, "If I don't make things sound complicated every once in a while, y'all won't be impressed."

That was encouraging, I thought. A desktop was going to be in a den or home office. A laptop could be anywhere.

"Your best bet is probably here or here." She pointed to two likely candidates. "I'd check there first."

"When are you disabling his home cams?" Don asked.

"Between twenty-thirty and twenty-one hundred," she said. "I'm going to spoof a power surge so it looks like an accident. But again, if you're detected, it's probably not going to fool anybody."

"I'll turn the computer on once I've located it," I said. "How long will it take you to break into it?"

She said, "Assuming his wireless hooks up automatically, not long. I already know the relevant addresses and SSID. If he has a desktop login, it might take another couple of minutes, no longer."

"And you're going to find what we're looking for?" Don asked.

"This isn't a goddamned research paper," she said. "I'm not going to open a bunch of files and peruse them over a cocktail. It's a data dump. I'm mirroring his entire hard drive to a cloud server hosted in Finland."

Don looked at her, then me. "Finland?"

"Anonymous hosting service," Charlie said. "U.S. has no jurisdiction."

I said, "And I'm on standby in case you need me to copy something immediately juicy."

She nodded. "I doubt that'll be necessary, but the mirroring process takes some time. If I see something we definitely don't want to lose, I'll tell you."

"Like a document that says 'Map to Mike Clarke,'" Don said.

"Don't hold your breath."

I said, "If everything works out, I should be in and out pretty quick. Once I reach the signal point, I'll contact Don to come pick me up. Whole thing shouldn't take more than fifteen minutes. Tops."

"After which I turn the street cams back on," Charlie said. She didn't say it, but I knew she'd leave Hammond's off to maintain the idea a power outage knocked them out.

There was a pause as the three of us looked at each other. "Is that it?" I asked finally. "Are we forgetting anything?"

"Does he have an alarm system?" Don asked.

She nodded. "ADT. Won't be a problem."

"Why not?"

"His particular system is several years old," she said. "There are several known exploits which I've ... exploited."

Hanford's house flashbacked to me and I said, "They don't have a dog, do they?"

Charlie said, "There are no pet licenses on record for them with the City of Houston, and nothing in their bank records about visits to pet stores or veterinarians."

"Thanks," I said. Knocking a dog out would complicate

matters.

Don said, "What's the actual plan if Cy calls for help?"

Charlie and I looked at each other. I said, "Assuming I'm not dead, I guess getting me the hell out of there as fast as possible."

"What about the kayak?"

"Paid cash for it off a burner Craigslist account eight years ago," I said. "Pretty much untraceable."

"You didn't carve 'Cy + Emma' on it at some point?" he asked.

"Just my Trapper Keeper," I replied.

"Is the GPS in the Range Rover disabled?" Charlie asked, ignoring us.

"It doesn't have it. Bluetooth either."

She nodded again. "Then I guess that's it."

I checked my watch. "Okay, about time to saddle up."

Don grunted and rose to leave. "Seems to me I don't get to do any of the fun stuff."

"And I hope that doesn't change," Charlie said.

He left and Charlie and I stood there for a moment.

"Be careful, asshole," she said.

"Just get the data, dipshit." This was pretty much as close as we got to sibling affection.

FORTY

It struck me that I'd had several opportunities for self-reflection in the past few days. First there was the hospital ledge, and now I was paddling in the Houston twilight on my way to commit a felony against a government official. Maybe this also happens on average felony-committing nights, but being out on the water is definitely a good way spend some time alone with your thoughts.

Said thoughts can assume a variety of forms. For example, might any choices you made as a youngster have kept you from going down this path? Maybe if I'd tried for a soccer scholarship, gone to school on one of the (other) coasts, or asked Sandra Miller out in the tenth grade ... maybe then I'd have avoided this sordid turn of events.

And maybe Mike would never be found.

Anyway, I mused as the waves lapped against the kayak and grackles cawed overhead in the trees lining Buffalo Bayou, it's not like I'd be leaving any widows or orphans behind if things went sideways. Hell, I didn't even have a dog.

The closest non-family connection I had was with Emma, and we'd been broken up for months.

I debated calling her before we left, but opted not to, based on both the "non-family" thing and the fact I'd already involved her to an extent that might cost her professionally. For being a bunch of soulless bloodsuckers, lawyers had a lot of rules. The hell with it, I thought; if this plan works and we find Mike, I'll give her a call.

"Testes, testes, one, two … three?" Don's voice crackled in my ear. "Didn't get lost, did you, chief?"

I smiled at the expression in spite of myself. "I'm about to enter radio silence," I said, checking the luminous dial of my watch. It was 2050 hours, ten minutes before I hit the bend and cut off active comms.

"I'm pulling into the Starbucks now," he said.

"Try to blend in," I said.

"Have any suggestions?"

"How well can you pull off the dead-eyed suburbanite look?"

He laughed. "How about if I just stay in the car like we discussed?

"Sounds like a plan."

"Did we ever decide on the panic word?" he asked.

"We did not." He was referring to what I'd say if I required his intervention. It was a worst-case scenario kind of thing, in the event I was in deep shit.

He said, "Lay it on me."

I said, "It should be something I don't say often."

"How about, 'Don is my favorite brother'?"

"Bit cumbersome," I replied.

He thought for a second. "What about 'poppycock'?"

"It's always about the cocks with you," I said.

"Gotta make the best of the situation," he said.

"'Poppycock' it is," I said.

After a pause, "Seriously, don't do anything cute, Cy. Get in, turn the computer on, and get the hell out."

"Ten-four." His connection dropped and Charlie came on.

"Five minutes to radio silence," she said, "assuming you two are done yukking it up."

"I know and we are," I replied. "What's Hammond's twenty?"

"His phone's GPS shows him at the office," she said. "And his wife doesn't get back into town until tomorrow night. You should be all clear."

"Roger," I said.

It was a peaceful night, minus the birds and the inescapable traffic noise. This stretch of Buffalo Bayou was far enough from streetlights you could actually make out a few constellations. Rare indeed for Houston.

"Don was right about one thing," Charlie said. "Get in and turn the PC on. Don't fart around."

I said, "Aw, I was thinking of rearranging all his photos just to fuck with him."

"That would be unwise."

"How long will it take you to mirror the hard drive?"

"Depends on the connection and how much there is to copy," she said. "Assuming I don't have any issues logging on, maybe fifteen minutes."

That was a long time to cool my heels, I thought. To Charlie, I said, "Cool, plenty of time to rearrange photos."

"I'm serious, Cy," her tone was muted, and I realized just how concerned she was.

I said, "I know. I'll be careful."

"Radio silence in three, two ..." she said.

That was it, I clicked the earpiece off — it wouldn't come back on unless I was calling for help — and paddled harder. Fortunately, there hadn't been any significant rain for about a week, and the bayou was low and moving slowly against me, without much current. I rounded the bend and was at a spot parallel to Hammond's house in less than three minutes.

Up yours, Don, I thought, maturely.

There was no pier or anything similar on the bayou at this location, so I tied the kayak off beneath a low-hanging live oak. It would be largely invisible to any but the most diligent observer. I didn't see anyone on the trail as I scanned the park between me and Hammond's house (he did indeed have a fence), so I dashed across the grass, keenly aware of the exposure of running across open ground.

The fence was eight feet high but otherwise unremarkable, and I scaled it swiftly, dropping to the ground on the other side and taking in my surroundings. Like most homes backing up to a waterway in Houston, Hammond's yard was pitched on a steep grade as it sloped up to the house. I wondered idly how he'd fared during Hurricane Harvey, when most of this area would've been underwater.

Taking a deep breath, I pulled the ski mask into place, strapped on my knapsack, and started up to the house.

Charlie was as good as her word, and even though I saw contact points for the security system on the door, the house remained silent after I picked the lock, put on my gloves, and opened it. I entered the house, finding myself in a small mudroom I recognized from the floor plan Charlie had downloaded. Shutting and locking the door behind me, I moved through the darkened kitchen and into the house proper.

Hammond's house was a fairly sprawling ranch style that thankfully only had one floor. The computer was in the second room I checked, a home office (as we'd suspected) with various photos of Hammond with local dignitaries and some printed awards he'd seen fit to frame and line his wall. I hadn't so much as hung my diploma up in my house, and the only framed picture I had was an autographed photo of pitcher Nolan Ryan famously punching Robin Ventura after the latter had unwisely rushed the mound after a brushback. The very definition of "rookie move."

The desktop was, no surprise, on Hammond's desk. It was an older model HP, just as Charlie had said, with a newish-looking webcam on top of the monitor. I felt around the base of the computer tower until I located the power button and clicked it on. I immediately heard the hum of the hard drive coming online and the accompanying whir of the fan.

So far, so good.

Though it would be breaking radio silence to do so, I knew Charlie would ping me if she had any problems. Still, I wanted to give her ample time to get up and running, so I decided to check out Hammond's desk.

I glanced at the various letters and papers strewn upon it. Hammond wasn't very fastidious, and while I doubted he'd notice if any were moved slightly, I was careful not to disturb anything.

It was mostly the usual office crap: an honest-to-god landline phone, receipts to be filed, letters both official and otherwise, pens, a checkbook. It looked like Hammond still got his bills in the mail and paid them the same way.

Paper receipts? A landline? I could almost hear Charlie's laughter from here.

The desk wasn't locked, so I opened the drawers to see if anything useful was in quick view. Hammond didn't seem like the kind of guy who'd leave sensitive information about the crimes he was committing in more-or-less plain sight, but people also put their passwords on Post-It notes next to their computers. It's hard to maintain 24/7 diligence in these difficult times.

I hadn't brought my phone, but that's what the little camera was for. I hated calling it a "spy camera," because it made me sound like one of those guys who tried to impress women by telling them he worked for the CIA. Then again, I'd purchased it at a place called the Spy Emporium on Bellaire, so the name fit.

I rolled the ski mask back up into cap configuration and took a few pictures. We really were putting all our hopes in Hammond's hard drive, but it couldn't hurt to check this stuff out later, just in case.

After closing the drawers, I went to a bookshelf situated against the far wall to check for items of interest and came up short again. There was little of interest next to the usual corporate tomes and arid businessman biographies that must be issued along with your AARP card when you turn 50.

I still wasn't entirely convinced anyone had actually read that book about the habits of highly effective people.

It was while perusing the shelves that I heard the front door open. I checked my watch: only five minutes had passed. Checking the perimeter of the room, I saw with a sense of impending doom there was no place in his office to hide.

I heard a set of keys landing somewhere. It was a Saturday night, I thought, maybe he wouldn't come into his office at all.

The doorknob turned and the door began to swing inward. Shit.

I looked at the computer. The power light was on at the base, but the monitor was still dark. Fortunately, the model was old enough you still had to power each component on separately. There was one other light visible, however, that of the webcam.

I swiveled it around so it was facing the doorway, just as Hammond entered. Hopefully Charlie would be monitoring the feed and could update Don. I didn't want to use the panic word until we had the hard drive, so I had to stall Hammond.

An idea formed as he walked in and saw me.

"Son of a bitch!" he exclaimed.
This was going to hurt.

FORTY-ONE

How to Annoy Someone into Violence, Part One: Talk Shit Disproportionate to Your Actual Tactical Standing.

"Well, look who decided to drop by." I said.

"What the hell are you doing in my house?" Hammond bellowed, with somewhat less panic than I'd hoped. This was likely due to the pistol he had pulled on me.

I looked around the room (after moving out from behind the computer in the hopes he wouldn't notice it was booted up). "Is this your house? It's hard to tell without any obvious signs of asshole habitation. I assume your wife cleans up after you."

"Phone," he said, holding his non gun-toting hand out.

"Didn't bring one."

He crossed the room quickly, jamming the pistol into my ribs. He frisked me and found the .40 in the holster at the small of my back. He gave me a shove after removing it, then glanced around, possibly to verify I was alone. "I could shoot you, you know. This is Texas."

"It sure is," I agreed.

"Cops would just slap me on the back." He took a step forward. "Hell, you're even dressed like —"

"Like a burglar out of central casting?" I suggested.

"Yeah, that," Hammond still wasn't sure how to play it. I helped him along.

"You shoot me and everything I've found about your

robbing freight shipments goes to the press," I said.

He stopped, uncertain and squinting at me. "I don't know what you're talking about."

I rolled my eyes. "You're a better thief than a liar. How long has it been going on, Dave? Did you really think nobody would notice?"

Finally deciding on his course of action, he walked toward the desk. "I'm calling the cops,"

"Call the cops and it still gets leaked," I said. "Just tell me where Mike is."

His hand hesitated over the phone. "I don't know," he said.

"But you know why he split," I said. "Because he and Ramirez both figured out what you were up to."

He shook his head. "Your brother *split* because he murdered a fellow agent. That's the only explanation there is, or that anyone needs to know."

"Bullshit. Ramirez was killed with a rifle shot from long range, not Mike's weapon," I said, "unlike what you conveniently reported."

He stared at me, his expression unreadable. Time to step it up.

I continued, "That's on the official autopsy report that you had suppressed, by the way. It's all part of what goes to the media *and* the Director of Homeland Security if anything happens to me."

"What do you want?" he said flatly.

"I want my brother, you fucking idiot," I said. "Why is that so hard for you to comprehend?"

"I already told you —" he began.

"You don't know where he is," I continued. "Yeah, this is getting boring, Dave. Maybe I'll just call the cops for both of us."

I reached for the phone on his desk when Hammond said, "Wait."

"Why?"

He licked his lips. "Maybe we can cut a deal."

Oh dear. "Why would I make a deal with you, you sack of shit? Tell you what, why don't you tell me why you do it and we'll go from there."

"Ever worked for the government?" he asked.

"I used to be a cop," I replied. "But you knew that."

"A cop," he sneered. "City police. You weren't even in for ten years. You have no idea."

"Let me take a stab at it anyway," I said. "You got tired of being a career desk jockey, right? Watching all that good shit seized from bad guys, it must have driven you nuts, how easy it would be to get a piece of the action."

I held my hand up when I saw him about to protest and continued, "Stop me if I start getting warm, but I'm guessing when you combine that sense of bureaucratic impotence with a good helping of Lone Star machismo, it was only a matter of time."

His face was turning red, which was good in the sense it was working. Bad for me in what was about to happen next. "You can't talk to me like that."

"What did I get wrong? The macho thing?" I laughed. "Like that H2 you drive? You can't even overcompensate right. I've seen your type a hundred times: you think you're a fucking cowboy when all you are is a crook. Hell, you're worse than a run-of-the-mill thief; at least my taxes don't pay their salary."

If the impotence thing lit the fuse, the taxes thing must have hit the detonator, because he pivoted away from the wall and swung, connecting with my jaw.

How to Annoy Someone into Violence, Part Two: Keep Them Talking.

I went down on one knee. Hammond stood over me, fists clenched. Depending on your definition of the word, things were going well.

"Was it something I said?" I spit mostly blood and some saliva onto the floor.

"You don't have any idea what the hell you're talking about," he growled.

"Don't I?" I stood up, rubbing my jaw. "Tell me you haven't been illegally seizing freight. And worse."

He punched me again, in the stomach this time. It was solid; not the worst I've taken, but I sold it well and doubled over with dramatic flourish.

"Oh, I've been doing it for years," he said, smiling. "Do you know how much comes through the Port of Houston every year? How many *tons*? There's no way any agency could keep tabs on all of it. And I can take my pick."

"Not just," I sucked wind, "not just contraband for you, huh?"

He laughed, then hit me again. A sharp jab to my nose. My vision flashed white for a second and I felt blood starting to flow freely. *Gonna stain those hardwoods, Dave.*

"Why stop there? Like I said, there's more cargo than anyone can keep track of."

I wiped my nose on my sleeve, the blood showing slightly blacker against the material. "What about the women?"

He leered, and I wished I could put a bullet in his head right then, but I hadn't gotten everything out of him yet. "Those are the best part! Blondes, brunettes, Asians, Europeans, Latinas … I can take my pick from all over the world. And you wouldn't believe how easy it is to move them when you have a federal badge."

My head was spinning but I couldn't back off now. "Wife's that lousy a lay, huh?"

He kicked me in the crotch and light flashed behind my eyes as a nauseating wave of pain roiled through me. I dropped to my knees and groaned. Unfortunately, no dramatics were necessary this time.

Leaning down, he said, "I can get a different girl every night. Hey, how about I pay a visit to that sister of yours after I get rid of you?"

That made me laugh, even though it hurt like hell to do so. He looked confused, and I didn't have the heart to tell him he'd pull back a stump if he ever tried to lay a hand on Charlie.

I rolled onto my side and propped myself up with one arm, shaking my head to clear it. So close now.

"Ramirez found out something, didn't he?" I guessed. "And because he was a good agent and respected the chain of command, he made the mistake of telling you."

"Yeah, but that's not why he died," Hammond said.

Here we go. I sat up as best I could and in my most puzzled voice said, "No?"

He smiled. "Ramirez came to me with his 'findings,'" he said, doing that annoying air quotes thing around the word, "and I said I'd look into them."

"Which you didn't," I said.

"Of course I didn't," he snapped. "Should've been the end of it right there, but the bastard had the stones to go over my head to *my* boss. That wasn't a good idea, which he found out right quick."

I was getting a bad feeling. "You didn't order Ramirez killed." I wracked my brain for the name and it came to me. "Morris. Director Morris is your boss, and he's in on it, too."

"See, you're not such a bad private detective after all," he said.

"So Morris orders the hit," I said. "What sucker did he get to carry it out?"

Hammond seemed offended. "I did, of course."

In spite of myself, I was impressed. "Autopsy report says Ramirez was killed by a .300 Winchester round, fired from a distance of five hundred yards. Not too shabby."

He smiled. "Aw, that's nothing. I've dropped a target from twelve hundred before. Just gotta put in the time." He looked at his watch. "Which is something you're about out of, friend."

I glanced at my own timepiece and saw fifteen minutes had passed since I booted Hammond's computer up. Knowing Charlie, she'd finished ten minutes ago and was making tea while searching for new episodes of *The Great British Bake Off*, but I had to be sure.

I got up on one knee, then stood. It was a little wobbly, but I made it.

"What about Hanford?" I said.

Another voice from the hallway, one I didn't recognize, said, "Stop talking, Hammond."

Hammond turned but didn't seem surprised when a man walked in the room. He could've been anywhere from 45 to 60 years old and moved with authority conferred by long years of military and government service.

It couldn't be anyone but Director Morris, Hammond's boss. Things had just taken a dangerous turn.

So I said, "What's all this … poppycock?"

FORTY-TWO

"Is this him?" Morris asked Hammond without taking his eyes off me. "The pain-in-the-ass brother?"

Hammond said, "That's him."

"Where's his gun?" Morris asked.

Hammond grunted and handed him my .40. Morris palmed it, racked the slide and checked the chamber, then stuck it in his waistband.

Damn, I thought. I liked that gun.

"The one and only," I said, extending my hand. "Cy Clarke. Real pleasure to meet you, Mr. Morris."

He looked at my hand like I'd just picked my nose with it. I dropped it and smiled as amiably as my blood-slicked teeth allowed.

"Why is he still alive?" This time Morris did look at Hammond.

"I don't know if killing him is a good idea," Hammond said, his bravado diminished in the presence of his boss. "Everyone knows he's been nosing around the Guerrero raid, looking for information about his brother. If he disappears —"

"If he disappears, the good people of this city will be concerned for exactly a day and a half, then some celebrity will say something stupid or another maniac will shoot up a school and they'll forget all about him," Morris said. He seemed like a cheerful guy.

"He's right," I said to Hammond.

He ignored me. "He says he has proof."

"Bullshit," Morris said.

I piped up, "No, it's true. Altered shipping manifests, transfer orders, even the original Ramirez autopsy report. Not sure how you managed to suppress those, though. Need to look into that a little more."

"Shut up," he said. To Hammond, "Shoot him."

"Bad idea, Dave." I said, silently hoping there wasn't any traffic between that goddamned Starbucks and here.

Morris said, "Shoot him. Bad enough to admit killing Ramirez, but you implicated me, and that can't leave this room."

Boy are you in for a surprise, I thought. At least I hoped so.

Hammond raised his pistol and aimed it at my chest.

"I wasn't kidding about the Feds, Dave." I was totally kidding about the Feds. "They're going to come sniffing around here when I don't turn up." I looked around the room, then pointed to the drops of my blood on the floor. "I don't know about you, but I've seen *C.S.I.* They're gonna black light the shit out of this place. Hope you know your way around a bucket of bleach."

He hesitated for a second, then raised the gun so I was staring at the barrel. This was escalating quickly.

"That's even worse," I said, trying to sound indifferent instead of panicky. "Do you know how hard it's going to be getting my brains out of this fine wood siding?"

He was still hesitating. It wasn't much, but every second gave Don more time to get there and execute whatever genius tactical plan he'd devised to save my ass.

Then I remember Don was the same guy who once ran through a wall of sheetrock rather than wait for my mom to pick the lock to the bathroom door.

I might be doomed.

"You guys have a real hard-on for my family," I said.

Hammond still had the gun on me, but that got Morris's attention. "How do you mean?"

I shrugged. "Killing me so soon after killing my brother. That's how those Sicilian vendettas get started."

Hammond said, "We didn't kill Mike."

"Bullshit."

Morris said, "No, it's true. But now I wish we had."

Hammond said, "Mike cosigned the report Ramirez sent me. Truth be told, I was supposed to take out both of them, but your brother's a smart bastard. Ramirez had barely hit the ground before he was out of there."

My head whirled, and it wasn't entirely due to lingering crotch pain. Mike was still in the wind, but short of his coded emails he'd made no attempt to contact me or Charlie or anyone. And he'd sent those before the Ramirez shooting anyway.

Where the hell was he?

"And the dead guy?" I said.

"Which one?" Hammond and Morris said simultaneously. It would've been funny if we weren't, you know, talking about murder.

I said, "The one posing as Chet Hanford in what I'm guessing is a front house."

They looked at each other. Morris shrugged. "I don't remember the name. New guy who drew the short straw that morning, I guess."

Cold bastard, I thought.

To Hammond, Morris said, "What are you waiting for?" He was getting impatient.

I said, as calmly as I could, "He wants you to shoot me because he knows his name's still clean. Your signature is on those manifests, and it's your ID attached to those altered shipments, not his."

Morris shook his head. "He's reaching. We're both in this."

"Then why kill me?" I said. "So you can both go down when the Feds get my stuff?"

Morris said nothing, but I noticed he had my gun out. It was pointing at the floor for now, but it added another layer of menace.

Hammond's gun lowered. "He's right, Hank. What about the information he says he —"

"There is no information!" Morris yelled. "He's bluffing and you're falling for it like a goddamned GS-5 rookie!"

A government insult, I thought. That's low.

I said, "That's what he wants you to think, Dave. You'll take the fall for this. Worst he'll get is an official reprimand for not realizing his direct report was a thief and a murderer."

"Shut up," Morris said. Now his gun was up. Speaking in net terms, this wasn't an improvement.

Hammond was no longer looking at me, "That's been your plan all along, hasn't it, you son of a bitch?"

Morris didn't take his eyes off me. "What are you talking about?"

"You don't have any skin in this game at all. It's why you ordered me to do Ramirez, even though you're supposed to be a better shot."

Not really what I wanted to hear right now.

"You need to stop talking," Morris said. "I can't believe you're having an attack of fucking conscience *now*, after everything else that's happened."

"Well, I am." Hammond reholstered his gun. "There's a better way to do this."

Morris looked incredulous. His eyes flickered to Hammond, and for a half second I considered making a move. The better part of valor convinced me to wait and see how this played out.

"Are you out of your mind?" Morris said.

"We don't know where his brother is," Hammond said. "We can't take the risk."

I don't know what happened to Morris at that point. Something passed behind his eyes, like a threshold — a Rubicon for those of you into classical references — had been crossed. I had no perspective on how years of thievery, trafficking, and murder affect a person. Some probably adapt to it easily, finding it scratching an itch in their souls they didn't know was always there. Others might experience conflict between the acts they're committing and their upbringing.

From his bearing, the fact he held a high position in DHS, and the anecdotal information about his shooting ability, Morris must be ex-military. They swear an oath to defend the Constitution, which is generally interpreted as frowning on criminal acts.

Or maybe Ramirez's was the first murder he'd ordered, and he'd finally come to a place he'd managed to avoid all these years. Knowing what I know about trafficking and the cartels, that seemed highly unlikely. If nothing else, living a double life for so long takes a psychic toll. I mean, just look at Batman.

These thoughts occurred to me in the instant of time it took for Morris to turn his (my) gun away from my chest, point it at Hammond, and pull the trigger.

He shot Hammond in the chest, the power of the bullet sending him back two steps, though incredibly, he didn't fall. He just stared at Morris, confusion and anger crossing his face in equal measures.

Oh, you stupid, stupid man, I thought.

Morris apparently wasn't the patient type, because he shot Hammond again, this time in the head. Hammond's left eyes disappeared in pink mist as the back of his skull blew outward, spattering his neatly framed commendations with blood and gray matter.

"Shit," I muttered.

"Yes," Morris said, turning the gun back on me as he walked over to Hammond's corpse. Treading carefully, so as not to disturb the body or step in blood, he retrieved Hammond's pistol from his holster. Bringing that one up to aim at me, he tucked my .40 back in his waistband.

"You knew I was bluffing," I said.

He snorted. "I'm not an idiot. However, you definitely have access to information you shouldn't. I suspect that's thanks to your sister."

"What makes you say that?"

"She's clearly the brains of your little operation," Morris said, then sighed. "Looks like I need to pay her a visit after this as well."

I laughed. "You wannabe cowboy assholes need to come up with some new scary threats, because this 'maybe I'll pay your sister a visit' shit is straight out of a *Lethal Weapon* movie."

He said, "It's not a threat, and whatever ... proclivities my dead subordinate may have displayed toward her aren't my concern. She, like you, is a loose end I need to clean up."

Maybe it was my sense of optimism, but I thought I saw a shadow move in the hallway. I kept my eyes on Hammond.

Stalling for time, I said, "What about Steranko? Was he ever involved?"

He smiled. "Another useful idiot. When we learned you

were looking into him, we naturally tried to encourage that line of thought. Pity you didn't bite."

"I see how you're going to get clear of this." I looked around the room. "It'll look like I confronted Hammond, then shot him, but he got one off and killed me before my second shot. Is that about right?"

Morris nodded. "It's not perfect, but it'll work. Homicide cops in this city are overworked as it is. They won't dig too deeply when both murder weapons are right in front of them."

"You've done this before." It wasn't a question.

"You have no idea." He smiled.

Don emerged from the shadows of the doorway and crept silently up behind Morris, a silenced pistol leveled at his skull. He raised his eyebrows, a silent request as to how he should proceed. My face must've given something away, because Morris started to turn around.

A couple things happened just then. Don turned his gun around and swung, hitting Morris in the back of the head with the butt. Morris pitched forward, unconscious, but not before reflexively squeezing the trigger.

I felt searing pain in my chest even as the shot knocked me into the desk. Through increasingly tunneled vision, I saw Don rush over to me.

"Hang on, bro. Hang on, I got you," He said. A second later, he had me in a fireman's carry and we were moving through Hammond's house.

He was talking, I assumed to Charlie, "Spartan, I repeat, Spartan. Evac proceeding from Constellation."

Charlie must have responded, because Don just said, "Out," and kept moving. We were out of the house now and running up the street. Dimly, I could see the Range Rover up ahead.

"Stay with me, Cy," Don said, as he bundled me as gently as possible into the back seat. Gently or not, I was about to pass out from shock and the pain.

"Don?" I said as he climbed into the driver's seat and started the engine.

"Yeah bro?" He peeled out. The neighbors wouldn't be pleased.

"Those are dumb code words," then I passed out.

FORTY-THREE

I drifted in and out of consciousness for the next day or so. It was my second trip to an emergency room in less than a week, only this time I was the patient. It'd been a while, and it still sucked.

They took me into surgery almost immediately after Don brought me in. I couldn't be certain of the location, but given how fast he got us here, I suspected we were in the Memorial City Medical Center. I'd have preferred Ben Taub, which has a better trauma center, but thoracic gunshot victims can't be choosers.

The first time I realized I wasn't going to die (not soon, anyway) is when I groggily came to in a hospital room and daylight was streaming through the windows. As my vision cleared, I saw Charlie arguing with Roy DeSantos next to my hospital bed. He was there in an official capacity, or so I assumed, given the presence of two uniformed cops in the room with him. I drifted off again before seeing any resolution.

My money was on Charlie, though.

Some indeterminate amount of time later, I woke up to a nurse checking my vital signs. It was night again.

"Am I going to live?" I croaked. My throat was parched.

"Depends on which law enforcement agency gets their hands on you," she said.

Interesting. I dozed again.

Daylight again. I shifted my position slightly and discovered that the pain in my chest had faded to "nearly unbearable" while my entire head throbbed dully. Only one eye was capable of opening, and with it I saw Charlie sitting next to my hospital bed, an expression of relief on her face.

"Ugh," I said.

"You scared the hell out of us, you asshole."

"I guess I'm not dying."

She shook her head, "Who goes on a mission like that without wearing a vest?"

"We didn't anticipate a firefight," I said. Wary now, I looked around.

Charlie answered my question before I could get it out. "Room's clean. I swept for bugs earlier this morning."

"How long have I been here?"

"Four days."

Jesus.

I rubbed my face. At least my arms still worked. "What's the damage?"

"Collapsed lung. Luckily the bullet missed any major organs," she said.

"Since when is a lung not a major organ?" I said.

"Please, you don't need both of them."

I attempted to sit up, but a wave of pain put an end to that plan. "I guess the shit really did hit the fan."

"You could say that," she said. "Don and I have been taking turns running interference for you against at least four agencies of interest."

"Homeland Security?"

"That was an easy one."

"FBI?"

"Two for two," she said.

"Houston PD?" I asked. "I thought I saw you arguing with DeSantos at one point. Or did I imagine that?"

Charlie smiled. "He took offense at your freelance operation. Apparently he took you at your word when you said you were going to back off."

"There goes my last friend on the force," I said.

"Oh, I doubt that."

I looked at her. "How come?"

"Never mind that," she replied. "You still haven't guessed the fourth."

I thought, but the effort was already starting to tire me out. Customs? No, they're part of DHS. Coast Guard? Men in Black?

"I give up," I said, finally.

She said, "None other than the Central Intelligence Agency."

The hell? "That doesn't make any sense."

"Don talked to them. They were here the second day, but I haven't seen them around since."

In what was becoming a common occurrence, I was completely at a loss. The CIA wasn't law enforcement and had no domestic agenda. This was an entirely new can of worms, and even the idea of unraveling this new wrinkle was exhausting.

Sticking with what I already knew, I said, "What did you mean about DeSantos? About his still being a friend?"

"I called him the night you got shot," she replied. "He's getting credit for the arrest, whether he wants it or not."

"Roy went to the house?"

"Yep. He's the one who found an unconscious Morris next to Hammond's corpse."

"And my blood everywhere," I added.

"Give your big sister some credit," she said.

I frowned. "If Roy got there right after Don took me out, how did you manage to clean up the scene?"

She smiled in that maddening way she had when she knew more than I did, which was often. "Just let the gears do their work."

"Any word on Mike?"

For the first time since I woke up, her face fell. "No. Nothing."

"Morris isn't talking?"

"No idea. He's disappeared into a black hole. Don and I haven't heard anything else."

I yawned. "What have you guys told Mom?"

Charlie rolled her eyes, "The truth? You think we could hide you getting shot again away from her?"

"Hope springs eternal, as they say."

"The good news is, your name's being kept out of things. So far." She looked around. "Press coverage is focused on Roy and the cops, and HPD is letting them run with that for now."

"But that doesn't mean they won't come after us," I began.

She glanced at the door. "There's been an FBI agent posted outside the room since you got out of surgery."

"Maybe they're waiting to see if I live before they arrest me."

"Probably want you healthy for the lethal injection," she agreed.

I wanted to argue the point with her, but I didn't get the chance. The door opened and a tall drink of water in a gray suit entered the room.

"He awake?" His clipped tone matched his crew cut.

"Are you?" Charlie asked.

"I guess it's too much to ask for the last week to have been a dream," I said.

The suit approached my bed, pulling a wallet from his jacket pocket and flipping it open to show the badge within. "Special Agent Winston, Mr. Clarke. I have a few questions."

"Not without his attorney present."

Emma walked in the room and my day improved one thousand percent.

"That'd be you?" Winston was pretty quick for a Fed.

She nodded. "If you have any questions for Mr. Clarke, you can submit them to me in advance. Any questioning takes place in my presence and at no other time."

Winston looked at her, then me. "You don't really think you're going to get away with this, do you?"

"Get away with what?" I asked, in the tone of voice that got me out of at least half the detention I should have been assigned.

Winston sneered and left the room. Emma walked to the side of the bed Charlie wasn't currently occupying.

"Hey," she said.

"Hey yourself." *Smooth as usual, Clarke.*

Charlie cleared her throat. "I'm going to go see if I can find Don. It looks like the sharks are closing in."

She walked to the door and I called after her, "Hey, Charlie?"

She stopped and turned. I said, "Thanks for everything."

"Anytime, little brother."

"Two goddamn minutes," I muttered as she exited. Then I looked into the face of Emma, my ex-girlfriend/current attorney, anticipating the glow of relief and affection on her face.

"I should knock the shit out of you," she said.

FORTY-FOUR

"Nice to see you, too," I replied. "You talk to all your clients this way, or only the ones you used to date?"

"What the hell were you thinking?"

"You look great, by the way." This was true.

She just stared at me.

"Mike's been missing for over a week now," I began. "The cops had no leads, and we had clear evidence Mike's boss was committing crimes that Mike found out about."

"Why not turn that information over to the police? Or Homeland Security?" She asked.

"Is this conversation covered by attorney-client privilege?"

Emma glanced back at the door. "Of course."

"I couldn't exactly go to the police with information we'd obtained illegally," I said.

"You could've sent it in anonymously," she countered. "Let them work on it from there."

"And waste even more time." It wasn't a question. "Police have procedures to follow and policies to adhere to. Charlie and I don't have that problem."

"Interesting to hear you refer to obeying the law as a 'problem.'"

"I'll remember that next time one of your siblings goes missing."

Emma sat down. "And how did your way work out? You're laid up in a hospital with a gunshot wound to the chest, no fewer than three law enforcement agencies are out for your blood, and Mike is still missing."

I sighed. Could I convince her my actions were necessary? That I wasn't just satisfying my own ego?

Maybe try being honest.

"I couldn't sit by while people kept trying to kill us," I said at last. "Or take the risk they might come after you."

She seemed taken aback by that. "Was that really a possibility?"

"Maybe? For all I knew, whoever was behind Mike's disappearance did a cost-benefit analysis and figured the cost of coming after Charlie and me was too high. You, on the other hand …"

"You went after Hammond to protect me?" She seemed dubious.

"That was an unexpected bonus," I said.

"I guess thanks are in order."

She took my hand. Unexpected, but I wasn't complaining.

We stayed that way for a moment, then the nurse had to come in and ruin everything.

"Time for your medicine," she said, producing a syringe and injecting its contents into my IV.

"Your timing sucks," I said.

"I get that a lot."

She left the room and even before the door shut behind her I started feeling the sedative's effects. Emma started getting her things together.

"Hey," I said.

"Hey yourself."

I smiled, but felt the drugs working. "Look, I know things have been … tense between us for a while."

"Have they?" She asked.

Ignoring her, I said, "But I just wanted you to know I never gave up on us. I always thought, if I got another chance, that we could make it work."

"I've thought the same thing."

"I appreciate all your help," I said. I was fading fast now. "Even if we don't find him, I appreciate all you've done to help look for Mike."

She grabbed my hand again. And as I slipped into unconsciousness, she said, "Hold that thought."

Daylight again when I woke up. The TV tuned to *Family Feud* and my mother sitting in the chair next to me. And now we've come full circle. She commanded me to tell her everything, and I did so.

"That pretty much brings us up to date," I said. I'd tried to ignore Mom's increasingly disapproving looks throughout the narrative, but it's no use lying to mothers; they're going to find out anyway.

"Unbelievable," she said.

"I agree," I said. "After all that, we still never found out what happened to Mike. Morris and Hammond said they didn't know where he is, and the thing is, I believe them."

Mom had a look I couldn't interpret on her face. She said, "No, I mean how you managed to get yourself shot *again* after you left the police force. Maybe you should consider another line of work."

Blinking, I said, "I think it's too late for me to become a doctor, Mom."

"I don't think that's even a good idea," she said, raising an eyebrow. "Apparently you can have shootouts in hospitals these days."

"You haven't seen many John Woo movies, I guess."

A voice I recognized but hadn't heard in weeks said, "Stick with *The Killer* and *Hard Boiled*, Mom. Whatever you do, don't let him show you the Jean-Claude Van Damme one."

I turned (painfully) to the doorway. There, as if he'd just returned from stepping out to go to the restroom, was Mike. He smiled and walked into my hospital room, followed by Charlie and Emma. For possibly the first time in my life, I was speechless.

Mom must have noticed the same thing. "Told you he wouldn't know what to say," she said.

"I owe you five bucks," said Mike.

Charlie said, "How are you feeling, little brother?"

"What the actual hell is going on?" I said.

"He's fine," Emma said.

"Where have you been? We've been going nuts trying to

find you and you just waltz in here like it's no big deal?"

"Calm down," Mike said. "We didn't want to cause you any more stress."

"More stress than thinking my brother was dead?" I asked.

He pulled a chair up to the bed. "Cy, I want you to know … the lengths you went to find me, it means a lot. I'm sorry I couldn't let you know where I was."

"Where were you?" I asked. It seemed the obvious question.

Emma laughed. "The Feds."

I looked at her, then back to Mike, "The FBI?"

Mike nodded. "When Ramirez's report got buried by Hammond, I knew something was going on. Ramirez wanted to go to over Hammond's head. I recommended against it, but he insisted on following the chain of command."

"And look where that got him," I said.

"Yeah," Mike said, with real sadness, "I had my suspicions about Morris already — Hammond never struck me as the mastermind type — so I went to the Bureau. Turns out they were up on the two of them already. They were going to move in on them in a couple weeks, so they told me to keep my eyes open." He paused. "Nobody realized Morris had already made up his mind about what to do with us."

I said, "That's when you sent the emails. Smart move, by the way."

"My sum knowledge of encryption comes from the DHS's four-hour Introduction to Cybersecurity training, so I was happy when Charlie told me it worked."

"How did you know to mention *Enemy at the Gates* if the sniper hadn't killed Ramirez yet?" I said.

Mike said, "Dumb luck, really. I was trying to tell you Steranko — the Russian — was actually not your enemy."

I said, "He's not dirty?"

Mike laughed. "He's dirty as hell, but he's smart enough to know the DHS and the FBI are focused on terrorists and human trafficking, so he steers clear of those. He also wasn't paying off Morris."

"The enemy of my enemy," Emma said.

"Pretty much."

"So you ran," I said.

"Tactically and strategically, it was the wisest course of action," Mike said. "I'm a good shot, but trying to take out a sniper with a .45 from a quarter-mile away is a little out of my league."

"You went back to the Feds," I said.

Mike shrugged. "It seemed like the best option. I didn't want to endanger you guys by showing up unannounced." He looked at me. "But it looks like you didn't need my help."

I laughed and immediately regretted it, as pain lanced through my torso. "You thought your family was just going to sit on its hands while you were in the wind?"

"I thought it'd take you and Charlie a little longer to almost get murdered," Mike said. "The FBI and Justice were set to go, and then the two of you came along. Serves me right for underestimating y'all."

I said, "How's the Bureau taking the news?"

Emma said, "They aren't exactly pleased."

Charlie said, "There were some agents here again yesterday, but I told them to get lost."

"They just wanted to ask him some questions," Mike said. "They're not going to arrest him," he frowned. "I don't think."

"You don't think?" I asked.

"They've had FBI agents stationed here ever since you were brought in," Mike said. "I don't think there are any plans to take you in, but I'm pretty sure they'd have preferred not to explain a high-ranking DHS corpse."

"What's the *official* story?" I asked, emphasizing the second to last word.

Charlie spoke up. "Well, since Hammond's dead, the narrative is that he was arguing with Morris about his cut of their ill-gotten gains. Tempers flared, guns were drawn, bada bing."

"That's it?"

Mike said, "People will believe it. Government corruption never goes out of vogue."

"They're not going to let Morris off the hook to save face?" I asked. "Even back at the house, he was careful not to say anything to incriminate himself."

Mike and Emma looked at each other. "About that," she said.

"What?"

Emma said, "That was a good move turning Hammond's webcam around."

"I was trying to keep you in the loop, in case things went south." I gestured to my supine form for emphasis.

Mike said, "It did more than that; she recorded everything. Morris may not have admitted to robbing container ships, but he's on tape murdering Hammond and planning to frame you for it."

"Then they must have Don on there as well," I said. "Why isn't he in custody?"

Charlie clucked her tongue. "Tragically, the feed cuts out right after Morris outlined his devious plan to set you up."

"Technology," Emma said, shaking her head ruefully.

"Unfortunately, it doesn't actually show him shooting you," Charlie said. "But the end results aren't difficult to extrapolate." She mimicked my gesture at my inert form.

"Where's Morris now?" I asked.

"In a very dark hole." Jim's voice blared from an iPhone next to my mother.

"Sorry," she said. "I should've told you he was on speaker."

I said, "Hey, man. Did your *State Department* sources tell you that?"

Jim didn't take the bait. "Standard FBI procedure for a suspect who is a high-ranking government employee and happens to be an extreme flight risk is to immediately ship them to Washington, DC. Director Morris isn't going to see natural light until his trial, assuming there is one."

"You think he'll cop a plea?" Charlie asked.

"Depends on how far up the chain this goes," Emma said. "If someone else is pulling the strings, maybe he flips and goes into WITSEC. If he's the top dog, and he's on tape murdering Hammond, maybe he admits to everything to avoid getting the death penalty."

All of us in the room looked at each other the way we always did when Jim explained things to us.

"How do you know all this?" I asked.

"It's all public information."

Mom said, "It was nice of you to check in on your brother,

dear."

"No trouble whatsoever," Jim said. "But now that it looks like you're out of the woods, I need to be going. Let me know if I can be of any help, Cy. And good work, to all of you."

"Thanks for checking in, spook," I said.

He hung up.

Charlie looked at me. "You thinking what I'm thinking?"

"Now we know why the CIA was sniffing around," I replied.

"It'd explain how he stays up to date even when he's 3,000 miles away."

"If he's even in Europe," I said.

Mom cut in, "Enough of that. Your older brother is an ... interesting   person."

EPILOGUE

In the end, the FBI never arrested me or Charlie.

Houston police detective Roy DeSantos did indeed end up getting official credit for Morris's arrest, after Charlie's phone call. This not quite anonymous tip led Roy to discover a dead Hammond and a concussed Morris (turns out Don thumped him a lot harder than I thought), and landed him on the front pages of those papers nobody reads for a couple days. All the local networks referred to him as a "hero cop," which he'll undoubtedly make sure I never hear the end of.

Charlie still hasn't agreed to a date with him, though she appears to be softening her stance on the issue.

Clarke & Clarke Investigations is still going strong out of my old ramshackle house. For while Roy may have received all the attention for the DHS case, word of mouth got around about Charlie's and my role. We weren't going to be driving Ferraris ourselves anytime soon, but I'm only eating Top Ramen once a week now.

Don's still doing the executive security thing. I'm not sure why he never gets any shit from Mom about the dangers of *his* job — escorting kidnap-prone oil company big shots to the Middle East and South America carries some risks, after all — but I'm half-convinced it's because Don had convinced her "executive security" means he works the door at ConocoPhillips headquarters like a nightclub bouncer.

Whatever, it's not my job to rat him out. Until it's

advantageous for me to do so, that is.

Mike stayed with the Department of Homeland Security and was actually promoted to associate director (which may or may not have been a backhanded apology for almost getting murdered in the line of duty by his boss). He and Kayla are still up in The Woodlands, meaning I still hardly ever see him.

It turns out Morris wasn't the only one involved in the trafficking ring, though he may have been the highest ranking. The FBI investigation is still proceeding, and happily, both the Feds and the DHS are satisfied no one in the Clarke family was involved.

Jim was as good as his word and has been overseas ever since he called me at the hospital. The odds on what his actual job is have pretty much leveled out, with "CIA" being the favorite by a wide margin, though Charlie still has a theory he's working for a foreign intelligence agency like MI6 or Interpol. Whatever the case, "State Department" is about tenth on the list of likely candidates and falling.

I healed up as well as can be expected. Since the bullet didn't hit any "major organs" (thanks, Charlie), I was released from the hospital after about a week and told to "take it easy." Given the frenetic pace of the previous couple weeks, the instructions weren't hard to follow.

Which means I've been watching a lot of James Bond movies and going nuts with boredom.

Oh, and Emma and I are officially back "on." I took longer to ask her out than I care to admit, until Charlie politely told me that if I didn't quit hemming and hawing about it and ask her out already, she'd shoot me again.

Emma told me she wants to go sailing some time. Maybe I can convince Steranko to let me borrow his boat.

ABOUT THE AUTHOR

Peter Vonder Haar is 23 years into his starter marriage and has three starter kids (he also may not know what the word "starter" means). He's been reviewing movies and concerts and writing trenchant essays about the Spice Girls since 2002. *Lucky Town* is his first novel.

Made in the USA
Middletown, DE
25 September 2019